SHAKE IT UP, BEVERLEY

SUZAN HOLDER

One More Chapter
a division of HarperCollins*Publishers* Ltd
1 London Bridge Street
London SE1 9GF
www.harpercollins.co.uk
HarperCollins*Publishers*
1st Floor, Watermarque Building, Ringsend Road
Dublin 4, Ireland

This paperback edition 2022
1
First published in Great Britain in ebook format
by HarperCollins*Publishers* 2022
Copyright © Suzan Holder 2022
Suzan Holder asserts the moral right to be identified
as the author of this work

A catalogue record of this book is available from the British Library

ISBN: 978-0-00-852208-7

Printed and bound in the UK using 100% Renewable Electricity
by CPI Group (UK) Ltd

For Nod and Django – In my life I love you more xx

Chapter One

I'd crawled on my hands and knees across my living room and pulled the curtains closed across the bay window from underneath, keeping out of sight. Of course, that only proved to the baying mob outside that I was indeed at home, and they immediately started shouting and yelling, holding cameras and phones above their heads and taking pictures of my little terraced house as though I was a movie star or a serial killer.

Of course I am neither of those things, but on that particular morning I woke to find myself a household name, a national laughing stock and the punchline to countless "jokes" doing the rounds on social media.

Me! Mild-mannered Beverley Wilson; completely ordinary in almost every respect. A Liverpool lass, a widow, single mother of three, and a part-time estate agent.

Well, I suppose that's not quite the full story. Life had been fairly humdrum and ordinary for the vast majority of my fifty-plus years, but that all started to change after my Geoff died. It's been over ten years now since he's been gone… I can't quite believe that… Ten years? Where did they go? Well, mainly into bringing up my three boys and trying to get through each and every day the best way I can, exactly what most women in my situation would do, is the short answer to that.

I can pinpoint the first time I ever decided to do something *extraordinary*, something unexpected and just for me. It was when I spotted this house was up for auction and decided to go for it. Downsizing made perfect sense once my middle son moved out to live with his girlfriend and the eldest was away doing his final year at uni. Once I only had my youngest still at home full-time – and knowing he wouldn't stick around much longer – meant this little terrace was just the job, but it wasn't simply the financial advantages of running a smaller home that swayed me to do it.

I'd gone along to the auction at The Cavern Club down on Mathew Street clutching the particulars for 72 Western Avenue, Speke, in my hot little hand. The Cavern was renowned for being claustrophobic and clammy back in the day, when The Beatles were just a bunch of local lads playing to a Swinging Sixties crowd rammed like sweaty sardines into the basement club. Apparently, it stank to high heaven! I'd missed out on that scene – born a little too late to be one of the lucky Liverpudlians who could honestly say they'd been there – but there I was now, about to try and grab my very own piece of Beatles history.

I don't know how I found the nerve to raise my hand and bid the way I did. It was like an out-of-body experience. One minute I was Beverley Wilson, anonymous lifelong Beatles fan, the next I was the owner of Paul McCartney's childhood home and had been dubbed "Beatles Bev" in the report of the auction in *The Liverpool Echo*.

People are often surprised that I was able to afford a home once lived in by a Beatle. They hear the word "Beatles" and instantly presume it must have cost millions, but really it's just an ordinary little terrace in a Liverpool suburb. It's not ordinary to me though.

This place isn't the more famous Forthlin Road home where Paul lived as a teenager and started to write songs with John Lennon in the back room. That house is kept as a museum, not lived in and used as a regular home like this one. That was part of the attraction to me though. I mean, think about it… Paul McCartney actually lived here with his little brother, Mike, and his parents, Jim and Mary, and now it's my home. I truly get a tingle up my spine every time I walk in the door.

Once I'd sold the family home I'd lived in with Geoff and the boys I was easily able to afford this place and I've never regretted it. Yes, I needed to relocate to make a fresh start, but I'll be honest, the house really was the ultimate prize for an avid collector like me. Over the years I've amassed an amazing collection of Beatles memorabilia, from signed original posters and programmes, to limited-edition lunchboxes and rare Beatles perfume bottles, plus other stuff you can't get for love nor money these days. I can't claim all the credit though; the bulk of the early items used to belong to my big sister Deb. I treasured it once it all became mine, and have added to it religiously over the years.

Life settled back into comfortable obscurity once the flurry of interest in me buying the house died down. But suddenly that all changed and I found myself being hounded by the bloody press, who were beating a drum solo on my front door that would put Ringo to shame. I attempted hiding under the window, trying not to listen, but they kept on yelling at me.

"Mrs Wilson? Come and talk to us, Mrs Wilson…"

"Come on, Bev, it'll only take a minute. You might as well talk to us. We're gonna print the story anyway."

"Mrs Wilson, Beverley, love – you need to tell your side of the story. Talk to us, Bev, it'll make you feel better."

"Bev – is it true you've got a yellow submarine tattooed on your arse?"

That did it!

I told them all to sod off and leave me alone … and just for the record added that I did NOT have a yellow submarine tattoo on me arse, or anywhere else, for that matter. Also, I've never rummaged through George Harrison's rubbish bins. What a disgusting allegation; it was just a good viewing spot, that was all. Oh, and while we're at it I do NOT sleep with a lock of Ringo Starr's pubic hair under me pillow. Bloody *Daily Star*!

They all buggered off eventually, but not before they'd made a right mess of me rhododendrons.

I knew they'd be back though… It was obvious they weren't going to leave me alone that easily. It wasn't even this bad when I worked part-time at The Beatles Story down on the dock. I was well chuffed when they said I could train up to drive the yellow duckmarine tour bus. You'll probably remember the way that all ended … at the bottom of the Albert Dock! It wasn't my fault – that damn thing was hard to keep afloat, you know – but probably the least said about that the better, that's what the lawyers advised anyway.

The only thing I was really guilty of was wanting to stop being so safe and careful in my middle age. I was never like that when I was young, but life can do that to you, can't it? What was it John Lennon used to say? *"Life is what happens when you are busy making other plans."* So I simply decided it was time to shake my life up a bit.

It's always given me a thrill living here in Paul McCartney's childhood home. I've loved The Beatles from the first moment I saw them but it was always Paul for me. You know that feeling you get when you're young and you suddenly discover someone – a singer or a movie star – who makes your heart flip and your palms sweat? Well, that's how Paul made me feel; always did and always will. But even I knew we weren't likely to end up together, and after so many years on my own I started to think there might be someone out there – a real, live man – whom I could love and be loved by. Does that sound like I've lost my mind? Is it really so terrible that I wanted to meet a living, breathing bloke, and not simply share my life with a fantasy … or a ghost, or a memory?

In some ways I think I was chasing those feelings you only get when you're young – when the world is still waiting to be discovered and all your mistakes have yet to take place. I wanted someone to make me feel like a teenager again. Bit of a tall order, I know. In the end, I've found myself riddled with insecurity, feeling like the whole world is against me, and I'm constantly in a terrible mood – so as far as experiencing a teenager's life, job done, I suppose!

I think part of the problem was the fact that I'd only got Harry still at home and the moment was fast approaching when he'd be off, too. That empty-nest syndrome is a right kick in the teeth, isn't it? You spend your best years ricocheting between toddler tantrums and history homework only to wake up one day to find they're off with barely a backward glance. I mean, that's fine – totally, completely fine – as it's what you've spent years working your fingers to the bone to create: independent adults ready to make their own way in the world. Marvellous. But let's be honest here, it's also just like someone has cut your heart out with a rusty old knife.

So that's how I found myself, Beverley Wilson – "Beatles Bev" – brought quite literally to my knees hiding from the gutter press. That lot just loved to write the most bloody outrageous lies about me. I went from being a woman who usually feels invisible in me own house to someone they talk about on daytime TV! They had a phone-in, for cryin' out loud! A bleedin' phone-in! People I've never met ringing in to give their opinions on MY life! Cheeky bloody beggars.

You wanna know how it all started? How someone who always believed that "All You Need Is Love" realised she "Should Have Known Better" and wished she could just "Get Back" to "Yesterday"? Well, read on...

Chapter Two

Four months earlier...

It had been a very ordinary Thursday in the estate agent office and I had just one last appointment in the diary. I double-checked the address of the property and made sure I'd got the right set of keys before I left Gratwick & Griffiths. I figured I'd be able to shoot straight off home from there once I was done.

It was only when I was halfway to Allerton that I realised there was not very much to be gained from an early dart. As usual, there would be no one at home waiting for me; no one to share a glass of wine with while cooking tea; no one to laugh with when a contestant on one of those teatime TV quiz shows demonstrated they didn't know their Shakespeare from their show tunes.

I know I was probably idealising day-to-day married life – I've got mates who do nothing but moan about their husbands – but sometimes it's having someone to do nothing with that's the thing you miss most. Like when you're sat watching telly and you just get a grunt of uninterest because you're wittering about wallpaper and they're pretending to be fascinated by the latest fracking debacle on *Newsnight*. Well, you don't half miss it when there's no one there grunting.

Harry was hardly ever home in the evening either. You can't blame him, he's eighteen and always off somewhere or other, often with his guitar slung over his back. That's one thing I'll take some credit for; Harry has picked up a real love of music from me. Not that he thinks I have any actual musical taste, of course. Or any taste at all. Apparently, the only thing I'm an expert in is being a complete and utter embarrassment. And I nail that without even trying. Seriously, the way he reacts to me singing along to the radio I might as well do a full-on Lady Gaga and pop on a meat dress to nip to the post office... I'd give it a go just to prove a point but I lean more towards a veggie diet these days.

I pulled up outside the house I'd come to value, a white-painted semi with a small overgrown front garden. There was a driveway big enough for one car behind a pair of low metal gates but I parked my car on the road. I wanted to take a few pictures and I didn't want my trusty VW Polo making an appearance in those.

It was a nice house on a pleasant street but it looked a bit unloved. I knew how it felt.

The owner of the house had been an elderly lady who'd lived there alone until she'd recently died. Mrs Malkin's family dropped the keys into our office a few days before and asked if we could give them a valuation. I'm used to doing viewings at properties without the owner being present as most people ask us to show prospective buyers around – I think they'd rather not hear any rude remarks about their interior design choices – but it was unusual for me to be inside a house completely on my own.

As I let myself into the front hall, and felt the door push against a small pile of mail on the mat, I suddenly felt a little apprehensive about being there. I gave myself a shake and a bit of a talking to; there was no point freaking myself out when there was a job to do. I intended to have a good look round, take some snaps, make a few notes, and with luck I'd be home in time to impress absolutely nobody with my extensive general knowledge whilst simultaneously shouting at the TV and cooking pasta.

I moved from room to room looking past the old-fashioned furniture and dated decor. I was concentrating on the room sizes, how the house was laid out and what features it had that a buyer would be looking for. I decided the first thing a young couple would want to do was knock through the two downstairs reception rooms to open the ground floor up and make it a much more usable space. The kitchen was a decent size, with room for a breakfast table but no separate utility area, which a lot of people ask for these days.

I opened a door I suspected might be a walk-in pantry but was pleased to find it had actually been converted into a downstairs cloakroom with a toilet and small handwashing basin. That was a bonus.

Upstairs, the two smaller bedrooms had a distinctly unused air as the beds were made up not with duvets but candlewick bedspreads. I felt a twinge of sadness for the old girl who'd lived there. How long had it been since anyone came to stay with her, I wondered? The cold rooms were overfilled with large pieces of dark wood furniture, cumbersome dressing tables, and wardrobes that looked like they held the secret entrance to Narnia. I edged around the bed in the back bedroom as there was hardly enough room to move, and tugged open one of the wardrobe doors. It squeaked loudly on its hinges and I was instantly hit by a strong, musty smell; clearly no one had looked in there for a very long time. As I peered inside I almost laughed out loud. There were a couple of huge fur coats hanging from the rail, just like you would find inside a Narnia wardrobe. I resisted the temptation to clamber in to see if I could also find a lion and a witch.

The sun had started to set and the bright afternoon had given way to a gloomy half-light in the empty house. There was just the old lady's bedroom left to assess now and I was conscious I was putting off the moment when I had to step inside. I can't remember now what I was so worried about.

As I turned the handle of the master bedroom door, I was aware I had the lyrics from the song "Eleanor Rigby" nagging at me inside my head, begging for an answer to the question of where all the lonely people in the world do come from. I had no idea what Marjorie Malkin's life had really been like, but the sense I was getting as I poked around her home was that in her old age she spent a lot of time there on her own. I knew that her son, who seemed to be the only family she had, lived on the other side of the country – that's why he and his wife left the keys with me for the valuation – and he'd made it plain they wanted to sell up quickly. No one had even started clearing out the old dear's belongings; they probably intended to employ one of those house-clearing firms to come in and give one price for taking the lot. I had an image in my mind of poor old Marjorie being just a face at her own window, sitting in her drab, draughty house day after day, watching the world go by without her. I wondered how many people had gone to her funeral … or if, like Eleanor Rigby, nobody came?

That morbid train of thought was really giving me a spooky sensation. I hesitated on the threshold of Marjorie's bedroom and steeled myself as though I was about to confront the ghost of the old lady herself, sat up in her bed, furious with my intrusion into her home.

The bedroom door swung inwards and I stepped forward onto the tufted Wilton patterned carpet. The dark curtains were partially closed across the bay window so it took a moment for my eyes to adjust, but the sight that suddenly materialised sent a shockwave of horror through me as I shrieked in fear and stumbled backwards.

A stark, pale face with a shock of white hair was staring straight at me through a pair of glittering eyes in deep, dark sockets.

My heart hammered in my chest and my hands fluttered to find the door frame so I could steady myself. What horrific nightmare was this?

As my breath came in short gasps my eyes never left the evil glare that was being levelled at me. Then sense slowly dawned. It was not a cadaver or a ghost. The unblinking gaze I had been confronted with was that of a large porcelain doll sitting upright, her legs sticking straight out in front of her from beneath the ruffles of a Victorian-style white lace dress. She was propped in the centre of the pink satin eiderdown, her blonde hair fanned out on the pile of pillows behind her.

I shuddered in relief and swept my eyes around the rest of the bedroom from the sanctuary of the doorway. There were dozens of similar dolls all around the room, sitting in groups on a bedside chair, on a dressing table, even on top of the wardrobe. They were everywhere I looked. They varied in size and colouring but all shared the same blank expression and slightly accusatory air of the first doll.

My sympathetic feelings towards poor old Marjorie Malkin morphed into irritation as I wondered why on earth anyone in their right mind would collect such an array of creepy dolls like these. How had she slept at night surrounded by so many pairs of staring eyes? As I moved towards the window to open the curtains and let in a little more light and sanity, I was aware of how those eyes followed me around the room. It was enough to freak anyone out.

I took my notebook from my bag and resolved to pull myself together as I began to write down the dimensions of the room and some of the original features I was able to spot in between the dozens of dead-eyed dolls: a small fireplace, original coving, an ornate ceiling rose above the centre of the bed… As I scribbled the details as quickly as I could I noticed my fingers were still trembling. I'd be lucky to be able to read half of those notes back later.

I gave the room one last look around. The collection

might end up being worth quite a bit of money, but I decided I'd be glad to never see a porcelain doll again for as long as I lived.

I'd taken a single step towards the hallway when there was a sudden and distinctive sound of breaking glass from downstairs. I froze immediately and racked my brains for what could have caused such a noise. Could something have fallen in the kitchen? I hadn't spotted anything that looked precarious when I was in there; in fact, the work surfaces were fairly uncluttered, unlike the rest of the house.

I was holding my breath but before I had chance to exhale, a further noise confirmed what I now know my subconscious had been dreading; the distinctive rattle of the handle on the back door to the garden and the shuffle of a footstep entering the house. It was almost like I could sense rather than hear the invasion of another person into the property. Someone had broken in.

My body took over while my mind stayed on pause. Instinctively, I took a silent step towards the bedroom door and pushed it gently shut. As I heard the intruder beneath me move into the dining room I moved quickly to the far corner where there was a gap between the wardrobe and the wall just big enough to wedge myself into. I pulled my mobile out of my cross-body bag and dialled 999.

I honestly have no clue how long I was standing, pressed up against the floral wallpaper, terrified and trembling. The noises from downstairs left me in no doubt that Mrs Malkin's home was being thoroughly ransacked. I hadn't heard any voices but I couldn't be absolutely sure there wasn't more than one thief on the premises. I didn't want to know. The eyes of the dolls now seemed to be staring at the closed door of the room we were all trapped inside; like me, they were waiting to be discovered at any moment.

Three sharp bangs from below thudded through the house and my body simultaneously. Were the intruders smashing the place up? Then, out of nowhere, a deep, loud voice yelled, "POLICE!"

Still I couldn't move, I stayed exactly where I was, frozen to the spot, literally shivering with fear.

The police officer who found me a little while later guided me out of the bedroom and down the stairs, talking to me all the while like I was a small child.

"Just a couple of kids," he said. "They didn't get away with anything as they dropped the bag of stolen stuff in the garden when they ran. They're on their way down to the station now."

I sat, still shivering, on the chair in the front bay window where he'd perched me, while from the kitchen he kept up a running commentary that was meant to be reassuring. He boiled the kettle to make me a cup of tea and informed me there'd been a spate of break-ins in the area. He added that I'd done a great job of calling the cop shop while the little buggers were still in the house.

"Caught 'em red-handed, thanks to you," he said with a friendly grin as he handed me a china mug, adding, "I put a couple of sugars in, to help with the shock." And then, I can't be absolutely sure – my faculties had been numbed by the whole experience – but I could have sworn the detective constable actually winked at me.

I sipped my tea then and took a moment to look at him properly.

DC Collins, he'd said his name was when he introduced himself, was rather good-looking. Fit, both in the athletic and the fanciable sense. He was wearing a very smart dark grey suit, white shirt and a navy-blue tie. His black leather brogues were polished and shiny, but he looked like the sort of guy who would be more comfortable in a rugby shirt or a knitted Aran sweater and walking boots. I've never been one for the great outdoors but if a hike up a hill with DC Collins was followed by a pub lunch at a country inn beside a roaring fire, I decided I might be persuaded.

I snapped out of my fantasy to notice DC Collins's dark eyebrows were furrowed slightly as he looked at me in concern.

"Are you okay?" he asked.

I stuttered a reply, and my fingers fumbled for the cup of sweet tea I'd placed on the side table next to me. I couldn't work out whether I was all of a dither owing to my recent brush with crime while trapped with the creepy doll collection, or if it was the close proximity of DC Collins.

It was definitely highly unusual for me to feel attracted to a man in such a way. Perhaps I just don't get out enough, but I really couldn't remember the last time I'd fancied someone. In fact, I'd go so far as to say I really felt there was some sort of connection between me and DC Collins. It could have had something to do with the fact he'd just come to my rescue, like a knight in shining armour, or it could simply have been down to his lovely broad shoulders and the distinct twinkle in his dark brown eyes that he was using to great effect on me.

I looked down and felt relieved I was wearing my second best pair of black trousers – they fit me well and together with my leopard-print shirt and black ankle boots I didn't look too bad, all things considered. I ran a hand through my blonde hair and hoped it wasn't too much like a bird's nest. I also wished I hadn't left my black leather jacket in the car; it would have given my outfit a more modern vibe. People tell me I don't look my age, and I'm damn sure I don't feel it, but I wasn't sure how old DC Collins was. He could easily have been several years younger than me; it was hard to tell.

I fluttered my eyelashes as I sipped my tea and gave him my best smile. "I'm good, thanks to you," I said with what I hoped was a note of flirtation in my voice.

He gave me a warm smile in response but then said something that to this very day chills me to the bone.

"Have you lived here long?"

The question hit me like a kick in the guts. He thought that I lived there, in that old lady's house, with swirly patterned carpets, floral wallpaper and old-fashioned furniture! There were even antimacassars on the armchairs and doilies on the nest of tables. No one under the age of eighty-five would have such things and … oh my God, the dolls! He'd found me hiding upstairs and so must have seen the macabre spectacle of those ghoulish dollies in every corner of what he had clearly presumed was *my* bedroom! What kind of batty old woman did he think I was?

"I don't… This isn't … my… I don't live here," I finally stammered, sounding more than ever like a doddery old dear. Seriously, could this day have got any worse?

It took a little while to sort out the confusion but DC Collins eventually understood my role as an estate agent and even seemed to find it all quite amusing that he at first assumed I was the lady of the house.

I was struggling to see the funny side of the mix-up. Just as I was casting myself in the role of femme fatale and entertaining the idea of attempting to seduce a hunky, darkly handsome detective, I discovered he actually saw me as a decrepit grandma with a passion for porcelain playthings. I know I am out of practice with the opposite sex but that didn't just take the biscuit – it took the whole damn packet of Jammie Dodgers!

Luckily, a neighbour from next door came to my rescue by popping round to see what all the commotion had been about and offering to board up the back door. Thank goodness I didn't need to stick around any longer.

As I made my hurried excuses for a quick exit, DC Levi Collins handed me his card in case I remembered any further details to add to my statement. I shoved it into my bag and in a final act of utter madness told him I had to dash as I had a belly-dancing class to get to. Belly dancing? Where that notion came from I have absolutely no idea, but I was so desperate for him to see me as a vibrant and youthful woman instead of a wizened old hag. By the look on his face, I think I only managed to revolt him more and who could blame him; the thought of me gyrating my pelvis in diaphanous harem pants would be enough to scare off even a beefy busy used to confronting drug-dealing gangsters.

I left DC Collins looking rather bewildered standing on Mrs Malkin's driveway. Once in the safety of my car I punched Julia's number into my phone and talked to her on hands-free as I made as quick a getaway as was possible whilst being closely watched by an officer of the law.

"Jools, I'm heading home to drown myself in booze. D'ya fancy coming over?"

Julia is a good friend, the best mate anyone could have. She didn't wait for further explanation. Instead, as always, she cut straight to the point and answered, "Hold on, girl, I'm on my way."

Chapter Three

Half a bottle of red wine down, I was *almost* able to see the funny side of the house-of-horror story myself, though I don't think I will ever find it quite as hilarious as Jools clearly did.

"Ow ... ow ... it hurts," she shrieked, clutching her sides while wiping tears of mirth from her eyes. "Tell me again about the dead woman's dollies!"

I could see where she was coming from but I patiently explained, yet again, how she was missing the point that the entire experience had given me the heebie-jeebies, not just because of the dolls and the robbers but because it had been a truly horrific glimpse into my own lonely future.

"You're not gonna end up living alone surrounded by dollies and doilies!" Jools snorted.

I was not so sure.

However, Jools refused to listen to my theory that I was not too far off a lonely existence, with only my music and Beatles memorabilia for company. In fact, she had a counter-theory that my experience in Marjorie's mausoleum actually proved I was ready to hit the dating scene.

"Sorry … what?" I goggled at Jools in disbelief.

She has always been a bizarre contradiction of romantic and cynic. I think it's linked to her job. She owns a bridal shop on Bold Street called "Bold Brides", which is typical Jools. She spotted a gap in the market for weddings with a strong hook and went for it. Forget demure, dewy-eyed and virginal, Jools attracts customers who want to have a wedding outfit that suits their real personality, whether that's a stunning trouser suit or a frock with a more rock-chick vibe. She's also great at suggesting unusual wedding venues and has loads of offbeat ideas for flowers and food and all the other paraphernalia that go with a wedding these days. Her success with the shop makes perfect sense to me; she works bloody hard and it's a great idea. I've never understood why perfectly sane women suddenly have an impulse to dress like Little Bo Peep on their wedding day. Everyone else turns up dressed in their finery and there's the poor bride in a crinoline, looking like she's lost her bloody sheep!

Jools was now looking at me like I was a dumb animal, peering over the scarlet frames of her spectacles, which matched her spiky red hair.

"You said yourself that the dashing detective was giving you the fanny flutters," she said.

"I said nothing of the sort and that's a revolting expression!"

Jools just giggled like she was twelve years old but then fixed me with a determined look. I always know I'm in trouble when Julia Gillespie zeroes in with those beady eyes.

"All right, I take back 'fanny flutters'," she said, somehow managing to apologise for the horrible phrase while repeating it just so she could see me squirm all over again. Hilarious. She carried on. "But I'm right about you having the hots for him. Don't try to deny it! You said as much and anyway you wouldn't have been half as bothered about him thinking you were the batty old bird who lived there if you didn't fancy him."

I couldn't deny she had a point there.

She went on for a bit about how much she lusted after Idris Elba but I'd have said Levi Collins had more of the look of Adrian Lester ... but as I had zero chance of pulling him, whichever actor the detective resembled was neither here nor there.

Jools was ploughing on with her argument anyway. "So if, even for just a nanosecond, you considered coppin' off with your cute copper, I reckon it's time you got yourself out there and back in the dating game, Beverley Wilson."

Now I thought she was seriously stretching the point, but I also know that when she's in that mood it's almost impossible to throw Jools off her charted course.

We've been friends a long time. She was one of the mums I met, back when standing in the school playground waiting for the kids to come out was the highlight of my day. Rain or shine, a little knot of us would huddle together for a gossip before we'd each gather up our gaggle of kids and head home to put the tea on. After a while Jools and I started arranging to meet up for coffee away from the playground and became proper mates. I lost touch with most of the others as the boys moved classes and eventually left school. The friendships were based on coincidence and convenience, as the only thing we had in common was that we had kids the same age at the same school. Julia, though, was someone I could talk to and she could always make me laugh.

I don't know what I'd have done without her when Geoff died. It was so sudden and completely devastating. A heart attack. She looked after the boys, made pots of Scouse to keep us fed and helped with the mountain of paperwork that threatened to bury me as I struggled to deal with banks, building societies, mortgage companies and utility suppliers. They don't make it easy for you when your partner dies, you know. Simply explaining that your entire world has collapsed as your other half – the father of your children and the person whose name is on every legal document that governs your life – has died, is no longer with us, is deceased … makes absolutely no difference to a jobsworth on the other end of the line, no matter how you put it. More than once I was tempted, as I became increasingly hysterical, to begin acting out Monty Python's Dead Parrot Sketch... *"Let me try and make this clear for you Ms 'Computer-Says-No'... He is no more, he has ceased to be... He has expired and gone to meet his maker."* It wouldn't have helped, obviously, but when I told Jools and we ended up laughing until we cried, that actually did help, quite a lot.

Now she was stabbing at my iPad while giving me a rundown of names of various online dating apps and agencies, I wasn't really listening but suddenly she stopped with a loud "AHA!"

She looked at me with a fresh gleam in her green eyes. Framed by her bright red glasses it was a bit terrifying, and I was beginning to miss Mrs Malkin's dollies.

"You're not going to believe it. There's one based right here in Liverpool called 'Lonely Hearts Club Dating Agency'!"

"You're making that up."

"I'm not! Look…" She flashed the screen towards me and I just saw a brief glimpse of the website's homepage, mocked up to look a bit like the album cover of The Beatles' *Sergeant Pepper's Lonely Hearts Club Band* with dozens of figures standing around the name of the agency spelt out in red flowers. Clever.

My mild interest spurred Jools on and she began looking at what you had to do to join.

"Right, you need to think of a nickname. It needs to be a mix of letters and numerals and they don't want you to use your real name … for protection." She nodded eagerly and I knew it would all be over a lot quicker if I just went along with it.

I thought for a while and then said, "Penny4 … as in Penny Lane, penny for your thoughts … penny for the *Guy*. Pretty smart, huh?"

Jools barely looked up as her fingers tapped furiously at the keys. "I think you're misunderstanding what men are looking for on these sites. It's not necessarily witty wordplay."

Charming.

"Right," she carried on, barely skipping a beat, "first question: name three things you couldn't live without."

Sulkily I offered, "Food, water and oxygen."

"*Beverley.*" Jools was using her stern "mum" voice.

I sighed and tried harder to enter into the spirit of it. I really didn't want to live the rest of my days all alone, and I knew I would love to find someone to be with, go out with, stay in with. The events of that day had shaken me up a bit but perhaps what I had to do now was shake my life up completely. It wasn't that I was bored – I kept myself busy – but I must admit I did sometimes feel lonely and I knew if I didn't do something it was never going to get any better. Jools was still looking at me expectantly.

"I don't know what to say…"

"Stop trying to be funny. You're not gonna get anyone interested by trying to prove you're a laugh a minute. Just be honest," she answered bluntly.

"Right, how about … me kids, me friends, and music," I offered.

"Better," she replied. "Ooh, here's a good question: list the things you wish people noticed about you."

Ignoring her direction to be less amusing I suggested, "That I've the same witty repartee as Mae West and I'm the same dress size as Marilyn Monroe." I took a congratulatory swig of wine, pleased with my clever cinematic answer, but once again Jools punctured my bubble.

"Bit of an age giveaway there," she observed but she tapped it into the online form anyway. "Next: what are you looking for in a man?"

The answer to that didn't take much thinking about. "A

kind, understanding man who's up for fun and a bit of adventure."

Jools snorted and exclaimed, "Take-me-now-I'm-desperate" as she typed. I made her delete that immediately.

"I'm *not* desperate but I want a man who's smart enough to talk to about stuff on the news … but daft enough to make snow angels in the park. Who might whisk me to Paris, but could also be happy with a game of Boggle in front of the telly. Who'll tell me my cooking is delicious, even when it's not, surprise me with a choccie bar when he goes to fetch the papers and will, just occasionally, hold my hand."

Jools was looking at me with something of a grimace on her face as I came to the end of my monologue. "Ahh, the elusive ideal man," she said with a slow shake of her head.

"Is it too much to ask for?" It was a serious question. I was now wondering if I was simply wasting my time.

"I'll let you know if we ever find one," Jools said curtly and turned her attention back to the screen to see where we were up to in the process.

Next they wanted me to describe the kind of things I like to do. That took a bit more thought but eventually I came up with the following: "You should contact me, Penny4, if you like home cooking, country walks, watching *Columbo*, visiting comedy clubs and going to the cinema."

Julia wrote it all down carefully as I dictated but then leaned back and folded her arms as she translated my words into her own version. "Don't bother if you live surrounded by pizza boxes and never go outside. Or if you can't follow the most basic detective stories, think Roy Chubby Brown is a comedy genius and your favourite movie is *Conan the Barbarian*."

"Do you think that's what we should have said?" I was worried now.

Jools just shrugged and answered, "Probably."

In the end we decided to stick with my version and hoped it wasn't too subtle to put off any anti-social junk-food addicts with an appalling sense of humour and a taste for violence. Fingers crossed, eh?

We pondered the online profiles of suitable and unsuitable men over the next couple of hours and did our best to weed out the more obvious nutters. Anyone calling themselves "Mr Grey" got fifty shades of "Get Lost". There were absolutely dozens of those, the dirty buggers.

Jools was now concerned I was setting my standards very high but I hardly thought weeding out the dirty mac brigade made me too demanding!

The whole exercise did help me understand what my instant turns-ons and turn-offs really were though. For a start, it was a no to ramblers, real ale drinkers, Dungeons and Dragons fanatics or Morris dancers. I mean, that last one was just pure common sense.

Reading carefully through the descriptions guys had written about themselves I also dismissed anyone who couldn't spell properly. Now, don't get me wrong, I'm no literary genius. If it was simply too many n's in "unnecessary" or a bit of a mix-up in the middle of "definitely", well, we can all be guilty of that sort of thing now and then. But this one bloke, he had spelt elephant with an i. El - eye – phant ... E-l-i-p-h-a-n-t? I won't go into exactly *why* he was going on about an elephant – use your imagination – but who the hell was this guy who didn't know how to spell "elephant"? You're trying to make a good impression, mate; read it through, use spellcheck. No thank you. So it was a flat no to buffoons, baboons or anyone who struck me as downright-crazy-bonkers-stalker-psycho-la-la-Looney-Tunes.

"Any other stipulations?" asked Jools with an arched eyebrow.

I told her to pass on anyone who claimed to be ex-SAS. The first rule of the SAS is you don't tell anyone you were in the SAS... Even I know that! Muppets!

"Oh yeah," I added, talking to Julia's back as she had her head in the fridge, looking to see if we'd got anything she could snack on, "we should also avoid all the firemen."

She instantly snapped her head in my direction. "*All* the firemen?"

I'd been scrolling through dozens of profiles while she'd been foraging in my fridge and I'd found there were sooooo many firemen, or men who claimed to be firemen, on the site.

"It's a wonder this country isn't one big smouldering ashtray with the number of firemen who are posing on this website, stripped to the waist in front of a gleaming pole or a large hose," I told her, only to find she'd skidded across the kitchen floor and was now right behind me, looming over the laptop with her eyes on stalks.

She caught me smirking at her and feigned indifference. "Hmmm, well, there is something about a man in uniform… You can't get arrested for it, you know!" Jools shrugged but then added, "Don't forget, you were the one who got all hot under the collar faced with a copper and he was in plain clothes. Anyway, I think we're just about done. Look out, Lonely Hearts Club dating website – here comes Penny4!"

And with that she leaned right over me and hit send on my profile. Whether I liked it or not my heartfelt plea to "Love Me Do" would soon be live on the internet… Help!

Chapter Four

I was amazed that any men responded to my dating profile but there were quite a few, and it happened so quickly, too. That was an ego boost, I can tell you. There was life after kids after all, who knew? Spurred on by Jools, I arranged to meet a man called Peter in a local coffee shop – that seemed a sensible approach, somewhere public and familiar where I could make a quick getaway if necessary. In the end, that wasn't what I should have been worried about.

I'd taken ages choosing what to wear and doing my hair and make-up. I felt pretty good about myself and was more excited than nervous considering this was the first actual "date" I had been on since Geoff and I were courting back when I was a teenager.

The butterflies did start once I got to the café. It was late afternoon but the spring sunshine flooded through the glass windows, making it hard to see properly inside. I peered around like a myopic mole as I came in through the door, trying to see if Peter was already there. We'd decided on a pretty stereotypical system for spotting blind dates and agreed we should both be either wearing or carrying a red carnation. Yes, yes, all a bit embarrassingly obvious, but it was tricky to think of a better way.

I couldn't see anyone adorned with a red flower so I found an empty table and ordered a cappuccino. I hadn't been able to bring myself to wear the carnation, as it would have felt too "mother of the bride" to pin it to my navy spotty dress. I'd toyed with the idea of tucking it into my hair but I was worried that would give off an "ageing hippy" vibe. Instead, I held it and twirled it between my fingers. At least it gave my increasingly shaky hands something to do.

In the end, I spotted him before he saw me. A flash of something small and scarlet caught my eye as a man with sandy hair wearing a navy overcoat walked past the café window and then through the open door. Just like I had done, he stood squinting around as his eyes adjusted and didn't spot me for a good while. His gaze panned over me and then back again and I had time to register that he looked quite nice.

I took a deep breath and gave a little wave. "Hi! Hey, over here, Peter... It is Peter, isn't it?" I gave him what I hoped was a reassuring smile.

He was standing there, backlit by the sunshine, the red carnation in his lapel clearly there for all to see. His brow furrowed even deeper as he looked straight at me then and shook his head. "No, no, I'm not Peter."

His words made no sense to me as I sat there with a

matching flower held before me like a poor man's bride, but like a lemming headed to the cliff edge I carried on. "Oh … but you look so like your picture… I mean, you're even wearing…"

I didn't get to finish the sentence as he seemed to spot my carnation at the exact moment he realised his own flower gave him away. In that infuriating way some men have of always insisting they are right and you are wrong, despite clear evidence to the contrary, he even had the cheek to carry on denying it while reaching up, crushing the flower in his hand and shoving it into his coat pocket.

"Look, love, I think you've got your wires crossed," he said.

What did I do? Confront him? Argue the toss? Laugh it off? None of the above, I'm afraid. Instead, I took the worst option ever – I apologised.

"Ah, right, silly me, of course… Sorry to have bothered you."

A look of relief, perhaps even pity, flashed across his face. "Don't worry about it, love," he said. "We all make mistakes."

As I sat there afterwards, slightly stunned, my coffee went cold as I ruminated on the fact that we do indeed all make mistakes and my first one was to presume that I was the only one with high expectations! Clearly my appearance had not made the grade with Peter the petal-crusher.

It took a good few days before I could consider taking another look at the Lonely Hearts Club dating app. But when you are panning for gold, even I know you can't expect to find a nugget at the first attempt. I've never been a quitter and I'd come this far so I felt I had to try again.

It was much harder to decide what to wear for a date the second time around. I'd gone for my favourite blue polka dot dress before, but the only occasion *that* dress would be attending in future was a date with a charity shop. Eventually, I settled on jeans and a soft cream jumper. Something about the fluffy wool made me feel comforted, as though I was already enveloped in a lovely hug, no matter how this date panned out.

We arranged to meet in a different place to where I'd met Peter. There are so many lovely cafés and bars to choose from in Liverpool, although I hoped I wasn't going to be stood up in all of them!

I was early, again, and the knot of nerves in my stomach was much worse as I tried to wait patiently for Juan. He had told me he was originally from Spain but now worked in a big hotel in town. His picture showed he had slicked-back black hair and a bright white smile. I didn't suggest any props to help us recognise each other this time. I wouldn't be making that rookie mistake again.

Juan arrived in an explosion of Spanish charm, double kisses and spicy aftershave. He gave me what appeared to be an approving look up and down as he took his seat at the table, but then rather spoiled it by giving the young waitress a lascivious wink as he ordered a double espresso.

He threw back his coffee as soon as it arrived and raised

his hand to immediately order another. He seemed to be in a tearing hurry.

"You do ze right sing asking to meet somewhere like-a zis," he said, looking around the room rather than at me as he spoke quickly, his Spanish accent making his words slur together. Then he leaned in towards me and added, "You can't-a be too careful nowadaze."

Quite.

I smiled and nodded, and also signalled the waitress for an espresso. I felt I might need it to match his energy.

"You done-a zis sorta sing before, eh?" He jutted out his chinful of designer stubble as he asked.

"Well, let's just say it's not my first date since joining up," I answered, adding with what I hoped was plucky positivity, "but you can't fall at the first hurdle, can you?"

He seemed delighted with this and erupted in a short, sharp laugh. "Ha! Jesus Christ, no. I 'ave ad-a some verrry bad ones, I can tell-a you."

I did not find this statement reassuring in the least, and to add to my unease, in one swift movement Juan stood and flipped his chair around, straddling it like he was riding a horse, saying, "Like-a you say, Chica, you just pick-a yourself up and get right-a back in ze saddle." His movements on the chair like he was riding a bucking bronco started to attract looks from some of the other café customers. I attempted to calm him by saying we should probably put the horse-riding comparisons to one side.

"Que?"

He appeared not to understand what I was saying about his equestrian analogy and I desperately wanted to move the conversation along. "So, Juan, how many women have you actually met through Lonely Hearts Club?"

I have no idea why I thought this was the right direction to take things.

Juan now had a dreamy, faraway look in his eyes as he leaned onto the back of the chair. "Ahhh, mucho … mucho…"

I blundered on, not knowing how to stop myself. "I see. 'Mucho', you say? And how many would 'mucho' be, exactly? A dozen … more than a dozen?"

Juan looked insulted as he repeated, "A dothzen?" looking at me as though I had cast the most terrible aspersions on his manly prowess. "I can 'ave a dothzen in a week, baby!"

Seeing the look of horror on my face, Juan then felt the need to add further detail of the humanitarian work he obviously felt he was carrying out in the community.

"Do you know 'ow many desperado women-of-a-certain-age zer are out-a zer?" he said, sweeping his arm wide to take in the café, the street and probably the whole of Liverpool and surrounding areas.

I hadn't had a clue up until that point, but thanks to Juan I was beginning to realise.

———

You might think these early experiences would make me delete my Lonely Hearts Club dating profile altogether, and instead begin a search for a nunnery to join. However, like I say, I am not a quitter and, if anything, these experiences actually spurred me on to set up several more dates. This might seem odd but bear with me… My reasoning was that if I was going to find the man of my dreams I was going to have to increase my chances by stacking the odds in my favour. Like I always tell my kids, if you really want something, you have to work for it. Therefore, the more men I met up with … the more likely it was that my perfect partner might be one of them. As a theory, it made perfect sense.

Unfortunately, the result was that I was subjected to a series of increasingly disastrous dates with men I'd describe as "Nowhere Man", as opposed to my ideal man!

There was the well-spoken professor type who appeared utterly charming until he launched into a wordy monologue on why monogamy is completely impossible for a man to maintain; something about it being *"a relatively recent concept in the history of human relationships"* and therefore *"unsustainable"*. He actually argued that men are programmed differently to women and that it wasn't their fault they couldn't keep it in their trousers. He said it was in their DNA and all down to science.

I had a one-word response to all that, beginning with F… No, not that one, I simply said, "Fascinating" as I got my coat.

Then there was the guy who was glued to his phone for the entire date. He couldn't leave it alone every time it beeped or vibrated. He made out it was all enormously important work stuff, but unless he worked for a top comedian, I couldn't imagine why all of his texts would be so hilariously funny. I called time on that date when he started taking pictures of himself. I'm pretty sure that at least one of those selfies has a clear image of me rolling my eyes in the background.

I switched venues to a local pub to meet up with a guy called Barney who sounded like a fun, adventurous sort, as there's only so much coffee a girl can drink. I was feeling better about this one, although that may have been down to the double vodka tonic I downed while I was waiting at a table by an inglenook fireplace.

The first sign of trouble actually occurred on that date before Barney even appeared. There was the distinct sound of a revving motorbike engine from the direction of the car park, followed by a series of loud explosive bangs as an exhaust backfired. I didn't think too much of it until a figure dressed in a battered flying jacket and voluminous plus-fours appeared in the doorway. On his head he had an ancient Biggles-style leather helmet that fastened under his chin. As he removed his enormous goggles, he announced to the pub in general in a broad West Country accent, "Eeee, it's never easy to park when I've got the side car attached to Betsy!"

I mean, seriously, you have got to me kidding me!

So by the time I arranged to meet Andrew, I was ready for anything … or so I thought. It all started off okay. He was already sitting at the table when I arrived at the café attached to the Royal Court Theatre. He was slim, with short, dark hair and spectacles, wearing a raincoat over his suit. He seemed more nervous than I did so I immediately tried to put him at his ease.

"So, Andrew, how did you get here today?"

The glass-fronted theatre café is right next to the bus station so I presumed that would be how he had come into town, but Andrew surprised me.

"I drove," he said. "I managed to find a car park round the back of the shopping centre."

"You drove?" I said, and then before I could stop myself added with a nervous laugh, "a car?"

Andrew looked a bit confused but confirmed, "Yes. It's just a Volvo; nothing fancy, I'm afraid, if that's what you're into."

Oh lord, he thought I wanted to know if he drove an expensive car and had pots of money, so I tried to convince him that wasn't what I meant. "Oh, no, a car … any car … that's great!" I said, a bit too enthusiastically.

Andrew was determined to make sure I understood how very ordinary his car was in case I was some sort of gold-digger. "It's a good few years old, with quite a few miles on the clock, to be honest, but it gets me from A to B."

I was nodding like the proverbial nodding dog by now. "No, honestly, that sounds absolutely great, fabulous. I mean … so long as it's not got a sidecar!"

Andrew just looked at me like I was some sort of lunatic. You couldn't blame him, really.

"A sidecar? What sort of Volvo has a sidecar?"

It was too difficult to explain so I just told him to ignore me as I was talking gibberish. He seemed to accept that and we then sat nursing our drinks in silence for a little while.

Eventually Andrew decided to take the initiative and reached into a leather satchel I hadn't spotted hanging on the back of his chair. He produced a small brown paper bag and slid it towards me across the table with a bashful smile.

"Well, anyway, I brought you a little present," he said.

I was taken completely by surprise. No other date had brought me anything. Modern men didn't seem to believe in showering dates with gifts of flowers or chocolates. In the olden days, a boy wouldn't dream of turning up to take you out without bringing a small gift of some sort, but I'd quickly realised that wasn't the way it was now. Perhaps Andrew was more old-school, more of a gentleman? Things were looking up.

"A present?" I was so delighted by this turn of events and Andrew looked chuffed at my reaction. "Really, there was no need. That's so thoughtful of you," I said as I reached into the paper bag and pulled out … a pair of tights. I was confused. "You've bought me a pair of tights?" I said, even though I was holding the very evidence of this fact in my hands. "You shouldn't have…?" I said with real uncertainty.

Andrew's face fell slightly as he asked, "Are they not the right size?"

I looked at the tights and then back at Andrew. The size wasn't really my issue. "You've bought me a pair of tights," I repeated, not knowing what else to say.

"Is it the colour?" Andrew was looking more distressed now, as though he couldn't work out why I wasn't leaping for joy. "So many women have stopped wearing American Tan, I know, but they're my favourite."

At the risk of turning into a performing parrot I repeated, "American Tan are *your* favourite?"

Andrew leaned forward then, as if to add emphasis to his words. "It's all leggings nowadays, isn't?" he said in a voice dripping with disdain. "Or those rubbish black opaque hold-ups with the ugly elastic tops. What you need though, you see – what you get with a product like this – is a proper gusset."

The final word of his speech hit me in the face like a slap of wet fish.

"Do you know you just said the word 'gusset' out loud?" I asked, hoping no one nearby could overhear this conversation, but my reprimand had the opposite effect to what I'd intended.

Andrew's eyes practically rolled back in his head and he licked his lips as he answered breathlessly, "Does it turn you on if I say the word 'gusset'?"

"NO!" I had forgotten to care who could overhear us now as the realisation dawned on me that the word "gusset" was clearly turning *him* on! Ewwwwwwww.

Andrew was pretty much drooling by this point as I sat before him still holding the offending packet of American Tan tights in my hand.

"So if we start our next date with you wearing the tights," he said with a distinctly lewd expression, "then I can wear them later on."

I jumped up from that table quicker than a scalded cat and threw the damn packet of tights at Andrew for good measure. There would be no second date with that pantyhose pervert!

Chapter Five

"I mean, I'm not a prude, but you have to have a pretty strong stomach for this online dating lark!" I bit into my cheese and pickle sandwich after updating Jools with my latest "hilarious" escapade.

Jools was supposed to be helping a customer choose a suitable outfit for her upcoming wedding in the tropical Palm House at Sefton Park, but both of them had ceased looking for a slinky gown suitable for a steamy greenhouse setting and were focusing on me and my pickle ... both cheese- and relationship-related.

"I don't get it," Jools said with a shake of her head. "What's the deal with the American Tan tights?"

Lisa, the bride, joined in at that point. "Oh, there's whole websites devoted to that sort of thing," she said knowingly.

"What sort of thing?" Jools asked while I tried not to choke on my sandwich.

"Men who pose wearing women's tights ... with nothing on underneath," Lisa explained. "They take pictures of themselves wearing women's tights, you know, close-ups of their tackle all squished up inside the nylon. Most of them look like a mouldy old bag of potatoes."

Jools shrieked in disgust while I coughed up a lump of cheddar that had gone down the wrong way.

Lisa just nodded sagely. "Thank heavens I'm a lesbian," she said before giving me a cheeky wink from beneath her heavy black fringe.

Lucky Lisa, I thought, although I wondered what a lesbian had been doing on kinky websites showing perverted pictures of men in hosiery.

I stopped coughing long enough to be able to tell them, "Then there was the guy who sent me a WhatsApp picture of his ... bits." I'd never met Lisa before but it felt like we'd bonded, so in for a penny. She didn't seem at all surprised by the revelation and simply sighed as though she'd seen many such pictures in her lifetime.

"They're called dick pics," said a disembodied voice from behind a rail of rainbow-coloured dresses in the far corner of the shop.

We all turned our heads towards the new voice and a stunning Black woman with a shock of blonde hair stepped out from behind the rail. "Hi, I'm Viola," she said. "Lisa's fiancée." She was wearing a floor-length satin dress in a shimmering emerald green.

"Oh, Vee," Lisa said on a gasp, "you look incredible."

She did indeed and we all enthusiastically agreed before the conversation reverted back to the matter in hand, or rather the matter in some weirdo's wanking hand. Yuck.

"I mean, what reaction are they expecting me to have?" I

carried on, putting my half-eaten sandwich to one side. "Is it meant to send me weak at the knees? Make me overcome with lust? Hah! I mean, I wouldn't mind, but as it popped up halfway through me breakfast, so to speak, it's a wonder the rest of me breakfast didn't come back up to join it."

According to Viola, "dick pics" are a common form of communication between the young people nowadays. A sort of "try before you buy" philosophy, I suppose, where you get to see the goods before wasting any time on actually getting to know someone.

"And they say romance is dead," Jools deadpanned as she carried on flicking through the rails looking for an outfit for Lisa that would match the exquisite perfection of Viola's emerald dress.

I hoped Jools wouldn't think our conversation was bad for business. It had been my half day at work so I'd decided to drop in unannounced after picking up my lunch from Greggs instead of heading straight home.

I love it inside Bold Brides. The deep cream carpet and the twinkling glass chandeliers make it feel both opulent and cosy. Unlike most bridal boutiques, everything isn't wall-to-wall white. Jools has one section of white and cream dresses and suits, as they are hugely popular, but then another rail is full of colour, from pastel pink through to electric blue and everything in between. Enormous mirrors in gilded frames are on walls decorated with metallic mint-green wallpaper patterned with shimmering hummingbirds. I was sitting on one of two high-backed gold thrones towards the front of the shop, suddenly aware that my cheese and pickle sandwich and pornographic conversation were probably not creating the sort of ambiance Jools would like for her loved-up customers.

I started to gather up my stuff and pick up my half-drunk take-away coffee cup but Jools whirled around and glared at me, barking, "And where do you think you're going?"

"You're obviously busy, and you don't need me cluttering up the place, banging on about my own personal dirty mac brigade," I hissed out of the side of my mouth. A bit late to be mindful of all that, I know, but better late than never… That should be my life motto!

But Jools hissed right back at me and told me I wasn't going anywhere and to sit back down. She removed my cold cardboard coffee cup from my hand and dropped it into the bin behind the counter, saying we both needed a decent cup of tea and then we were going to "sort this all out".

I wasn't sure what that meant but the cuppa sounded good so I settled back onto the golden throne.

Lisa and Viola disappeared behind the far rail of clothes then, still hunting for the dream outfit for their tropical theme nuptials.

I felt like I was about to receive a telling off from Jools, which would be fair enough after my impromptu foul-mouthed lunchbreak on her premises, but that's not what was getting Jools's goat.

"We've gone about this all wrong," she said as she leant on the shop counter nursing her mug of tea, after handing me mine.

I was about to heartily agree but then Jools said she

thought we'd been so focused on trying to find the ideal man that we hadn't put enough effort into describing *me* properly.

"I don't think that's the problem," I began to say, but Jools interrupted to insist that if we didn't pitch "Penny4" correctly then we were bound to attract the wrong sort of men. It was a thought, I supposed, but I wasn't sure which part of my profile was to blame for the procession of feeble candidates for my heart. I was also not at all sure that I even wanted to continue the search; it all seemed a bit pointless.

On hearing this Jools instantly changed tack. "Don't look at it like that," she said. "You are funny, clever, a good cook, a great dancer... There's some lovely man out there who is looking for someone just like you. Do you really want that kind, sensitive man – who is also red hot in the sack, by the way – to live his life alone because you gave up too early?"

I couldn't help but ask why, if she knew of such a man, she didn't just call him up there and then and have done with it? Why put me through all the online dating humiliation?

She ignored me.

"You need to show the real Bev, let them see what you're passionate about. That's the way to find your soulmate, I'm sure of it," she said.

She told me I needed to include my love of music and The Beatles in my profile, to give the guys a real insight into what made me tick, but I wasn't sure how to feel about that. I've loved The Beatles with all my heart from when I was a child – they are a huge part of my life and I wasn't sure any man would ever understand and accept that. Geoff certainly struggled with it. He'd get proper jealous if Paul ever came on the TV, and go off into the kitchen, banging pots and pans around so that I'd struggle to hear what Paul was singing or saying. He also never took any interest in my memorabilia collection, calling it a load of old rubbish. He didn't intend to be mean, I'm sure – Geoff wasn't like that – but I didn't ever feel comfortable leaving pictures and records lying around like I do now. He certainly wouldn't have put up with living in Paul McCartney's old house, that's for sure. Would any man?

Jools was still talking, explaining that I might find a fellow Beatles fan, someone who loved them as much as me and might come with me to gigs by tribute bands or on Beatles-themed weekends. I *did* like the sound of that.

Jools seemed to sense my opposition weakening and said, "There are loads of guys who are equally as mad on The Beatles as you. Just imagine if you found one?"

Lisa and Viola emerged from the changing rooms just then. Lisa was wearing a gorgeous silvery metallic trouser suit with a lacy silk camisole, the exact same shade of green as Viola's emerald dress, peeping from underneath the tight-fitting jacket. They looked so beautiful together. They had also overheard the last part of our conversation.

"Ooh, just imagine," said Lisa, not realising the irony of that remark in itself, "you could have a Beatles-themed wedding! Jools could organise it, couldn't you, Jools?"

Jools agreed enthusiastically but I wasn't clear what a Beatles-themed wedding would involve… Holding the ceremony on a yellow submarine? Getting married in the style of a Beatle perhaps? Macca got hitched in a London register office with both Linda and Nancy, his first wife and his third, but hired a remote Irish castle for his wedding to Heather Mills. That would be amazing, but then look how that turned out! John and Yoko got married in matching white outfits – very cool and very Sixties – and followed that with a bed-in in a hotel in Amsterdam, but I couldn't really see anything like that being on the cards for me.

Jools was already in professional wedding planner mode. "You know Liverpool does have its very own Beatles-themed hotel called 'The Hard Day's Night'? That would be a great venue for the reception."

I pointed out she was getting rather ahead of herself.

"Fair enough," she said, "but just think, what if on your very next date the guy looks like Paul McCartney, has the sensitivity of George Harrison, the humour of Ringo Starr and the wit of John Lennon?"

She looked so pleased with herself I didn't have the heart to mention how unlikely a scenario that really was. It had made me think though. Maybe I had been too hung up on what I wanted to avoid and I'd forgotten to emphasise who I was and what I was looking for.

Jools was certainly right about one thing. Ultimately, I needed to find a man who shared my outlook on life, my interests and my passions. I agreed to go home and tweak my profile – not a euphemism – and see if that yielded better results. What could possibly go wrong?

Chapter Six

Julia's advice rattled around in my brain for days after our lunchtime chat. I concluded that she was right, I did need somebody ... but not just anybody. I might never have needed anyone before but now it was time to change my mind ... and open up the door.

So now I was clear that if I wanted to succeed in finding a soulmate, I had to help myself. I adjusted my online profile accordingly – this time making sure I included my love for The Beatles – and then scoured the responses for signs that any prospective date shared my passion for music.

It took a little while to find anyone I wanted to set up a date with. Several times bitten by my bad date experiences, I was shy of making yet another mistake.

Luckily I was busy at work, so that kept me occupied and stopped me obsessing over the dating app during the day. There had been a lot of interest in Mrs Malkin's house, so I was juggling offers from several potential buyers while overseeing the emptying of the property by a local house-clearance firm that we had used many times before.

As usual, I also had to handle the wide-ranging variety of requests for help from the boys, which never failed to come in thick and fast. Once kids become teenagers and young adults you tend to take on the role of Executive P.A. as opposed to "Mam". They may not be helpless in the same ways as when they were little, but that doesn't make them any less demanding … or is that just my lot? From helping to find suitable gifts for girlfriends, to booking dentist and optician appointments, to taking their car for an MOT because they are "too busy" at work, through to dealing with lost parcels, health emergencies, unpaid bills and general life admin, I always think I could become a highly effective personal assistant to an international business tycoon with the skills I've acquired over the years. Not sure how I'd write it all up on my CV though.

But in the evenings, I would find myself returning again and again to the Lonely Hearts Club dating website and scrolling through the profiles to see if anyone had made the grade and matched my expectations. I didn't hold out much hope, in all honesty, but the haunting strains of "Eleanor Rigby" and lyrics about lonely people kept playing on repeat in my head, so I kept on looking.

Late one night, I flicked off the TV in sheer frustration at the number of late-night dating shows. There seemed to be a different one on every single channel. Some of the programmes showed couples getting together over dinner in a restaurant, fair enough, but others had them meeting each other through an improvised interpretive dance. Huh?

One show even had people standing in front of each other stark naked so they could judge each other's naughty bits before they'd even said hello. I Kid. You. Not! Is that what the future of dating and relationships has in store for all of us sad singletons? Standing in the nuddy while a prospective partner assesses your lady garden to see if they like the way you've trimmed your bush? Sod that!

Online dating seemed completely sane and rational compared to all that so I pulled out my laptop and looked to see if there had been any new matches for "Penny4". And that was when I first saw Scott.

His picture made him look both friendly and fanciable, he liked to cook, travel and go to music gigs – this was looking good! – and then there it was, the line that made all the difference in the world. He'd ended his profile description with the line – "there's only one thing I believe in this life … *All You Need Is Love*". Bingo!

———

Just a couple of days later I found myself hiding around the corner from The Quarter, an Italian coffee shop and bistro in the Georgian Quarter. I was already late but my feet wouldn't seem to walk the few extra steps to get me to the entrance. I looked across the square towards the large sandy-coloured building there, The Liverpool Institute for Performing Arts, a sort of "fame school" for singers, actors, musicians and technical arts students. I could hear strains of music drifting from one of the open upstairs windows, meaning a rehearsal of some sort was taking place.

I wondered for just a moment if it might even be a masterclass being held by Sir Paul McCartney himself. He used to go to school in that very building before it was LIPA, when it was just called The Liverpool Institute, and George Harrison was a fellow pupil. Paul is lead patron and founder of the arts college and I knew very well he attends each and every graduation and occasionally teaches masterclasses, but I thought it was highly unlikely he would be in there at that point, sharing his songwriting tips with a lucky group of music students. I do live in hope of bumping into him one day, and as I was standing on Hope Street there couldn't be a more likely location.

Behind me was the Philharmonic Pub, and I knew Paul popped in there sometimes when he was in the area. I gave myself a little shake and asked myself: Was I really going to spend the rest of my life hanging around the haunts of my hero in the hopes he might one day show up? Wouldn't it be better to force my legs to move so that I could meet the *real* man who was actually waiting for me right at that moment?

I found my knees had turned to jelly as I walked around the corner and past the windows of the café. I could see it was busy inside, as always, but I thought I spotted a smartly dressed man with silvery blond hair and a healthy-looking tan, as though he'd just flown back from a foreign holiday, sitting at a table on his own. He was reading the menu so didn't see me looking in, trying to find a last-minute reason not to carry on to the doorway and go inside.

By the time I made it to his table I'd worked myself up into quite a tiswas. "I'm so sorry I'm late," I said before he even had a chance to register my arrival. "I bet you thought I wasn't comin'; it's a wonder you waited. I hate being kept waitin'. I'm never late, normally, but it's just been one of those mornin's, you know – toast in the washing machine, marmalade in me knicker drawer…"

I was talking ten to the dozen while trying to unwind my floaty scarf from around my neck. Consequently, I was making absolutely no sense and almost strangled myself in the process.

Scott simply smiled warmly at me and said, "No harm done and you're here now."

I finally released myself from the grip of my scarf and tried to slip off my denim jacket so I could put it on the back of my chair. I was so hot and bothered I couldn't get the damn thing off fast enough, but one arm got completely stuck in a sleeve and so I carried on blabbering while I tried to tug it free. "I expect you were thinkin' all sorts. That I'd had second thoughts, changed me mind, was even checkin' you out through the window."

What was wrong with that jacket? And why couldn't I keep my embarrassing confessions to myself?

Scott was doing an impressive job of pretending not to notice I was in utter meltdown. He looked towards the window where I had been standing just moments before and then back at me as I finally sat and said, "I would say checking me out before you came in would be a very sensible thing to do in this day and age."

Oh no! He'd seen me! I could tell from the amused expression on his face. I'd blown this date even before it started.

"Oh, look, sorry," I said. "Don't worry if you just want to leave. It's perfectly fine and I completely understand."

For the first time a frown furrowed his brow as he looked at me. "I'm not sure I do," he said.

"Huh?"

Scott sat back in his chair and looked at me for a long moment with his clear blue eyes. "Do you really want me to leave?" he asked in a reasonable voice. "Or would it make more sense if we actually had a drink together first? That was the plan and we are both here now after all…"

He made a very reasonable point in a very reasonable way. I could hardly be completely unreasonable and argue with that.

———————————

I probably should have avoided caffeine given the jumpy state I was in before the date had even started, but somehow being with Scott made me feel calmer and more confident than I had done in a very long time. He was so nice and friendly, and, well, after my recent dating disasters, most importantly … normal!

As we had one coffee, quickly followed by another, I decided he was pretty easy on the eye, too! Someone you would call a "silver fox". His hair was a great shade of gunmetal grey that complemented his tanned skin really well. Bright blue eyes with a distinct twinkle and a dimple in his chin put me in mind of a young Kirk Douglas. Forgive me for looking so closely but I really could not find a visible flaw; even his eyebrows and nostrils were evenly spaced, which meant he wasn't the slightest bit sinister or snuffly. He was good company and also a great listener.

I only realised quite how good a listener he was when he began ticking off on his fingers all the things he already knew about me from just this one conversation … that I was a mum of three, a part-time estate agent, the youngest of two sisters, born in Liverpool and had lived here all my life, but would love to own a holiday home in Tuscany.

"But above all that, the most important thing to know about you, Beverley" – I held my breath as he hesitated. What was he going to say? He smiled and nodded as he concluded – "is that you are a massive Beatles fan." He grinned at me then as he added, "However, there is one thing that marks you out as a highly unusual Liverpudlian."

"There is?"

"Oh yes" – he had a mock serious expression on his face now – "amazingly you do *not* claim to have gone to school with one of the Fab Four or say you ever saw them play live at The Cavern."

Ahhh he was teasing me, I got it. "Ha, you mean coz every other bugger from Liverpool claims a personal connection to The Beatles?" I said, laughing. He was right; it's like a disease in this city. Of course, I did have my own little links to the band, but I didn't want him to think I was some sort of nutter so I kept those to myself, for now. Anyway, I was more worried about how much I'd rattled on. I didn't want to bore the poor man to death. "Tell me something about you now?" I asked.

He put his head on one side while he considered this for

a moment. "Me? Umm, well, I actually used to play in a band myself when I was younger."

"You did?" I almost jumped out of my seat. "Oh wow, really? Would I have heard of you? Did you have any hits?"

Scott shook his head but was still smiling, "Oh we never troubled the charts. We did have quite a few fans though, for a time – a loyal little gang that would follow us all over the club circuit. We were part of that whole 'New Romantic' scene, hair so high we were six-foot-four in our pixie boots."

I was hanging on his every word by this point. I could just picture it.

"It looked like we were gonna break through at one point" – a wistful look passed over Scott's face – "but showbiz is a tough world. I'm just an *old romantic* now, I suppose."

I tried not to swoon too obviously. "Ahh but that's amazing. What did you say you were called?"

"I didn't," he answered with the amused look of someone who knew very well I was trying to catch him out.

"Oh, go on," I wheedled. "I might have heard of you."

He waited just a beat but then answered, "Scott Smith and the Silhouettes."

As soon as he said it I knew it sounded familiar and asked if there was any footage of them on YouTube. I was dying to see Scott strutting his stuff on stage; how cool would that be?

"Afraid not," he said with a slight grimace. "We were well before those days. Feel free to Google away but there's nothing to see, thank goodness… I'm not sure the purple eye-shadow was ever a good idea."

We both burst out laughing then at the memories of outlandish Eighties fashions and the sorts of highly styled pop videos that were all the rage back then. I wondered if Scott's band wore androgynous clothing like most pop stars at that time, or sharp suits like Ultravox, or perhaps he dressed as a dandy highwayman like Adam Ant? The images from the era were so easy to recall – bright neon colours, flashing light effects, crazy camera angles, everyone's hair gelled into elaborate and ludicrous shapes.

We swapped our musical memories of those days for a good while. I was just having the best time.

"Well," said Scott when our conversation paused for a moment, "I think we have identified something we definitely do have in common."

"Oh, really? Can you play 'Mull of Kintyre' on the accordion, too?"

I have been told that I have an odd sense of humour sometimes and Scott clearly didn't get why I had veered off onto such an unexpected tangent. I think it happens when I'm nervous or over-excited. I tried to cover it up by joking how that particular skill of mine clearly hadn't been mentioned yet, and anyway, I can only actually perform it if I'm a bit squiffy.

He seemed somewhat reassured by that explanation and gamely carried on. "Ahh yes, well, what I was going to say was … I've always loved The Beatles, too."

Honestly this was the Best. First date. Ever!

He reached across the table then and his strong, tanned hand held mine. "So, do you think we should let The Beatles determine our fate and 'Let It Be'?"

It was the perfect way to ask for a second date but my jitters were still there, just below the surface, so I couldn't help but answer with another little joke. "Mmmm, maybe," I said. "But The Beatles also said, 'I Am The Walrus' while livin' in a 'Yellow Submarine', so it's probably best not to rush into anythin'."

Scott looked at me and smiled warmly. This time he seemed to get the joke completely. He was a fast learner for sure, and he obviously wasn't going to be easily scared off, and so we both stood to leave, each of us certain we would be seeing each other again very soon. That much was understood.

As he helped me on with my denim jacket, slipping it up my arms and around my shoulders with complete ease, I was already longing to know how it would feel to be taken into his arms and held tight. I just knew in my heart it would feel so right.

Chapter Seven

We didn't rush things but it was amazing how Scott "got" me right from the start. My sense of humour, the fact I constantly talk nineteen to the dozen, my love for The Beatles … he took it all in his stride. He also told me he loved the way I made him laugh. Being with someone so in tune with me and the things I cared about was intoxicating. I've never been much of a drinker but in those very early days I felt I was drunk on Scott.

After our first meeting at The Quarter we arranged to meet there again for lunch a few days later. Following that, we had our first evening date with dinner at Beppi's Bistro. We were taking our time getting to know each other, seeing each other every few days, maybe one or two times in a fortnight. Scott's work involved a lot of travelling, which meant he was often out of town, but we were always texting and FaceTiming each other in between our dates.

On our first date Scott told me he was a "property

manager", which didn't sound all that interesting, but it turned out he worked for an events company, managing a huge portfolio of concert halls and gig venues all over the UK. He explained that his job was to oversee repairs and refurbishments at all the various buildings owned by the company, but I was fascinated to find out he practically worked in showbiz! After all, he was working to create the perfect environment for performers to entertain their audiences, and he even admitted that he sometimes bumped into famous people backstage. Amazing! I'd never really given much thought to the buildings you went to see shows and concerts and the like at before, but now I realized how hugely important all that area of the business was. From overseeing old dressing-room fit-outs to designing new front-of-house foyers or theatre marquees, Scott could be up and down the country several times a week. He seemed to like the fact that I was interested in his work and always let me know if something interesting happened when he was away, like coming across a band doing a sound check, or an actor doing weird vocal warm-ups in his dressing room. Once, he even caught Kenneth Branagh backstage doing a complicated yoga pose with Greta Scacchi!

I understood how busy he was when he was away, and then, when we did meet up, Scott always managed to make it feel so special.

He was great at suggesting fun things for us to do, or places to visit. One afternoon we walked the length of Crosby seafront, awed by the one hundred cast-iron figures all along the beach gazing out to sea. It was a weekday afternoon and apart from a couple of dog walkers we had the breezy beach to ourselves. I'd brought my two younger boys, Richie and Harry, here a few years ago when they were driving me mad cooped up inside on a gloriously sunny day at half-term, but being here again with Scott was very different. Walking from statue to statue and really taking in the spectacle of the way some had the waves lapping around their feet, while others were submerged up to their knees, made me think about what it's like to feel alone in the world and how quickly time ticks by. It also made me feel so grateful to have someone to share these thoughts and feelings with, especially when Scott took off his scarf and wrapped it around one of the statues and did a silly voice pretending the figure was thanking him as it was "brass monkeys weather". It was very funny. Maybe you had to be there.

On another afternoon we went to the pictures, which felt naughty in itself, like we were playing hooky from school. We went to see a showing of the classic film *Citizen Kane* and Scott couldn't believe I'd never seen it. We didn't go to one of the big, soulless multiplexes in town where I sometimes drop Harry off, we went to a proper old-fashioned cinema in Woolton called The Picture House. Scott said it was the oldest working cinema in Liverpool and that was easy to believe with its plush, red velvet tip-up seats in the quaint auditorium. They also stopped the film halfway through for a proper interval so you could get an ice-cream, which definitely made me feel like I had stepped back in time. It was only as we were making our way out and talking about picking up a chippy tea to complete our vintage experience that I spotted a framed article on the wall in the foyer. It said the Woolton Picture House had been used as a location in the movie *Nowhere Boy*, made about John Lennon's life. We were really excited to discover that. Scott said he'd had no idea when he'd booked our tickets, and the coincidence really made the day extra exciting.

One of our most bonkers dates was the night Scott took me to Bongo's Bingo at a nightclub called Camp and Furnace in the city. I'd heard people talk about Bongo's Bingo, but I'd never really understood what they were going on about. I thought bingo was for old ladies and clubbing was for bright young things. As I fell into neither category, I was confused by the whole idea, to be honest. It turned out that Bongo's Bingo is a regular event that attracts enthusiasts of all ages, but it's not all about multi-coloured dabbers and "two fat ladies, clickety-click". It's bingo crossed with a rave, if you can imagine such a thing. The bingo cards look familiar and the game is played properly, with everyone trying to match a line, get a spot prize or shout "BINGO'"when they get a full house. But there are also impromptu games, lots of silliness, and thumping music to get everyone whipped up and excited. At one point we all had to jump on the benches along the length of the trestle tables we were sitting at and join in with the Macarena. Someone on the next table won a joke prize of a box of Coco Pops and decided to spray the contents into the air like they were a racing driver on the winner's podium exploding a bottle of fizz over the crowd. I would never have gone along to something like that if it hadn't been for Scott, but I was so glad I did; it was a right laugh.

Over those first few weeks, as Scott and I chatted about anything and everything, I tried to find ways to casually drop into the conversation certain things I thought he should probably know about me. He didn't seem the sort to scare easily but I wanted to dial down the crazy after my ridiculous panic attack on our first date when I hadn't been able to take my own scarf and jacket off without almost doing myself a mischief.

When I eventually did casually mention the fact that I lived in a house once owned by the McCartney family, I was relieved to find Scott didn't look either appalled or consumed with jealousy. He was genuinely interested and said not only was it fascinating, but also probably a very good investment, and complimented me on being such a clever businesswoman. That was a first.

For reasons that never became clear, there was a life-size cardboard cut-out of Phillip Schofield on the stage at Bongo's Bingo. That prompted me to also tell Scott about my four full-size figures of The Beatles. He took my ownership of a two-dimensional set of the Fab Four in his stride, too, once I'd made it clear that I didn't keep them all lined up at the end of my bed!

However, I never managed to get round to admitting to the fact I had a yellow submarine dressing-up costume in a box up on top of my wardrobe. Well, a woman is allowed to retain a certain air of mystery after all, and I've only ever worn it once. I got it for a fancy-dress party thrown by Julia for her husband Mickey's birthday. Typical Jools, the party had a fun musical theme, and she got Mickey a white Elvis Presley jumpsuit to wear that I'm not sure he's ever forgiven her for. She looked great in comparison, with a cropped denim jacket over a tight black leather dress and a spiky, blonde Tina Turner wig. Mickey said she looked more like Rod Stewart, but I think he was just sore because the jumpsuit showed off his little pot belly. At least he wasn't the most ridiculously dressed person there with me blundering about with a huge yellow foam submarine suspended from straps over my shoulders, my arms sticking out of the red-rimmed port-holes and a big daft periscope on my head! And I wondered why I was single for so long?

That wasn't the situation I found myself in now though, thanks to Scott. We had really clicked. In fact, there was so much clicking it was like everything we did had a backing track of castanets.

It was a revelation to be with a man who seemed to understand me and accept me for who I really was. No, not just accept, who actually seemed to be *impressed* by me. Can you imagine? Scott was so supportive of my decision to buy the McCartney house and my love of all things Beatles. It was the first time I'd ever been with anyone who saw my admiration for the band as a positive personality trait, something that made me a bit more interesting, rather than a hobby I should have grown out of years ago. I had always yearned for someone to understand that side of me and not feel threatened by it. My love for John, Paul, George and Ringo seemed to alarm every other Tom, Dick and Harry … but not Scott. He was a mature man, secure in his own worth and attractiveness, and therefore he not only accepted but also agreed with my strong belief that The Beatles were the best band *ever*, and their music was an important gift to the world. As we shared our mutual love and respect for the band, I could feel those emotions growing between us, too.

As we became more involved, he gradually divulged more details about his own past loves and losses. Everyone has a past, don't they? I don't believe in being jealous over the women that went before. I know a lot of people can't handle the thought of their partner ever loving someone else, but I find that a ridiculous notion. How can you be envious of something or someone that happened to your partner before you even met them? Even if you did feel the odd twinge of jealousy, I just don't believe it's fair to have a bad attitude about it with your partner. It's not their fault, after all. I expect Scott was waiting to see how I dealt with things like that before he opened up fully about his own background.

It was while we were walking along the windswept beach at Crosby that he started to tell me about his wife and how she had died. He didn't give too many details at first, and I could understand that completely. I'd lost Geoff ten years earlier but some days it was still too difficult to talk about, and it had been even less time for Scott to get over losing Meg. I could tell by the way he spoke about her that he had loved her very much. No wonder he had been so sensitive and empathetic when I spoke about my own loss; he really did understand it all.

I remember gently slipping my hand into his as we

looked out at the white foam cresting here and there on waves the colour of grey granite, small eruptions breaking through the vast expanse of Irish Sea before us. We stood in companionable silence and I thought how our view of the sea in that moment was very much like my own experience of grief; at times so relentless and overwhelming, but then sometimes tiny waves of hope and happiness could surface. As Scott squeezed my fingers, and the wind whipped my hair across my face and made our eyes water, I imagined he was feeling exactly the same – that now we had found each other we should never let go.

Scott was also a proper old-fashioned gentleman. I don't mean he wore a monocle and had his newspaper ironed by a butler every morning, but he wasn't some sort of caveman only interested in his carnal needs. In fact – well, to be completely honest – taking it slowly and showing me some respect was all very nice, but I was beginning to wonder if he was *ever* gonna make a move? You know … *sexually*!

The dating rules are all different now, aren't they? What you should say, what you should do… Decent blokes are too scared to pat a woman on the knee in case they're accused of assault and the *indecent* ones want to share your underwear! It's a bloody minefield.

But then I met Scott Smith. Lovely Scott. Nice, polite, well-mannered, thoughtful… Sod that though! I mean, holding hands walking along the beach and sneaking kisses in the cinema is all very well and good, but what I wanted to know was, when would we get to the part when he ripped me clothes off?

I hadn't really given much thought to the mechanics of

that side of things before. I suppose I just presumed it would all just "happen". After we'd been dating for a little while though, I was beginning to wonder if I was doing something wrong. Not to say I wasn't terrified by the whole idea of sex. Taking my clothes off and being naked with a man, well … it's not something to be done lightly, not by a woman of my generation. Maybe he was nervous, too? Do men get nervous about that sort of thing? I couldn't imagine any of the men on my earlier dates being so backward in coming forward, so at first I was glad Scott wasn't rushing me, but as time went on, well … something had to give.

As I always say to my boys, *"Life is what you make of it"*, and in my particular case that included my sex life!

After giving it some thought, I decided I would take matters into my own hands and give him a bit of a nudge. He was probably waiting for some sort of overt sign from me that I was ready for all that sort of thing.

I finally decided that what I needed to do was pretty simple. I would invite him to mine for a nice home-cooked meal, a bit of music, some wine… Well, in my case, I might need quite a lot of wine – it had been a while. So, I had my plan. But then, as I so often do, I started to overthink the whole scenario. You can hardly blame me; seduction hadn't exactly been part of my repertoire for the past decade or more.

You'll laugh when I tell you the thing that was worrying me the most at this stage. What was I going to wear? I mean, what the bleedin' hell do you wear when you are hoping for an evening of mama's home cookin' followed by a bit of how's-your-father? It's not like I was exactly planning to follow my lasagne with a dance of the seven veils, but it did all need very careful consideration.

You know, I'll wager you are exactly the same as me. Do you have a wardrobe bursting full of clothes but never the right outfit for the right occasion? I even have to use suitcases to help rotate my summer and winter clothes. But I will admit right now – and I know I'm not alone so I'm not even embarrassed to say it – I did not have a single, solitary thing to wear!

What I needed was something flattering yet comfortable. Something I could get out of without having to be Harry Houdini, and something that showed a bit of personality but didn't make me look like Su Pollard.

I bought an armful of magazines on the way home from work one day and flicked through them all, hoping for inspiration. Unfortunately, that backfired completely and the only thing that achieved was an overwhelming sense of desperation as I stared at picture after picture of impossibly glamorous women in outfits that appeared impossible to relax or move in.

I tell you what I quickly realised I did *not* need … a bloody jumpsuit! An item of clothing they use in Guantanamo Bay. An all-in-one piece that often fastens just out of reach, right at the back, and so you have to wriggle and jiggle all the way out of it whenever you need the loo. Even Elvis barely got away with the whole jumpsuit malarkey and the very last thing I thought Scott needed to be confronted with was a female Elvis impersonator badly in need of the toilet.

If I hadn't been so in lust with Scott at this point I could easily have talked myself out of the whole thing.

Instead, I did the only thing a woman can do when faced with the need to start afresh and give herself a chance to show the world what they've been missing. I went shopping.

Chapter Eight

I walked in and out of a dozen shops and a couple of department stores and eventually ended up in a small boutique in town that I didn't remember ever noticing before.

Why is it that when you have money to spend burning a hole in your pocket it's virtually impossible to find anything that you actually want to buy? Forget gravity and the theory of relativity, surely that is the most universal law of physics?

I am also very easily intimidated by snotty shop assistants. I wouldn't even dream of going inside some of the more high-end designer places. The way they look you up and down as you flick through the rails, you might as well have your current bank balance tattooed on your forehead.

In fact, I'd almost talked myself out of that shopping trip before it began. The night before, I'd decided, against all previous experience to the contrary, that there simply *must* be some sort of suitable outfit in my extensive wardrobe.

I pulled out dresses, jeans, floaty tops, tight-fitting tops, cropped trousers, wide-legged trousers and an assortment of skirts in a variety of lengths, and lamented that none of those things seemed to go together in any acceptable way. Just as I was at risk of drowning in a sea of multi-coloured fabric, Julia arrived.

She'd responded to a forlorn selfie I had sent her. A picture of me pulling an anguished face amidst my clothing mountain, which had now spilled from the bed and was creeping into all four corners of my bedroom as I held up each garment then flung it away in frustration.

"Having a clear out? Good idea." Julia breezed in and plonked herself right on top of a bright red blazer. I repeat … a *red blazer*. Whatever had I been thinking?

"I don't have a style, Jools," I wailed. "Why don't I have a *'capsule wardrobe of easy to wear basics'*, and what even is my *'signature look'*?" I'd let those magazines get to me and the result appeared to be that I had now lost even the most basic ability to dress myself.

Julia snorted in a way that made me think she was not about to be very sympathetic to my plight. Lifting her right buttock, she pulled out the red jacket she was sitting on and waved it towards me. "I never knew you had a job at Butlins?"

"Stop it." I groaned. "Can't you see I need help?"

Julia tried to calm me by arguing that I had already been on many dates with Scott so there was no reason to suddenly panic and overhaul my "look".

But I argued that my style of dressing was not doing anything to encourage Scott to rip my clothes OFF! Did he not find me sexually attractive enough? Was my lack of dress style leading him to believe I would not be good in bed? Did he, oh God … did he see me as "mumsy"?

"I think you are wildly over-thinking this," Julia said, sweeping her eyes around the room and surveying the clothing massacre that had occurred in my desperate attempt to find an outfit suitable for seducing Scott Smith.

But Jools is nothing if not a good mate, and so she set to work trying her best to help me pull together the ideal combination of clothes to put on when the ultimate goal was to be taking them *off* as quickly as possible.

We tried a wrap dress, thinking it would be easy to undo, but the only underwear that could decently be worn underneath was the ugly, practical sort. Anything more attractive and pretty would make me look lumpy and that would not be a good start, so that landed on the clothing mountain. I had a couple of nice sheer tops that were flattering to the figure but they only really worked with skinny jeans and the last thing I wanted to reveal were tell-tale ridge marks on my tummy and thighs once the jeans were removed. Anything that made me feel sexy presented some sort of barrier to easy removal, whereas anything that came off with ease was far too frumpy to be considered.

"You've got no choice, Bev," Julia finally conceded, "you're gonna have to go shopping."

She also made the point that this whole outfit conundrum was my way of sticking my head in the sand and putting off thinking about what I was ultimately trying to achieve. My focus was on what to wear at the start of the evening, instead of what sort of position I might find myself in at the end of it! Once again, Jools was totally right but I hadn't got time to think about that – I had an outfit to find.

———

The music playing in the high-street boutique I eventually found myself in was poppy but not too loud or grungy. I'm pretty sure places that play that sort of "*doof … doof … doof*" music do it to make sure shoppers as old as me know it isn't a shop for us and so turn back at the threshold.

The lighting in the store was nice; not too bright, not too dark. What is it with that one uber trendy clothing shop that's so gloomy inside you need a torch to see your way around? How are you meant to find the right size or work out what colour anything is? They ought to hand out night vision goggles to anyone wanting to shop in there.

I rifled through the rails, picking up items at random. I still wasn't at all sure what I was looking for. I grabbed a couple of armfuls and headed towards the girl standing near the changing rooms to ask if I could try them on. She was young and looked bored. She barely glanced at me, just cracked her gum as she nodded and jerked her head towards the nearby curtain.

Once inside, I was surprised to find there was no mirror. What good is a changing room without a mirror? Perhaps that's why Miss Congeniality was stationed out there, so that she could give her "expert" opinion. Heaven help me.

I was already second-thinking this whole enterprise as I

stood staring at all the clothes I'd brought in with me, not having the slightest clue where to start. I must have been standing there for a good while because suddenly the shop girl stuck her head inside the curtain.

"You okay in 'ere, love?" Clearly a local, she was Scouse through and through.

I nodded and stuttered a reply but she seemed to sense my unease. Despite her previous blank expression, she furrowed her heavy dark brows as I tried to explain that I wanted to update my look and said she knew exactly what I meant. That was encouraging, so I selected an item and began to pull it on.

The girl told me her name was Tina and to let her know if I needed anything, before withdrawing her disembodied head from my changing space. I felt quite connected to Tina now we had bonded in our little exchange through the curtain. She was experienced in this sort of thing. I should listen to her advice, use her like a personal shopper even.

"I need to find something just right, you see..." I called out to Tina as I wriggled into the first dress. "I really think it's time me and my fella moved things up a gear, if you know what I'm saying..." Now she was out of sight I felt emboldened to share perhaps a bit too much information.

Tina's voice drifted through the curtain. "Right, yeah."

The dress was on, but I was going to need Tina to tell me how it looked. That made me nervous all over again.

"You will be honest with me, won't you? You will tell me if it looks all right?"

There was a long pause but then Tina answered. "Yeah, yeah ... 'course."

She wasn't filling me with confidence now. In fact, she'd gone back to sounding bored out of her brain and I was twisting this way and that trying to see what I looked like before exposing myself to the critical eye of a girl half my age. Why wasn't there a mirror in there? It didn't make sense.

"Why isn't there a mirror inside the changing room? I've never been in a changing room without a mirror before."

No reply from Tina. Perhaps another customer had come in and she was off helping them?

"S'cuse me, Tina, are you there?"

"I'm 'ere. Where else am I gonna be?" She sounded a bit irritated now.

"Sorry, yes, yes, of course you are. It's just you didn't answer my question so, I didn't know if you were still there."

I'd started to babble and Tina was confused. "What question?"

"The question about why there isn't a mirror in here." Perhaps I was making too much of this. Tina clearly thought so.

"I did answer," she said.

"Oh right, yes, well, sorry, I just didn't hear you," I said.

"I don't know why we don't have one, so I shrugged," she added, as though this was perfectly acceptable. Was she having a laugh? Before I could figure out a way to reply, Tina asked if I had got the dress on, but I didn't want to show her now. I told her I didn't think it was "really me".

In an attempt to be helpful, I think, Tina told me the dress was "cut on the bias". It didn't help me much at all.

"What does that mean exactly?" I asked, trying to look over my shoulder to see if bias cutting made any difference to how big my bum looked in it.

But Tina's dress designing expertise seemed to have been all used up already. "I dunno," she said in a voice of resignation, "I don't think anybody knows."

I concluded that this dress was simply biased against me, and took it off. It was hopeless.

Tina thrust a hand through the curtain, proffering a glittery gold creation that was quite short.

"Oh, I think that's a bit over the top," I said.

Tina just thrust the dress further towards me until I had no choice but take it from her hand as her voice came at me loud and clear from the other side of the curtain. "Trust me, men LOVE that sorta thing."

I supposed I should listen to her, I thought, as she was bound to know far more about this sort of thing than I did. As if to underline the point, a pair of gold platform high heels were then also thrust through the curtain. "Put these shoes on as well; get the whole look," she said with a certainty that I couldn't argue with. She might be right. If I was trying to send a sexy signal, maybe I couldn't mess about being too subtle. Men responded to visual stimulus after all, didn't they?

The dress fitted, hallelujah, and the glitzy fabric pulled me in and made me feel a bit Jessica Rabbit. Who'd have thought it? I would never have selected this for myself; maybe this personal shopping experience would work for me after all. I screwed up the courage to totter out for a full appraisal from Tina.

"Wow!"

Yes, that was exactly the reaction I had been hoping for. I managed a nervous smile as I asked, "Really?"

Tina was emphatic as she looked me over, "It's very 'Real Housewives'," she said.

I took a chance. "Of Beverley Hills?" I asked hopefully.

"I was thinking more Cheshire," she said, not realising for a second how much that had crushed me. Oblivious to my new distress, she got as animated as I'd seen her. "You know, the one who's got the fat baldy 'usband? She came in 'ere the other week."

I'd like to say I had absolutely no idea what she was on about, but unfortunately I did. I could instantly picture the dopey meal-ticket husband and his hideous wife who spent all of her time on the TV reality show spending ridiculous amounts of his money and screeching abuse at her so-called friends. That was NOT the look I was after. Not at all. I tried to let Tina down more gently than she had me. "Hmm, yeah, good for her … but on balance I'm thinking … no."

Tina had the bit between her teeth now and was not about to give up on me.

"'Ere, try this one," she said, grabbing a dress with black and red panels and hanging it on the hook inside my cubicle.

It looked a lot more suitable than the glittery gold monstrosity. A bit unusual in design but at least it was knee-length. I'd come in here hoping to find a new look so the least I could do was give it a go, I thought, but unfortunately the dress had other ideas. As I struggled my way into it the dress fought me all the way. As I tried to pull it up over my hips, it snapped back and then clung to me, clamping my legs together. By the time I had hoisted it as far as my boobs I was panting for breath and had a slick of sweat running down my back. Determined not to be defeated by a frock, I made a huge effort and got both arms into the arm holes. The dress snapped itself around me like a boa constrictor.

"It feels really weird," I gasped, "It's made of really unusual material."

Tina sounded excited as she answered, "It's a scuba dress. It's the same sort of fabric they use in diving suits."

I was struck dumb by that. In fact, I found myself looking around the cubicle for a hidden camera. Was I on one of those TV prank shows?

I finally mustered enough breath to say, in what I hoped was a scathing tone, "Well, that'll be handy then!" My sarcasm was wasted on Tina. Even more annoyingly, I now had to get the damn thing off.

I felt like an overstuffed pork sausage about to split its skin as I tried to figure out how to get out of the scuba dress. Tina, sounding more cheery than ever, asked me how I was getting on so I just told her it was "a bit tight".

"If you've got it on at all you've done well, love," she said. The cheek of her!

I pushed and pulled, wriggled and tugged, taking my frustration with young, skinny Tina, in her tiny crop top showing off tanned, toned tummy muscles, out on the dress. "Urghh, ahhh, gah…" I was practically ricocheting off the walls of the cubicle and thrashing against the curtain and then it happened. With an almighty rrrrrrriiiiiiipp the fabric finally and fatally split, accompanied by the tell-tale noise of tearing fabric.

Tina said nothing. There was total silence outside the changing room.

"So, I've decided not to bother with that one," I said breezily as I stepped out of the ruined remains of the scuba dress.

I pulled my leggings and sweatshirt back on and emerged onto the shop floor to face Tina, who was wearing a more sympathetic expression than I had expected.

"We've got body-con dresses, bandage dresses and illusion dresses, but I don't think you're gonna like any of them," she said with a raise of her Scouse brow, as if she was trying to figure me out.

I tried to find a way to explain to her what I was trying to achieve. "I don't want to be someone I'm not," I started to say. "It's not that I don't like those dresses, it's more a case that they don't like me, I think. You can use every designer 'illusion' trick in the book, love, but you can't make a normal woman like me look like a size zero no matter how tight you pull her in or how many coloured panels you use. It's not even about that."

Tina was listening intently. I had her attention now.

"I don't expect to look like Audrey Hepburn" – a flicker of incomprehension passed over Tina's face and I spoke quickly before I lost her all over again – "or someone trendy you will have heard of." Phew, she was back in the room. "I just want to feel positive about looking like myself … but on a good day."

We started all over again, looking over the rails and making new selections. I found a couple of silky black dresses – one patterned with stars and another with a subtle feather motif. Tina then pulled out some super soft T-shirts and two pairs of trendy straight-leg lounge pants, black with a sporty green or white stripe down the outside leg. I liked the look of those a lot; they said "relaxed but fashionable". When she saw the dresses I'd selected she had a genuine lightbulb moment and realised they stocked other items in the same stars and feather fabrics. As soon as I saw a black, silky, kimono-style cover-up with its pattern of white feathers, I knew it would work so well with the sporty stripe pants over a fresh white T-shirt. I dove straight back into the cubicle and tried the whole lot on. That was it! I looked comfortable and youthful, like I'd just thrown the outfit on, but still totally pulled together. I could wear it with trainers, dress it all up with heels, or even just pad around in bare feet at home. Even better, it was easy to get on, and off, and wouldn't leave any unsightly marks on my seldom seen skin.

I emerged from the cubicle in my new garb with a huge smile on my face. Tina grinned back, looking just as delighted. "So how did you meet this fella of yours then?" she asked.

When I told her it was through an internet dating site you could have knocked her down with a feather. "Go way! I've been on Tinder for ages. God, you meet so many freaks!"

Interesting. So, youngsters found it just as bad as us oldies the. Who'd have thought it? I felt for her then and tried to offer her the benefit of my newfound wisdom. "Hang on in there long enough and a good one will come along," I said.

Tina looked a little comforted and said she hoped I was right.

"'Course I am," I said. "I never thought I'd meet anyone like my Scott. He used to be in a band, you know; he was the lead singer."

Tina looked well impressed, until I told her the name of the band, Scott Smith and The Silhouettes, and then she just looked blank again, but obviously they were well before her time.

I changed back into my own clothes then and she wrapped my new purchases in generous amounts of tissue paper and put it all in one of their lovely stiff carrier bags with ribbon handles.

The bill was expensive but worth every penny. The clothes felt such good quality and I don't mind paying more if I'm getting value for money. Just before I left I pulled out my mobile and showed Tina a text Scott had sent me the week before. It was the night we'd been to Beppi's Bistro and he'd put me in a cab home at the end of the night. I'd asked if he'd wanted to come back for coffee but he had an early start the next day so he said we'd have to take a raincheck.

Tina peered at the screen as I showed her the text, which said, *"I wanna hold your hand"*. I started to explain why it thrilled me so much, but she said, "Yeah, The Beatles, right,

I get it." Of course she did, you're practically born with an inbred knowledge of The Beatles in this city.

I couldn't resist being a bit naughty then as I answered with a wink, "Well, with any luck we'll be doing a lot more than holding hands on our next date." Tina's little face was a picture.

Chapter Nine

Outfit sorted for my planned night of seduction, I should have felt a lot more relaxed. But this is me, Beverley Wilson, and no one has ever used the word "nonchalant" to describe me. To be fair, I don't know anyone who has ever used that word to describe anyone, but that's not my point.

Once I'd solved the dress code riddle I immediately began agonising over the menu. Suddenly, I decided lasagne was too stodgy and filling; you don't want a tummy full of congealing pasta as you attempt to lure a man into your bed. Fish – too smelly. Shellfish – too risky. Steak – might be too chewy. In the end, I plumped for – ooh, bad choice of word; I'd been watching what I ate like a hawk. I might want to be "love-handled" but I didn't want Scott to think I had love handles! In the end, I selected coq au vin. Don't laugh, it wasn't until I mentioned it to Jools and she hooted with laughter about the suggestive connotations of "coq" that I realised what I'd done, but that wasn't what I was thinking at the time. I just reasoned chicken in red wine sauce would be easy and tasty, and I could serve cheesy mashed potatoes on the side but just nibble on a few green beans myself. I'd throw a pavlova together for dessert, pile some fresh fruit and lashings of whipped cream in a meringue, and even if it all went wrong, I could present it in a dish and call it Eton Mess. If it all went right, we might even be able to find something more interesting to do with the whipped cream!

So, I knew what I was going to wear and I knew what I was going to serve for dinner. I couldn't avoid it any longer; I now had nothing to distract me from thinking about actually having sex for the first time in a very long while.

That's when I found myself rooting round in my boxes of Beatles memorabilia looking for some cool things to show Scott when he came round. Well, I wanted him to have an interesting time as well as a lovely meal. It would be nice to have some good conversation starting points, wouldn't it? Yes, yes … I realise now that I was doing it again. Thinking about anything and everything other than what was really playing on my mind and giving me restless nights. But whenever life gets on top of me, or I'm upset or fretful, my Beatles collection always comes to my rescue. I can lose myself for hours at a time going through all the different stuff in various boxes, picking it up, turning it over in my hands, running my fingers over all the familiar items. As I do that, all the memories come flooding back; it's like coming home and it comforts me like nothing else in the world.

I might have been too young to experience the first flush

of fame when four lads from Liverpool began shaking the world with their music, but I'd heard about it so much from my older sister, Deb, it was like a series of learned memories. Even though I wasn't actually there at the start I knew precisely how it felt to cram into The Cavern Club for lunchtime concerts, or see The Beatles' first televised performances on an old flickering black and white TV set.

You see, my sister Deb wasn't just a little bit older than me, she was a good deal older. An only child until her teenage years, she was well past the stage of being jealous of a new baby sister by the time I came along. In fact, I think she welcomed me as a distraction that took my parents' attention away from her. Just at the point when she didn't want them to know how much time she was spending out watching bands, drinking, smoking or getting entangled with boyfriends, they suddenly had a new baby in the house to deal with.

I was an accident. My parents called me their "little surprise", but we all know that's just a nice way of saying accident. My mam probably thought I was "the change", as they called it back then. Well, I was a change all right!

Mam and Dad were older parents with traditional ways of doing things, but they were good, honest people. I presumed they'd been a lot stricter with Deb when she was growing up than they ever were with me. My arrival seemed to give them an excuse to relax a few rules for both of us, yet another reason for Deb to welcome rather than resent it.

With an older sister like Deb around you could say I was weaned on The Beatles. My earliest memories are filled with their music all around me, their faces looking down on me from all the pictures on her bedroom wall.

As soon as I could toddle I'd follow Deb all over the place, watching her put on her make-up and trendy clothes when she was going out. As I grew up, I only idolised her more. Her life was so groovy and modern, and if she included me at all I was made up. She'd sometimes dance around with me, singing along to the latest Merseybeat releases and teaching me the words. I loved it all as much as I loved her.

I rummaged around in the box in front of me and pulled out a metal canister with faded black and white pictures on the front, showing the boys in their Beatle suits and shaggy haircuts. It was a tin of talcum powder from the early Sixties branded with a red "Margo of Mayfair" logo. It probably only cost a few pennies when it was new but I knew stuff like this went for a fortune now. I sniffed the black stopper on the top of the tin and a distinct flowery scent filled my nostrils; the canister was still full of powdery talc.

The memories of my childhood came flooding back and swirled around my mind along with the perfume that had been designed to appeal to little girls like me who had loved the musical moptops.

Deb would probably not have bothered collecting so much of this kind of merchandise if it hadn't been for her annoying little sister trying to find a way to join in. She was far more bothered about grabbing the set list from the stage and getting as many of the guys to sign it as she could. She kept programmes and posters, ticket stubs and bubble gum cards. Any time she could find a way to push her way through a crowd to get an autograph scrawled on something, she did. But when it was my birthday, or at Christmas, she knew I would absolutely love a Beatles hairbrush or lunchbox.

My fingers found their way into another box and curled themselves around the neck of a small plastic guitar. The best birthday present I ever had. I remember the bubbling excitement I'd felt in my tummy as I'd torn the paper off and revealed the guitar for the very first time. Drawings of John, Paul, George and Ringo's faces decorated the tiny cream-coloured instrument and it was edged in vibrant red. The strings were only plastic, and it never sounded any good, but I bloody loved that guitar. I had carried it around with me all the time; I think I even tucked it up in bed with me for a while. Deb teased me about it at first, even though she had been the one to buy it from Woolworths in town, but I think she secretly liked the fact I was trying to be her very own mini-me.

Having a big sister like Deb often made me feel life was one big game of catch-up. She was glamorous and sophisticated, and I was always going to be the little girl trailing in her wake. It sort of made me feel I would always be late to the party and it's a sensation I've never really been able to shake off.

I was too little to know anything about The Beatles splitting up in 1970. I didn't read newspapers or listen to daily bulletins, and you weren't bombarded with information by social media back in the Seventies. It wouldn't really have made any difference to me at that point anyway, as I wasn't anywhere near old enough to go to a concert or be in the audience for a recording of a television show.

It obviously didn't even occur to Deb to tell me. She'd gradually drifted into preferring The Rolling Stones anyway. I think her disillusionment actually started when she found out George Harrison had married Pattie Boyd, because George was always her favourite. I wasn't so fickle. I kept the faith. As I got older, I happily stayed in my Beatles bubble, discovering more and more of their music and practising my signature as "Beverley McCartney".

John, Paul, George and Ringo spent so much time down in London or away in America, us Liverpudlians had got used to sharing "our boys" with the rest of the world, and feeling they weren't just ours anymore. I simply carried on playing their records, stopped to listen every time they were played on the radio, and went to watch their movies when they came on at the local cinema like all the other true fans.

Call me naive, but even when I finally realised they'd split up I carried on hoping for years that they'd get back together and I'd finally have my chance of seeing them play live. I suppose I didn't ever completely give up hope of that happening, not until December 1980. No one would ever understand why I cried so much that day, but I was mourning so much more than John Lennon's horrific murder and the ultimate end of the best band the world has ever known.

I made a couple of trips up into the attic, via the pull-down ladder I'd had fitted to the hatch, to put most of my Beatles boxes away, but kept a couple back with a selection of things I thought might interest Scott.

I wasn't sure if I'd be brave enough to show him any of this stuff when it came to it. It felt so very personal, like a real window into my soul. I might be considering baring my body, but sharing my Beatles trinkets and treasures actually felt like an even more intimate act. With that in mind, I decided I would have to wait and see what felt right on the night. I needed to listen to my inner urges and act accordingly. I'd come this far and I could feel I was on the brink of a new phase in my life now.

As I reached up to close the hatch above my head, one of my favourite Beatles songs came floating into my mind. I started singing the lyrics before I registered which song it was. When I realised, I couldn't help but chuckle to myself. Was my brain playing naughty tricks on me and second-guessing what might happen between me and Scott? I hoped we were destined for more than just the one-night stand described in the song and I'd be much more than his "Day Tripper". Oh, I hoped so; I really, really did.

Chapter Ten

When the evening I had come to think of as my "Big Night In" finally arrived, I opened the front door to find Scott Smith on my step looking absolutely gorgeous and holding a bottle of wine in one hand and a bunch of flowers in the other. That was a great start.

Despite my nerves, Scott did his best to help me feel relaxed as he settled himself in the living room while I checked everything was under control in the kitchen.

"Are you sure there's nothing I can do to help?" he called out.

"No, it's all under control," I called back, despite feeling rather less in control than I sounded.

As I popped the green beans into boiling water, John Lennon's voice suddenly floated in from the living room, saying something about a "Doris" who "gets her oats". That was a bit near the knuckle and I was glad my blushing face was hidden from Scott. I realised he had popped my *Let It*

Be vinyl album on the vintage record player and John's jokey ad lib intro was quickly followed by the opening bars of the song "Two of Us". Nice.

I was in a bit of a rush to get dinner on the table – for me the main event of tonight would hopefully not be the coq au vin.

Scott made lots of approving noises and said all the right things during dinner. I'm usually a pretty good cook but being all of a fluster I was worried I'd mess it up. Thankfully, I'd opted for a tried and tested recipe and he pronounced it all delicious. Phew. He even tried to help wash up but I assured him I was just flinging it all in the dishwasher.

My usual inappropriate joke mechanism kicked in as I rejoined Scott after clearing the dishes and I found myself suggesting a game of Boggle! Your mind is probably boggling at my irritating nervous tic but Scott just laughed, thank God, and didn't take my insane suggestion seriously. It gave me the breathing space I needed to pretend I just happened to have some Beatles memorabilia handy to show him.

"You'll probably think it's all a bit childish, really," I said to the top of his head as he bent over the box and rummaged inside. "I don't show anyone this stuff as a rule. Geoff could never be bothered with any of it so don't think you have to be polite by taking an interest."

Scott looked up with a look of astonishment. "It's absolutely fascinating," he said, lifting a couple of items out of the box and gazing at them with such a look of wonder it melted my heart. "I never knew you could get a Beatles lunchbox with a matching flask," he said in awe.

"Well, you probably can't anymore." I laughed. "They may look like just bits of blue plastic tat but they're from 1965."

"Wow," Scott said as he laid the lunchbox and flask reverentially back in the box.

He asked me then all about how I came to have such a collection and I found myself telling him about my big sister Deb and how it all started with her.

"You see, she really did hang out down at The Cavern back in the day, breathing the same air as The Beatles," I told him.

He laughed again then and teased me about the fact that on our first date I'd said I wasn't like all those other cheeky Liverpudlians who claimed a connection to The Beatles. He was clearly joking though.

I explained how Deb was so much older than me, already a teenager by the time I was born, and how I was probably a bit of an accident.

"Prettiest accident I ever saw," Scott said with a naughty twinkle in his eye.

I blushed furiously then and lunged for a black leather sleeve I could see poking up from the second box.

"Deb told me she actually hung out with Ringo Starr when he was in Rory Storm and the Hurricanes," I said quickly to cover my embarrassment. "One of her best mates even dated him for a while in those days! Deb wasn't too jealous though. She was actually sad when they kicked out Pete Best and replaced him with Ringo, as she reckoned

Pete was very dishy." I was holding the leather jacket, stroking it absent-mindedly as I spoke. "Oh, this is Ringo's jacket! Deb's mate Doreen let her have it after they'd split up. I think he'd left some gear at her place and she wanted to chuck it all out once he dumped her." Scott was looking at me with his mouth slightly agape. "I always thought I could give it back to Ringo one day, if our paths ever crossed, but funnily enough they never did," I told him.

As I shrugged Scott gave a little cough and said, "I think you did the right thing holding on to it for all these years. I doubt Ringo would have missed it. This stuff must... I mean, do you think this lot is worth anything much?"

"I suppose some of the stuff must be," I said as he carried on poking about in the boxes, ooohing and ahhhing over the contents. "I've never bothered having any of it valued or anything like that, but I'm sure the longer you keep things the more they're worth. That's one of the reasons I can't see the point of selling any of it, really. The longer I keep it, surely the more it'll be worth?" Scott nodded in agreement as I carried on. "It was my way of being part of it all when I was little, you see, my way of joining in and being a Beatles fan. Deb didn't care you could get socks with their faces on, or Beatles bubble bath, she was much more sophisticated."

"So that became your thing?" Scott was looking at me now with an expression on his face I couldn't quite place. A bit like he was seeing me with fresh eyes.

"I suppose it did, yeah," I said, feeling hot again under his gaze. "I joined the fan club, bought merchandise with my pocket money, asked for things every Christmas and birthday to add to my collection. I was so prissy about it all, keeping it all nice and not letting anyone open or ruin the original packaging. I never imagined back then anything like this would be worth money in the future, but those habits have paid dividends now, of course. I'm probably sitting on quite a pretty penny."

"Very pretty indeed," Scott repeated in a low murmur as he looked deep into my eyes.

For a millisecond I thought about leaning in for a kiss but I couldn't quite muster the nerve so I let the moment pass and carried on talking instead. "This isn't all of my collection, of course, there's loads more upstairs. I keep most of it safe up in the attic; stops the boys moving it around or messing about with it."

"Or working out how much they could get for some of this stuff off a man in the pub," Scott said in low mutter with a slight shake of his head.

I couldn't believe I'd heard him right. "MY BOYS?" I said in a high-pitched squeak, jumping to my feet. "They'd never do such a thing!" Did Scott really think my lads were the sort to plunder my precious Beatles memorabilia and sell off choice pieces for a few quid?

Scott immediately looked mortified at what he'd said and held his hands up in complete surrender. "Hey, I'm so sorry, Bev… I was only kidding. C'mon, Liverpudlians are known for their sense of humour … aren't they?"

He gave me a nervous smile, then patted the sofa seat next to him. I sat gingerly and as he gave me a quick nudge in the ribs I realised he really was only teasing and I didn't need to be so touchy.

We spent a little while looking at a few bits and bobs – signed dinner menus, faded posters and flyers, some of the earliest single releases still in their original paper sleeves. Scott sat back with an autographed publicity photo in his hand. "I don't suppose there were many kids who had the presence of mind to start putting a collection like this together and still have it pristine all these years later. You were ahead of your time, Bev."

If he was trying to make up for his little faux pas earlier, he was saying all the right things. I'm not used to taking compliments though so I went into classic defence mode. "Me? Ahead of my time? I can't say I've ever thought of it like that," I said, swatting away his look of admiration. "I'm hardly rock 'n' roll, not like you, playing in a band, up on stage in front of loads of adoring fans."

A small smile played around his lips as he raised an eyebrow at that and said, "There weren't *loads* of adoring fans." He waited just a beat before naughtily adding, "Some … but not loads."

"Oh … you!!" I tried to look outraged but couldn't stop myself from giggling.

He started asking me more questions about Deb then. I suppose I knew it was inevitable but I'd been dreading this moment. "So how come Deb let you keep everything? Surely some of this is still hers by rights?"

My mood dropped and I shifted uncomfortably on the sofa, and I found I couldn't quite look Scott in the eye. I really didn't want to get into all this now. He wasn't daft though and as I busied myself putting things back into place in the boxes he knew I was avoiding giving him a direct answer.

"Bev? What is it? What's wrong?"

"Nothing." I knew the quiver in my voice gave me away but I didn't know what else to say. I wasn't giving a very convincing performance. "This collection is all mine," I said, but I'd said it in a way that aroused his suspicions.

"Have you and your sister fallen out over all this stuff? Does she want a share of it now she knows it's probably worth a fortune?"

I shook my head violently from side to side. "No, not at all. It's nothing like that."

But he knew there was something and instead of questioning me further he leaned back on the sofa cushion, linked his hands behind his head and just waited.

My voice was so quiet when I eventually started talking I wasn't sure he'd be able to hear me properly. I told him more about my big sister Deb, like how she was always known as Deb, never Deborah, and definitely not Debbie. I described how from when I was teeny-tiny I loved to follow her around, clip-clopping across the kitchen floor in her stiletto shoes and smearing my toddler lips with her red lipstick. I told him all about how she wore her blonde hair short and wavy with little kiss curls across her forehead, and how she would sometimes tie my hair up in rags before I went to bed so that my long, straight, fair hair would be a mass of curls in the morning.

Scott never said a word as I gabbled on, telling him all about how gorgeous and glamorous she was and how, even when I got older, I always felt like the more ordinary, plainer sister, a pale imitation of her at best.

"It wasn't Deb's fault I felt like that," I said. I would never want Scott, or anyone else, to get the wrong impression of Deb. She never put me down or did anything to make me feel inferior. I don't remember anything like that anyway, it just sort of happened. "Mam and Dad used to describe her as 'a free spirit'," I said, remembering the way they would almost smile as they said that and then sigh to themselves as though they knew it wasn't something they could do anything about. "While Deb was carefree, I was always care*ful*," I explained. "That's just the way we were both made, I think. The thing we had in common was how much we both loved music and The Beatles. At least when she still lived at home, it was. After she moved out it was harder to keep a connection going as our lives were at such different stages." I paused then and the familiar ache washed over me, pulling me down as though I'd thrown on a cloak made of something dark and heavy. I took a deep breath and carried on. "She got a job at a music magazine down in London. It was just on the front reception but it was her way into the industry. She was ambitious – she really wanted to write for the music press, review gigs and interview bands, that sort of thing."

"And did she?" Scott was leaning forward now, eager to hear more about Deb, the way everyone always did. If Scott had met Deb instead of me I wouldn't stand a chance of keeping him interested, that much I was sure of.

I wasn't ready to answer his question though, not yet, so I carried on telling him all about the glamorous new life she made for herself in London. Sharing a tiny flat with a couple of other girls and working at a place where pop stars would regularly swing by and chat her up. She used to send me a letter now and then telling me all of her news, or at least the news she was prepared to share with her kid sister. I was working my way through high school, trying to conjugate French verbs and keep my acne under control. Some days I'd sit on the bus winding its long and weary way home, dreaming of the day I might be allowed to go and visit Deb in "that London" and sample some of her exciting life for myself. Of course, it never happened.

Deb was bound to be a huge success in London, everybody said so. She was right in the heart of things, rubbing shoulders with the rich and famous. She was talented and bright, and once they realised just how bright she would get her own column at the magazine and really start to make a name for herself. Dressed in all the latest fab fashions and hanging out at all the groovy clubs and bars in the city… No one was all that surprised when she hooked up with an emerging rock star and became his beautiful live-in girlfriend, the envy of all of his fans.

"Is that what happened?" I barely heard Scott's whispered question but I just nodded and said, "Pretty much, yeah."

"And then?" Scott was hungry to hear more of the story and I couldn't blame him. Even when she wasn't here Deb could fill a room with her personality and presence. No wonder I missed her so much every day.

I steeled myself and turned to face Scott. I almost felt sorry for him now, sitting there eager to hear more about

Deb Hopewell and her carefree, wonderful life. "And then," I said, "she died."

It never gets any easier to tell people something like that. Saying it out loud, making it real for someone else, is like hearing it for the first time yourself all over again. It's weird, you'd think I'd have got used to the idea of her being dead by now. In many ways I have, but then occasionally it comes up and hits me like it's the first time I've heard about it and then I'm back scrabbling around trying to make sense of it all.

"Way to go, Beverley, great way to create a romantic mood," I said, trying to make a lame joke of the whole thing, but Scott needed a minute to recalibrate while he took in my bombshell announcement.

"Of all the things I thought you were going to say, that actually wasn't one of them," he said in a voice full of both surprise and concern.

Of course I had to fill in the missing details then – the how, when and where. The fact she'd been killed in a hit-and-run while she was walking through Soho late one night. They never caught the speeding driver and I always wondered if they ever realised what they'd done. The police had arrived on our doorstep very early one morning to tell Mam and Dad as we didn't have a phone back then. I'd always seen Mam and Dad as being calm, rational people, always so in control of themselves, but I saw them both break into a million pieces that day.

I could feel the tears building behind my eyes but I blinked them back and thought about what Deb would say if she could see me now. I'd prepped and prepared for this night, dressing myself in my new laid-back and cool outfit, dishing up my best recipe, and hoping to end the night in the arms of this great guy who was now sitting next to me on my sofa. Instead, what was I actually doing? I was throwing my chance of a wild night of passion away as I plundered my maudlin memories. If Deb wasn't dead, she would kill me.

In the hope it wasn't too late to salvage the mood I fluffed up my hair with my fingers and turned to face Scott with a smile on my face. "Yeah, so I think we can say for certain that The Beatles memorabilia collection is definitely all mine now, and I like to think that it's what Deb would have wanted, you know?"

"Yeah ... I mean, of course, I'm sure that's right."

Poor Scott. How was a bloke meant to respond to this avalanche of personal baggage? I needed to move things along now, for his sake as well as mine.

"Me mam always used to say I was a slow starter compared to Deb," I told him then with an exaggerated roll of my eyes, taking the mickey out of myself. "'Slow and steady wins the race, Beverley,' she used to say, as though I was a blinkin' tortoise and Deb was the hare. Me dad always joined in then saying, 'Looks may attract a man but that's not what keeps him interested, our Bev,' which I always thought was the most back-handed compliment I'd ever heard." I took a beat while Scott seemed to be considering what the best response to all this might be. I didn't give him a chance to speak though, turning to face him and looking at him from beneath my lashes, giving him my best come-hither expression. "I can be wild and reckless if I put my mind to it though," I teased.

Scott took the bait and gave me a big grin, "I bet you can!" he said, clearly relieved we were moving back into safer territory. "Come on, confession time, what's the wildest thing you've ever done, Bev?"

Ahhh, well, there wasn't exactly a raft of examples to choose from ... but I'd made the claim and so now I needed to back it up. I really should think things through more before I jump in with both feet. I knew there was one particular thing I could tell him but I was a bit worried it might backfire on me. "I ... no, well, oh God, you'll think I'm dreadful. It's not even wild really, just a bit bonkers."

Scott was loving watching me squirm. He widened his eyes in mock horror and inched along the sofa away from me. "Should I be scared?" he asked, pretending to be properly alarmed. He was such a big tease.

"Well, I'll have to tell you now in case you're thinking something peculiar," I shot back.

I considered confessing to having a yellow submarine costume hidden away but he might have thought I was into fancy-dress fetish behaviour and I didn't want to scare him off completely so I avoided that. Instead, I asked, "Well, you know me boys – James, Richie and Harry?" Scott nodded. "Well, their dad, me husband Geoff, he never really liked how much I loved The Beatles. The soppy sod used to get proper jealous and give me so much grief. Anyway, I suppose I shouldn't be proud of this but I am really. When the boys were born he left it up to me to choose their names and he never had a clue what I'd done.

Shows how little notice he used to take of me goin' on about The Beatles all the time, I reckon. So anyway, me first boy I called James … that was for Paul. *James* Paul McCartney is his real name, did you know?" Scott simply nodded again and let me carry on. "Harry, that's short for Harrison, as in George, and Richie … Ringo's real name is Richard Starkey, so Richie is for him." I tried to look a tiny bit shamefaced but really I'd always been rather proud of my achievement.

Scott gave me a look as though he'd just found me with my hand in the cookie jar and gave a little shake of his head. "Even poor Geoff might have rumbled you if you'd had another," he said. I was sure I could see him trying to suppress a look of amusement.

"Not if it had been another boy and I'd called him Winston," I shot back. "Can you believe Geoff knew so little about The Beatles he wouldn't have had a clue that John Lennon's middle name was Winston?"

I was relieved to see Scott definitely looked like he found my "wild confession" funny but I needed to double-check. "D'you think I'm dreadful?" I asked, batting my eyelashes for all I was worth yet again.

Scott leaned towards me and I smelt the woody scent of his cologne. "I think you're deliciously devious," he said in a soft voice.

This was it, the moment I'd been waiting for, but instead of sinking into Scott's arms I bottled it again and reached for my glass and took a large swig. The wine had already gone to my head and together with Scott's voice, his aroma and the very nearness of him, I was feeling distinctly giddy.

So much for my Mata Hari moment, I was about as skilled in seduction as a dithering debutante.

Scott didn't seem to notice how hopeless I was at all this. He reached out and laid his hand on my shoulder, stroking his hand down the silky sleeve. "You're so funny, Bev," he said in a low voice just inches from my ear. "You make out you're someone life just happens to, when all the time you've got stuff going on." His words made me feel exhilarated and his hand slid down onto the bare skin of my arm as he spoke.

"D'you really think so?" I asked as his fingers continued to stroke my arm in tantalising circles.

"I knew it the very first time you came into the café," he said, although I was concentrating more now on the circles he was drawing on my skin and couldn't recall being the slightest bit impressive on our first date at The Quarter.

"Oh God, I was in such a flap." I winced as the memory came back to haunt me. "I was like a headless chicken in a KFC. I don't know why you didn't run for the hills."

Scott leaned closer, one hand caressing my arm as the other moved a strand of hair that had fallen in front of my eye. "Because I could tell straightaway…"

He paused and I was so desperate to know what he had been thinking when he first met me that I couldn't stop myself asking, "What?"

"I could tell you were a woman ready to make something happen in her life, shake things up a bit … and I was just hoping that something … could involve me."

Here he was at last, a man who found me exciting and

desirable, so I did it, I asked him, "Shall we shake … I mean … *take* our wine … upstairs?"

I held my breath then as Scott's eyes crinkled in the corners and he leaned even closer. I closed my eyes, ready for him to kiss me, but then heard him say, "You know I want to, Bev, but not just yet."

I snapped my eyes open and shot up from the sofa in one sudden move. "Oh, right, sorry, I don't know what came over me. It was all that talk about shaking! It's just … I don't usually, well … I don't ever…" My excuses tailed off as I stood there feeling like an utter fool. What on earth had I been thinking?

Scott was still sitting on the sofa, not looking at all fazed by my outburst and pathetic attempt at getting him into my bed. He stood slowly and went over to the record player – the LP on the turntable had finished a while back and he removed it and put it back in its sleeve. He flipped through the record stack as though he knew exactly what he was looking for and picked out an album. I saw it was *Please Please Me* as he carefully slid the record out, checked the label and flipped it over onto side two. He put the record onto the player, moved the arm into position, and pressed play.

Neither of us had said a word but watching him complete this ancient musical ritual had calmed my jangling nerves. As the familiar crackle played out through the speaker, and the record began to spin, he walked towards me and took both of my hands in his. "There's no rush, you know, Bev," he said softly. "Do you fancy a dance?"

The music started. "Love Me Do". I was charmed but still embarrassed. "Give over," I said.

Scott didn't let go of my hands. "Come on, Bev, dance with me." He drew me closer and started to sway me from side to side.

"Are you askin'?" I said.

"I'm askin'," he answered without missing a beat.

"Then I'm dancin'," I said, stepping into his arms.

And we did.

Chapter Eleven

I f I was to liken my first sexual experience with Scott to any particular Beatles song – bear with me – I think I would probably have to choose ... "Yellow Submarine". Nothing to do with anything or anyone "going down" – get your filthy minds out of the gutter, please!

"Yellow Submarine" is a perfectly *acceptable* song – jaunty and pretty memorable with a nice, regular rhythm. It's definitely not my favourite Beatles song by any stretch of the imagination, but when all is said and done it still *is* a Beatles song so it can never be judged too harshly in my book. *Any* Beatles song is better than *no* Beatles song, after all.

I suppose I'm trying to find a way to tell you about that first time with Scott in a way that doesn't make me feel too embarrassed. I know, I know, I shouldn't feel embarrassed about stuff like that – I'm a woman of the world, I've had three kids, for goodness' sake – but all that counts for diddly squat when you suddenly find yourself in bed with a new man. I'm also ashamed to admit that our "first time" didn't hit the jackpot like those first-time sex scenes in movies and romcoms so often do. But this was real life and that's how the real-life nookie cookie crumbles.

I wanted to feel sexy and alluring. I wanted to throw myself into unusual positions with wild abandon and leave Scott breathless with lust at my capacity for multiple orgasms. I *wanted* that to be the way it was; honestly, I did. The reality, however, was a lot more awkward and hesitant, on *both* our parts. He seemed nervous, too, and even getting naked turned into a bit of a comical farce. He pulled my T-shirt over my face, leaving me flailing blindly, and when I tried to undo his fly I got his boxers caught in the zip. Ouch. We did see the funny side and laughed about it before carrying on, but the tone was set to goofy as opposed to sexy, like we were a couple of clowns rather than a pair of lovebirds.

We eventually found our own rhythm, steady and regular, like the backbeat to the music that began playing in my head – *"We all live in a Yellow Submarine, Yellow Submarine, Yellow Submarine…"* – and for a while, just like that tune, we went around and around, coming back to the beginning and then starting all over again. I enjoyed it. It was nice.

I was a bit surprised that a former pop star like Scott hadn't thrown in some different moves; surely he must have picked up a few tricks along the way? But he kept to the tried and tested formula, bit of kissing, a couple of tweaks to my nipples and a ride in the missionary position until the end of the line. I mean, I didn't get to the end of *my* line, if you get my drift, but I figured there was all the time in the world to perfect a routine that would do that.

I was probably expecting too much from a first go. I decided to consider it a work in progress and aimed to develop our repertoire over time. "Yellow Submarine" was okay for your Beatles beginners, but ideally I'd include a raucous medley starting with "Please Please Me", a bit of "Twist and Shout" and we'd finally end up at "Come together! Yeah, yeah, yeah..."

Chapter Twelve

I awoke the next morning to find myself in an empty bed. For a second, I wondered if I had completely imagined the events of last night, but then I rolled onto my side and saw my favourite Beatles mug on the side table, the steam rising from it letting me know it was filled with fresh, hot coffee. I propped myself up on my pillows to sip the coffee and heard distinct sounds of someone moving around downstairs. Phew. Scott hadn't done a runner in the middle of the night after all.

I dashed into the bathroom to freshen up and check I didn't look like too much of a train wreck. I flung on my very best silky robe, the one I usually saved for rare visits to a posh hotel, and attempted to sashay my way down the stairs.

Scott was sitting at the dining table reading a newspaper, and he lowered the pages as he heard me come into the room and gave me a warm smile. The sight of him sitting there in the morning sunshine all real and manly punctured my intention to be sexy and sensual. Instead, I defaulted to my more usual setting of giddy and gawky. "Thanks for the coffee," I said, raising my mug as if I was toasting him and almost slopping the contents onto my bare toes. "Would you like another cup?"

Scott had an almost full mug of his own near his elbow but I couldn't stop myself from jabbering. How was I supposed to behave after what had happened last night? This was most definitely not the sort of morning I was used to. One where you wake up to find a handsome man you've had sex with for the very first time making himself at home in your living room. There's no advice in any of those daft magazines on how you are meant to handle this bit, and I've definitely never seen a daytime TV show cover the topic during a phone-in.

"It's no trouble," I insisted, nodding my head in the direction of his practically untouched coffee mug.

"I'm fine, honestly," he answered perfectly reasonably.

"How about something to eat? Oh … I've got some croissants, I bought them 'specially."

Scott put his paper down and looked at me then with his eyes wide and his brows raised. "How very forward of you," he said in the manner of an outraged schoolmaster.

"What?" Oh bloody hell, me and my big mouth. Why on earth did I say that? "Oh, no, I didn't mean… Well, it's just that I thought … well, you know…" As I stumbled and stuttered my explanation, trying to convince both Scott and myself that it wasn't *exactly* like it looked, I realised Scott was having to do his very best not to burst out laughing. "Oh … YOU!" I flapped my hand towards him and went over to straighten the curtains at the window so he couldn't see how embarrassed I was by my own foolishness.

Scott sat there, chuckling to himself, "It's okay, Bev, calm down... You are funny."

"Funny ha ha, or funny peculiar?" I questioned over my shoulder, trying my best to sound blasé.

"It's hard to tell," Scott said, the chuckle still unmistakable in his voice. "You tend to swing from one to the other in the blink of an eye."

I didn't mind too much if Scott found me amusing. Funny is good. I just didn't want him thinking I was some sort of idiot. I could cope with a bit of teasing and poking fun at myself – I knew what I was like, after all – and told him so. "Oh I know, what am I like? I don't know why I do it but it's just the way I am, I have to fill a silence and that can very quickly lead to me witterin' on."

Scott took a swig from his coffee mug and picked his paper back up. "Don't worry, it's more entertaining than breakfast telly," he said pleasantly, still smiling.

That set me off again as I scurried about looking for the remote. "Oh, do you want the telly on? I tend to leave it off in a morning. I can't be doin' with all the endless weather reports – local weather, national weather, international weather ... coming up soon, stay tuned for *more* weather! They interrupt politicians and movie stars to reassure us they will be coming back soon with yet another weather report. It drives me mad. Don't they realise we have windows?" I halted my diatribe to see Scott had disappeared behind the raised pages of the newspaper, which were shaking slightly as though he was silently laughing. "I'm doing it again, aren't I?" I said quietly.

Scott peeked from behind the paper and gave me a wink. "I can't say I noticed."

Ha ha, very funny. I gave him a rueful smile and plopped myself down on the sofa.

Scott folded his paper away and put his head on one side with a look of concern. "Bev, you are happy I stayed over, aren't you? I never wanted to rush things."

Sitting there with his shirt untucked and his socked feet poking out from beneath his trousers, Scott suddenly looked a little bit lost and unsure of himself. I instantly felt silly, not for being gauche but for presuming that I was the only one who might feel a bit anxious in this situation. Maybe that's why Scott was up and dressed. Perhaps he hadn't felt comfortable waking up naked in my bed. Women don't have the monopoly on sensitivity, I reasoned to myself. I wanted to reassure him that I wasn't regretting our night of practice passion. It wouldn't be very good for his ego if he thought I was uncomfortable with him staying the night or disappointed with his performance.

"Of course I'm happy you stayed over, that you're still here … of course. You didn't rush me, not at all. To be honest I'm still pinching myself; I'm not sure what I did to deserve you."

Scott looked comforted by that and told me not to be daft and then said something about how he felt like pinching himself because he felt so lucky to have met me. Seriously? I couldn't let that just go by so I asked him then how many other women he had met through the Lonely

Hearts Club dating site. He was noncommittal in his answer, muttering something about "one or two".

"Come on, Scott." I leaned forward on the sofa. "Now it's time for you to confess. Are you seriously saying out of all the dates you went on I was the best one?" I suppose it was blatant compliment fishing but given compliments have been as rare as rocking-horse poop in my life over the last few years I don't think anyone could blame me.

"Oh, Beverley," Scott said, "the day I met you I simply couldn't believe my luck!"

I needed some convincing about that and it took a bit of cajoling on my part but Scott did then reveal a few horror stories about some crazy women he'd been paired up with before meeting me. I certainly knew how that felt! He explained it was so hard to form a relationship with the amount he had to travel for work that he didn't feel like he'd had many opportunities to really connect with someone. I nodded understandingly as he began a rundown of several unsuccessful encounters. There was a very business-like executive type who conducted an interview rather than a date and managed to include a question about his sperm count in her interrogation. There was a flighty piece who'd clearly wanted to make her regular boyfriend jealous and achieved her ambition when the guy turned up mid-date, making Scott think he was going to get battered. One story actually made Scott shudder as he remembered a Sophie who was so determined to be a bride she had already booked the ceremony and reception and was simply looking for a man who was available on July 21 to fill the vacant groom role in her dream wedding. "She'd even chosen the wedding cake," Scott said, still sounding utterly incredulous. "It was fruitcake … of course."

I stifled a smile at that. Fruitcake sounded about right – poor Scott! It did make me feel a little better about all the disastrous dates I'd had to endure on my road to romance though. I wondered if any of Scott's dates drove a motorbike and sidecar?

Scott was now talking about a woman called Susie who sounded quite nice, sort of hippy-dippy and into baking, sewing and other crafts. "Oh yeah, she seemed very sweet," Scott answered when I said she sounded lovely, "until I realised she was a psychopath!" He rolled his eyes and grimaced as he described "sweet Susie" and her obsession with cats. Apparently, she had fourteen, which wouldn't have been quite so bad in itself until she dropped the bombshell that the furry hat she was wearing and the fluffy bag that matched it had been made out of a couple of her cats that had died after being run over! "I was basically trapped with a woman wearing roadkill," Scott said with an anguished expression. I tried to look sympathetic at this point but couldn't keep it up when he added, "And then she asked me to stroke 'Mrs Mittens', so I panicked and told her I was allergic."

I snorted at that point and tried to cover my laughter by pretending I was coughing. It seemed to jolt Scott out of his reminiscing and back into the moment, as he suddenly announced he had a little something for me and got up to search through the pockets of his jacket, which was hanging on the back of one of the dining chairs. That pulled me up short as a particularly nasty memory of one of my previous dates came back to haunt me.

"For me? Oh God, they're not American Tan, are they?" I said.

"American Tan? What are you on about?" Scott paused in his search and looked at me in confusion.

I really didn't want to elaborate and tell the full story about the creepy bloke with the perverted interest in women's underwear, so I took off on a tangent about tights. "Oh, well, you know, American Tan tights – they're the bane of every woman's life. Well, they were. Hideous orangey colour, always went baggy at the knees. They were a sort of primitive contraception."

I was on a roll but Scott was clearly baffled. "You've lost me," he said.

"Well, when I was a girl we always wore knickers, tights – most usually American Tan – and then another pair of knickers over the top." I was on my feet now, demonstrating the age-old practice of layering as I mimed pulling up knickers, tights and then more knickers.

Scott's eyes were on stalks. "Another pair of knickers over the top?"

I nodded and carried on with a completely rhetorical question. "No one does that anymore, do they? Might be fewer candidates for those shows with lie detector tests to find out 'Who's the Daddy?' if they did. It would take someone pretty determined to get through all that resistance. You don't need those extra knickers these days though, must be 'cause the Lycra or whatever is so much better now. You couldn't risk it in the old days."

Scott was doing his absolute best to keep up with my train of thought, bless him. "Couldn't risk what?" he asked in a hesitant tone as though he was a bit scared of what on earth I might say next.

"Well, if you didn't wear the extra knickers your gusset would be down by your knees by lunchtime." I demonstrated the way sagging tights could droop to just above your knees by swinging my hand between my thighs but then looked up to see a look of shock on Scott's face.

"Do you know you just said the word 'gusset' out loud?" he said.

It was a like someone had poured a bucket of cold water over me. What on earth had I been thinking? In my desperate attempt to avoid telling Scott about my embarrassing encounter with Mr Pantyhose Pervert I'd outed myself as some sort of bawdy stand-up comedian with dubious off-colour material. I clamped my hand over my stupid mouth and sat back down on the sofa.

Scott was immediately full of concern, asking if I was okay and saying I looked like I'd just seen a ghost. I shook my head and didn't trust myself to speak. Scott retrieved what he had been looking for from his jacket pocket and came and joined me on the sofa. He seemed to think now was as good a time as any to change the subject and I was most grateful for that. What he held in his hand was a flyer for a Beatles convention and he was asking me if I wanted to go and saying he wanted to come with me. Wow. The double whammy of my outrageous gusset gaffe followed by this amazing guy offering not only to indulge but also to share my passion for The Beatles was boggling my poor brain. It didn't fully compute. How the hell had I got myself here? Me, Beverley Wilson – Beatles Bev – in a real relationship with a generous, good-looking guy who didn't react to my quirks and foibles by wanting to run for the hills; who actually wanted to be my partner in every single way I'd dreamed of.

We chatted about the convention for a while and I told him I'd never actually been to one. I had supplemented my memorabilia collection with a few purchases from eBay and other online outlets in recent times and I'd picked up a couple of things from contacts down on Mathew Street before that, but an actual convention always seemed like a daunting thing to go to on my own.

"Well, now you don't have to," Scott said, taking my hand in his. He leaned in to kiss me then and I responded with an urgency that took the breath away from both of us. Scott slipped his hand inside my silky robe and brushed his fingers across my breast, I gasped as a shudder of desire ran through my body, and pulled him on top of me as I lay back on the sofa. This time, with the pressure off, it all felt a lot more natural.

———

Later on, as I quickly showered and dressed, I felt amazed at the way my life was unfolding. Scott had told me he had an appointment to get to this afternoon so we just had time to grab a quick brunch before he had to leave. Scott offered to "rustle something up" while I made myself decent, and joked he needed something to top up his energy levels.

I entered the kitchen to find him spooning creamy scrambled egg onto a couple of plates, the notorious croissants having been warmed and buttered to accompany them. This guy was definitely a keeper!

"Did you know 'Scrambled Eggs' was the original title of the song 'Yesterday'?" I asked Scott. He shook his head and looked confused so I told him how Paul McCartney claimed the tune had come to him one night in a dream. "When he woke, he added the first words that fit so he wouldn't forget it ... *scrambled eggs, oh my baby how I love your legs...*'" I sang and Scott nodded his approval, saying he much preferred my version.

We moved back into the living room and chatted easily as we ate with the plates balanced on our knees. It really felt like this sleepover had accelerated our relationship and not just in the physical sense. I didn't always feel able to share my stories and feelings about the loss of my big sister – it was always such a painful subject for me – so it had been a huge relief to talk to Scott about it and have him understand that part of my life. I told him as much as I popped the last bit of croissant into my mouth.

"I'm glad you felt able to share all that with me," Scott said as he chased the last of his scrambled egg around his plate. "Losing Deb like that must have been heartbreaking, although when you started to tell me what happened I must confess I thought you were going somewhere else entirely with the story."

I looked at him in surprise then. What did he mean by that?

"Can you believe I actually thought you were about to

tell me that your big sister had turned out to be your real mum," he said with a snort of laughter. "You finished?" he added, indicating the empty plate still resting on my knees. I smiled and nodded mutely, taking in the fact Scott had imagined my glamorous older sister had secretly given birth to me and therefore also believed the rest of the family could have colluded in keeping that from me as I grew up. "I mean, you hear about stories like that all the time, don't you?" Scott carried on as he headed towards the kitchen, adding, "Especially in those days. If an unmarried young girl had got pregnant in the Sixties, people would react in a very different way than they would nowadays."

I sat there turning Scott's words over and over in my mind. He was certainly right in what he said about people's attitudes to unwanted pregnancy in the mid Sixties, but of course it couldn't possibly be the case that teenage Deb had been my real mam. That was completely ridiculous! Wasn't it?

Chapter Thirteen

The seed that Scott had sown in my mind, that my beloved, glamorous older sister Deb was actually my mam, took root and sprouted little seedlings of its own over the next hours and days.

I turned the idea over and over, imagining the scenario in all sorts of different ways. It all seemed so plausible I couldn't now figure out why the idea had never occurred to me before.

My mam and dad were certainly at the older end of the spectrum to be parents. Nothing demonstrated it more clearly than the fact that my dad sadly died several years ago and my mam was now in a nursing home, and she had become increasingly frail and forgetful. Tom and Mame had always been wonderful to me and I felt disloyal to suddenly be doubting whether they were indeed my birth parents. Not as disloyal as they may have been to me, mind you, if they had really conspired to keep the truth from me all these years. The whole situation was definitely stirring up a conflicting set of emotions.

As for Deb, I mined my memories for any moments that might have given the slightest indication she was more to me than just a much older sister. The times she danced around with me singing Beatles songs; the nights she wove rags into my hair before bedtime so I'd wake up with curls; the little gifts she brought me linked to our shared love of the Fab Four... Were any of these actions clues that there was a deeper connection between us?

The one thing that meant I couldn't simply shrug off Scott's remark was how very much Deb had always meant to me. I had loved her so much and I always felt she really loved me, too. The connection between us had always been so different to those I had observed between my friends and their sisters. I'd always put it down to the big age difference between us. That marked us out as different, of course, because we weren't squabbling over toys ... or boys ... in the way other sisters of a similar age used to do. But in many ways our age difference should have meant we were more distant as siblings, had less in common, not much interest in each other at all. But Deb and I had not been like that. I had worshipped her and it had always seemed like she was a little besotted with me. I'd never questioned that before or wondered why we acted the way we did with each other, but now I was looking back at our whole relationship from a different angle. Was the reason we always felt so bonded to each other because we were really mother and daughter?

If Deb hadn't been killed, if our lives had unfolded the

way they were supposed to, maybe we would have grown apart, or fallen out over something along the way? Maybe, but I doubted it. If Scott had unwittingly uncovered the truth of my situation, would that fact have been revealed at some point and would I now know all about it? The thought was as tantalising as it was incredible. Was it really possible that my talented, beautiful, slightly wild big sister had been my birth mam?

All of my thoughts kept bringing me back to the one big question – why? If Tom and Mame Hopewell had decided to pass off their wayward teenage daughter's unwanted pregnancy as their own child – why? Why would they do that? Why would a teenager like Deb decide to go through with the pregnancy in the first place? That one was not too hard to figure out an answer to. Abortion would have been a huge decision and I could completely understand anyone finding that solution impossible to contemplate. Why not give the baby up for adoption? That plan was fraught with dilemmas and if a young girl endured nine months of pregnancy it's possible she could potentially change her mind about handing her baby to a stranger after the birth. So that would leave only a couple of options: the first being that a young mum, still in her teens, would have to have given up her education and any career plans to become a full-time mother to her new baby. The life she could have led would be gone. No more hanging out with her mates and people her own age. The boyfriends and the relationships she could have forged would no longer be possible, the opportunities and career choices no longer hers for the taking. Is that what had happened in Deb's case? Had Tom and Mame realised that my birth would have changed

Deb's life in too many negative ways? Had they consequently made a huge sacrifice for their daughter by deciding to bring up their grandchild as their very own?

The scenario was not too difficult to believe but I was going to need more than a passable theory now the idea had taken root. I was going to have to figure out a way to get to the truth. I resolved to confide in Jools before taking things any further. She might have some suggestions of how to proceed, and she was itching to hear more about how things were going with Scott anyway, so I agreed to meet up with her in town for a drink after work.

We arranged to meet at a tapas bar called Lunya in the city centre. It had long been a favourite place of ours and was popular with folk wanting to unwind after a hard day at work. Downstairs was already busy when I arrived, with people sitting on stools at the deli counter beneath hanging aged hams and wreaths of garlic. I knew Jools would have headed upstairs where it would be quieter and, as I thought, she'd bagged a table by the window overlooking the street below. There was a large glass of red already poured and waiting for me, and having eaten there so frequently I barely needed to look at the menu. We quickly ordered a selection of small plates of Spanish delicacies to share and, as always, added Lunya's speciality – a serving of Catalan-style Scouse made with chorizo.

"So?" Jools uttered the one quizzical syllable with an expectant look on her face as I took a large gulp of my wine.

I didn't want to behave like a naughty schoolgirl and gossip about "boys" as though we were behind the bike sheds. I tried to affect a more sophisticated demeanour and gave a casual shrug as I carefully replaced my wine glass on the table between us. "It was … lovely," I said simply. Forget the Spanish surroundings, I suddenly felt quite Parisienne, with my Gallic shrug and attempt at sexual confidence.

Jools wasn't going to be satisfied with just that, however. "The meal? The conversation? The sex? Which bit was the loveliest?" She was smirking as she spoke but I knew she was genuinely chuffed that my foray into internet dating had led to a real relationship. I wouldn't have ever met Scott Smith without her encouragement so I suppose I did owe her more of a detailed explanation.

"The meal was very nice, the conversation flowed easily and the sex, well, let's say we might need a little bit more practice to get the fireworks exploding … but it'll be a lot of fun trying, that's for sure," I answered honestly. There was no point trying to kid a kidder, and Jools would have seen through it straightaway. It wasn't like I was too disappointed with the slight awkwardness we had experienced the first night. Our encounter on the sofa the next day had been a step in the right direction but it would still take time to find our rhythm. I was a bit rusty, that was all, and I couldn't expect Scott to immediately be able to tap into both my deepest emotions and my secret physical desires.

I waited for a glib retort from Julia but instead she had a faraway look in her eyes, almost as though what I'd said made her sad. "Ahh, I remember how it feels right at the start." She sighed. "How wonderful to have so much to look forward to."

A few of the tapas plates arrived then and I tried to make Jools laugh by cracking our usual joke about *albondigas* – the word for Spanish meatballs – as it always made us giggle, but it wasn't having the same effect on this occasion. Jools seemed preoccupied with picking over the padron peppers, and though I tried to catch her eye she looked away as though she was embarrassed about something. I started to tell her how Scott wanted to take me to a Beatles convention, and that he'd booked us on a Magical Mystery Tour bus trip around Liverpool for the end of next week as he was away working until then, but Julia suddenly blurted an exclamation that things were not good with her and Mickey.

At first I was surprised – she and Mickey always seemed so solid – but then I realised that for Jools that was clearly the issue. My fledgling romance with a guy who had practically been a pop star must be making her marriage to a part-time DJ feel stale in comparison.

"Mickey loves the bones of you," I said, hoping to reassure her. I wasn't used to Jools looking down in the dumps; she was one of the most positive people I had ever met.

Now it was her turn to give a Gallic shrug as she bit down into a hunk of garlic bread. For the next hour or so she described the endless ways Mickey was failing to make her feel loved to her bones. Most of her complaints were the predictable sorts of things you would expect in a couple who had been married for years and had kids on the verge of adulthood, but then it strayed into more unusual territory.

"I actually think he loves Elvis more than he loves me!" Jools had downed several glasses of wine by this point and was definitely emotional. I opened my mouth to say something but before I had a chance she was off again. "He spends night after night watching old footage of Elvis concerts, and I've actually caught him trying to copy some of the Presley moves; you know, shaking his leg and wiggling his pelvis!" She looked completely appalled by the memory and I was having trouble picturing tubby Mickey with his little legs and bald head attempting any Elvis-style move. "He's even" – she took a steadying glug of wine before completing the sentence – "he's even trying to grow his sideburns."

She looked at me then with a *"what do you say to that?"* expression. What *should* I say to that? I was a little stumped, to say the least. It sounded like a bit of a mid-life crisis but Mickey had always been a music lover – it was one of the traits we shared that meant I enjoyed his company so much. His interest in music had always been pretty wide although I knew he was particularly fond of the old rock 'n' rollers. I hesitated before I answered Julia. It would be highly hypocritical of me to condemn a man for his affection for any music or musician, given my history with The Beatles. Just because Mickey was a man it didn't rule out the possibility that he felt a deep bond with an artist as incredible as Elvis Presley. I completely got that.

"It's not like he's seeing another woman though?" I said, although I was sure Jools had already factored that into her thinking and it hadn't helped her so far. She admitted then that she thought it possible Mickey *was* seeing someone on the side, pointing out he certainly had the opportunity as he was out several nights a week DJ-ing at a variety of bars, nightclubs and parties all over the north-west of England. She said she was worried he really was up to something.

I countered that I thought it was highly unlikely he was having an affair, but maybe the nub of the problem was she was spending too many nights home alone. Like me, her kids were older now and needed her less, and more time on her own meant time feeling lonely and abandoned.

We spent the rest of the evening talking it all through and by the time we decided to make a move for home it seemed that for Jools a problem shared had been a problem halved. For my part, I kept my mouth firmly shut about the unexpected issue that had raised its head the morning after my night with Scott. For now, the enormous, life-changing question as to who my real mother was would have to go on the back burner. Jools was not in the right frame of mind to deal with my historical drama now she had real-time problems of her own.

―――――――

Later that night I climbed into bed and reached for my iPad to check my messages. I knew Scott had a particularly busy week with meetings, and he was travelling all over, but he had promised to call when he could. A little *"night, night, beautiful"* text message popped up on my screen with a row of kisses. Such a simple thing but the warm glow it gave me would last until I heard from him again.

I went to close the screen but then found my fingers typing the words *"how to find your biological parents"* into a search engine. The results threw up a mixture of ancestry websites, which would presumably help you find out if you were related to Richard III or Anne Boleyn. Other sites had tips for people who knew they were adopted on what channels would reunite them with their birth parents, but there didn't seem to be anything for a middle-aged Beatles fan who may have been lied to all of her life because her sister was really her mother. I wasn't altogether surprised.

I waited until after work the next day to ferret out my birth certificate. I couldn't imagine it would tell me anything new, but I also couldn't remember ever giving it more than a cursory glance when I'd handed it over as a proof of identity to do things like renew my passport. I felt compelled to double-check the details.

I found it in the important drawer where all important things are kept – you know the one, everybody has it!

I sat at the dining table and smoothed out the yellowing paper, taking care not to tear it along the sharp creases where it had been kept folded. It was irritating how brittle it felt to the touch, like a piece of ancient parchment … not exactly good for a girl's confidence to have a physical reminder of the passing of time and how old I really was. I might like to think I looked good for my age but this certificate obviously told the true story.

My name was inked in loopy black handwriting. "Beverley Anne Hopewell". It reminded me of my nickname at school: "Humbug". Some wag had spotted my initials spelled BAH and therefore decided to call me Humbug, as in *"Bah Humbug"*, the phrase used by Scrooge in *A Christmas Carol*. Not that I realised that was the true reason for the name for years; I thought it was because my stripey socks made my legs look like those black and white humbug sweets. How naive I was.

Was I also so naive that I hadn't realised my old mam was actually my grandma? If so, the birth certificate was not going to be the way I found out the truth. As I suspected, the names of my parents had been filled in according to what I had always been told: Father – Thomas Hopewell; Mother – Mabel Ruth Hopewell, formerly Morrison. Or, as they were more commonly known, Tom and Mame.

I sat and considered the document before me. It didn't prove anything one way or another. If Tom and Mame had conspired to bring up their own grandchild as their daughter then of course they would have entered their own names, and not Deb's, on the birth certificate. The deception would have to be done properly if it was going to work.

Had I really imagined that Deb's full name of Deborah Jayne would be written there for anyone to see, in the column headed "mother"? And if it had been, whose name would have been inked into the space reserved for the father of the child? For the first time I let myself really consider the possibility that a mystery man could be my father.

Deb had never had a steady boyfriend that I was aware of when she lived at home. She was always getting dressed up to go out with her mates, or so I thought. Tom and Mame had always spoken indulgently about Deb, as though she was a social butterfly, too pretty to be kept inside and therefore allowed to flutter freely. Had their indulgent parenting style resulted in Deb falling pregnant with me by one of the young men she encountered in the clubs and bars of Swinging Sixties Liverpool? Could it even be someone she met while dancing to the music of The Beatles down at The Cavern Club?

Good grief! It hit me like a sledgehammer – how well had she got to know John, Paul, George and Ringo? Could one of *them* actually be my dad?

Chapter Fourteen

The week that followed seemed to last for ever as I counted down the days until I could see Scott again.

I tried to put all thoughts of Deb being my real mam to the back of my mind. Sometimes it seemed ridiculous how far my imagination had spiralled having been triggered by Scott's one off-the-cuff remark, other times I was practically convinced my entire life had been one big conspiracy and there was an enormous secret world I had been excluded from. Whatever had happened to my boring, humdrum life?

I now spent my time switching between my daydreams of my new romance with Scott Smith – he of Scott Smith and the Silhouettes fame, don't-you-know – and my new pet conspiracy theory. I knew what I really needed to do next was visit Mame in the nursing home, but I was putting that off for as long as possible as I just didn't feel ready. I wasn't getting much sleep, I was distracted at work, and all in all it didn't make for a very peaceful existence.

Scott had only called a couple of times during the week but I knew how busy he was overseeing the refurbishment of a concert hall in Birmingham and he'd sent several messages in between. It gave me time to ponder everything, at least. I decided I didn't want to let him know the quandary he'd put me in with his incidental observation. Anyway, I wasn't some silly schoolgirl who needed to be draped around his neck every minute of the day. I actually liked the fact he worked hard; I found it admirable. That said, I felt like a lovesick teenager on the day we were due to meet up again.

As soon as Scott had found out I'd never been on the Magical Mystery Tour bus trip around the city he insisted on booking two tickets. It was just one of those funny things. Despite my love for the band, and the fact I'd even worked at the Beatles Story tourist attraction for a short, if ill-fated, time, I'd just never got around to taking the tour. No matter how much I thought I knew about John, Paul, George and Ringo, I reckoned I was bound to discover something new, but my giddy excitement probably had much more to do with seeing Scott again than learning any new band trivia.

I thought it was incredibly romantic that Scott had suggested we both head down to the dockside separately and meet up by the Beatles statue on the Pier Head … like something out of *Brief Encounter*.

I arrived early and despite it being sunny and bright there was a chilly breeze down on the waterfront. It's always pretty windy down there, even on the warmest day, and I was glad I had a big, soft, cream scarf to wrap around my neck. I'd decided to wear my bright pink raincoat with the fancy floral lining in case of showers, but as cheerful as it made me feel it didn't offer much warmth.

I took a moment to stand and look at the statue of the four familiar guys cast in bronze. They were captured as if out for a stroll beneath the watchful eyes of the twin Liver Birds on the Royal Liver Building. Paul actually looked as chilly as I felt with his collar turned up and one hand shoved into a pocket of his coat. Ringo and George also had their hands deep inside their pockets. Only John looked unconcerned by the cold weather with his coat casually slung over the bag he carried in his hand.

I walked up to the figures and gazed into each face in turn. They towered over me, each man more than eight feet tall, which I felt befitted their status as true Liverpool giants. I was just pondering what pictures could potentially have been captured on the old-fashioned box camera Paul had tucked in his left hand when I suddenly heard a voice from behind me. "Excuse me, madam, are you ready for your day trip?"

"Scott!"

Wearing a stylish brown leather flying jacket he looked even better than I remembered. I breathed in the delicious smell of real leather mixed with a forest-fresh scent as he put his arms around me and pulled me in for a quick kiss. The memories of our night together flooded back and I briefly considered abandoning all plans to join the bus tour in favour of booking a nearby hotel room. Now was as good a time as any to get some more practice in, but I bit my lip and savoured the kiss instead. I wouldn't want Scott to think I only wanted him for his body, after all!

It was so good to see him. He took my hand as we walked to collect our tickets and started telling me a silly story about something that had happened in one of the many meetings he'd had to go to since he saw me last.

"...But then his mobile went off and his ringtone was 'Agadoo'. Can you imagine?"

To be honest, I hadn't been paying complete attention to what Scott had been saying about the officious building inspector with a surprising taste in music, as I was feeling rather overwhelmed by just the welcome sound of his lovely voice and the wonderful way his warm hand felt in mine. I smiled and nodded, which seemed appropriate, and before I knew it we were boarding the Magical Mystery Tour bus and taking our seats.

Beatles music was playing through tinny speakers while the passengers, mainly foreign tourists, climbed aboard, some of them already snapping pictures through the windows and of each other.

The bus took us on a fun whistle-stop tour of buildings and places relevant to the four members of the band and their rise to worldwide fame. We saw homes and schools, the site of Strawberry Field children's home – where a pair of distinctive red-painted wrought iron gates still stood – and St Peter's church hall in Woolton where John and Paul first met and a gravestone in the churchyard could be found inscribed with the name "Eleanor Rigby".

When we got to Penny Lane we all got out and tried to spot the landmarks mentioned in the lyrics of the song that inspired it. There was indeed a barber who was playing the Penny Lane game by showing photographs in his shop window. Tony the tour guide told us there used to be several high-street banks but only one now remained. Disappointingly, there was no sign of a fireman or any sort of fire engine; perhaps he was busy elsewhere keeping his machine clean. The reality of Penny Lane was certainly in my ears and in my eyes along with all the words of the song I knew so well, although the weather had now turned overcast so unfortunately there were no "blue suburban skies".

We wandered over to the "shelter in the middle of the roundabout", which used to be a bus terminus when The Beatles were boys but was now disused and had been allowed to fall into disrepair. The building was an unusual semi-circular shape, although the "roundabout" was more of a triangular piece of land in the centre of the busy junction. It struck me as a wasted opportunity not to do something more with this iconic building on such a prime spot that attracted hordes of Beatles tourists day after day. It turned out I wasn't the only person to think so as there was a man handing out leaflets and engaging with anyone milling around the old shelter. I noticed he was drawing a small crowd and I found myself drawn towards them, not least because there was something weirdly familiar about him.

Someone handed me one of the leaflets as I hung at the back of the group listening to the man talk. It was a homemade notice headlined "Save the Penny Lane Shelter" and claimed there were plans to tear the place down unless enough money could be raised to save it. I looked up just in time to hear the dark, handsome man say, "If you are able to support our crowdfunding page please do. We would love to create a community café here for Beatles fans to gather and preserve the heritage of this hugely important site." I recognised that voice and that face – it was Detective Constable Levi Collins from Mrs Malkin's house of horrors!

I stood there, a little stunned by the unexpected encounter, my mouth most probably unattractively agape. It was at that very moment, of course, that DC Collins's eyes found mine and he recognised me, too.

"Beverley! Er, Mrs Wilson, hello." For some unfathomable reason he looked pleased to see me.

He pushed his way through the bodies between us and stood in front of me with a warm smile and ready twinkle in his deep brown eyes. I felt myself flush to the roots of my hair, which I presumed was owing to the flashback I'd just had concerning the last thing I'd said to him about my fictitious belly-dancing class. Oh. My. God. With any luck he wouldn't remember that.

"Done any belly dancing recently?" he asked. Just my luck.

I opened my mouth to reply but noticed how his mouth twitched to suppress a smile and felt another flush wash over me as I realised all over again how attractive I found this darkly handsome detective. He spotted my fluster and immediately tried to put me at my ease by making a joke at his own expense instead of mine.

"Maybe you could give me a few lessons. I could do with getting in a bit more exercise." He slapped his hand against his flat stomach, which looked perfectly toned beneath his "off-duty" striped rugby shirt. I knew it, I just *knew* he'd suit a rugby shirt – collar flipped up, sporty but stylish. I'd thought that would be his casual look the very first time we met. He grinned a dazzling smile then and we fell into easy conversation about the shelter and his involvement in the campaign to save it. "I take it you're a Beatles nut too?" The question was rather unnecessary given our current situation, but I found myself telling him that I owned a childhood home of Paul McCartney and therefore fully supported a plan to preserve the shelter for future generations. He was well impressed with that. He told me he often spent his free time helping some friends of his who wanted to make the run-down shelter a real highlight of the Beatles tours. It sounded like a great idea to me.

"The Beatles have done so much to put Liverpool on the map," I told him, "the least we can do is make sure the landmarks connected to them are well looked after."

Levi said he couldn't agree more and was just saying something about maybe going for a coffee or a drink to discuss it all further when Scott suddenly appeared at my elbow.

"Tony the tour guide says it's time to get back on the bus," Scott told us in what I thought was a rather abrupt manner.

"Scott, this is…" I hesitated for a fraction of a second, not exactly sure what to say. But DC Collins wasn't standing on ceremony and stuck out his hand with a friendly, "Levi Collins, pleased to meet you." The two men briefly shook hands but Scott was preoccupied with getting back onto the bus before it left without us. I almost detected a note of jealousy from Scott that he'd found me chatting to another man. I couldn't be certain, of course, but it was a novel and not altogether unpleasant sensation.

I said a quick goodbye to Levi almost over my shoulder, leaving him once again with a quizzical look on his face as he watched me disappear. The poor guy must have had me down as a right flakey bake.

Back on the bus Scott began to grill me on how I knew Levi. I wasn't planning to mislead him but I had no desire to regale Scott with the embarrassing story of our first meeting and how DC Collins thought I lived like a little old lady in a house full of creepy dolls. He also didn't need to know how my lusting after the dishy detective had helped Jools convince me to sign up to the Lonely Hearts Club dating website in the first place. Without my previous encounter with Levi I might never have met Scott Smith, but somehow I had the feeling that Scott wouldn't see at as simply as that. While all those thoughts flashed through my mind Scott helped me out. "I suppose you meet a lot of people in your job," he said, already back to his more affable self as the bus sped through the streets on its way to our last stop. "Was he someone you met on a viewing?"

It wasn't exactly a lie. A viewing, a valuation … you say

"tomayto", I say "tomahto". It seemed churlish to split hairs so I just didn't bother to correct him.

"Mmm hmmm," I answered.

We were on our way back into Liverpool city centre now and The Cavern Club down on Mathew Street. Scott took my hand into his and gave it a squeeze. "Have you enjoyed it so far?" he asked.

I had indeed and I told him I'd particularly enjoyed seeing all the other homes included on the tour, particularly Ringo's childhood home on Admiral Grove, and George's very similar terraced birthplace on Arnold Grove. I was tickled to hear the tour guide say that George often used "Arnold Grove" as a fake name when he wanted to check into a hotel incognito once he was famous. We also had the chance to take pictures outside the most famous Beatle home – Mendips on Menlove Avenue, where John lived with his notorious Aunt Mimi – and also Paul's home on Forthlin Road.

I thought I'd probably return for a nosey around Mendips and Forthlin Road at some point. Both of them were National Trust properties and had been turned into mini museums so it would be interesting to see inside the recreated worlds. However, I hugged the knowledge to myself that I must be the only person on the bus who actually *lived* inside a former Beatle's home. Scott caught me smiling to myself and I felt compelled to explain.

"I doubt anyone else on this tour gets to go home to a house where Paul McCartney used to live," I said, trying not to sound too smug.

Scott nodded emphatically but then suddenly turned to

me as though he'd been hit by a thunderbolt.

"You should be *on* this tour," he said as though it was a revelation.

"I *am* on this tour," I said, not having the slightest clue what point Scott was trying to make.

He laughed then and went on to do a better job of explaining that he meant my little house could possibly offer something different to the tourists and fans on the Magical Mystery Tour.

"Go 'way!" I flapped my hand at him, thinking he must be winding me up.

But Scott had the bit between his teeth and his idea was that foreign tourists in particular would love to meet a *real* Beatles fan, have a chat about their heroes and hear from the horse's mouth, so to speak, what it was like to live in the very place a Beatle had called home.

"You're the real deal, Bev," he said earnestly. "I'm telling you, foreign fans would lap you up, getting their photos taken with 'Beatles Bev'. I'm gonna have a word with Tony the tour guide."

There wasn't much I could do to stop him, but anyway I didn't for a moment expect Tony to be the slightest bit interested in Scott's hair-brained idea. Shows how much I know. After chatting to us for just a short while Tony said he loved it. He reckoned it could work particularly well when they had big Chinese or American parties booked in, or a large group from one of the cruise ships. He took my number and said he'd give me a call. He thought we should maybe start off doing the occasional visit, just a couple of times a month, if that suited me.

I felt completely blindsided by the whole thing as we disembarked for our final stop and walked up Mathew Street until we reached The Cavern Club. I knew the basement venue was not the original venue the band had played in. For reasons that seemed unfathomable to me that place had unfortunately been demolished years ago, and this new Cavern had been recreated a little way down on the opposite side of the street. However, the fact still remained that Mathew Street would forever be linked to The Beatles and it was where my sister had thrown herself into the Swinging Sixties, although with quite how much gusto remained to be seen.

High on the wall above us was yet another tribute to Liverpool's most famous sons. This one had a faceless Madonna figure – some people referred to her as "Mother Mary" – cradling three infants in her arms. These, I knew, were meant to be Paul, George and Ringo. Over to one side another babe with a guitar was clearly John as it had "Lennon Lives" inscribed on a scroll above his little head.

I'd seen the sculpture many times before and I even remembered how it had been altered after Lennon's assassination in 1980. I'd always found it a poignant statue, if slightly macabre in appearance with its shrouded, blank-faced figure at its centre. It was captioned "Four Lads Who Shook The World" and on that day, more than any other time I had ever stood in Mathew Street, a place so synonymous with The Beatles, I felt the truth of that statement to my very core. My love for those guys, their music and everything they meant to me, shook my world and kept on shaking it.

Chapter Fifteen

Unfortunately, the earth didn't exactly move for me later on when Scott came home to Western Avenue and stayed the night.

Harry was out, staying over at a mate's house, clearly having decided to absent himself from the situation after I left him a voicemail giving him the heads-up that we were on our way home after stopping for a bite to eat on the dock. He had responded with a curt text letting me know he was out for the night, signing off, "See ya later", but I knew he was unlikely to reappear until he knew the coast was clear and there was no chance whatsoever that he might catch his middle-aged mother getting up to anything remotely sexual with her new fella. I can't say I blamed him.

I've never been a screamer – well, to be fair, I've never had much to scream about in the bedroom department – but that night I thanked God for the substantial old brickwork of my terraced home as my wooden headboard rhythmically pounded the bedroom wall. Scott seemed determined to give it his all – I have to give him credit for that at least; he got ten out of ten for effort – and it wasn't his fault that I was so out of practice, so I moaned and groaned in all the right places and hoped my neighbours might presume I had taken up midnight DIY if they heard any unusual banging noises. I know what Jeff and Mary next door might surmise should not have been uppermost in my mind as I joined in with gusto, but I found my mind wandering and imagining the Browns having to turn up their TV so they could hear *Question Time* over our energetic lovemaking.

Afterwards we lay spent and slightly sweaty as I pondered the quirks of fate that had brought us together: my initial meeting with DC Collins where I had made a fool of myself because I fancied him; Jools deciding my lust for Levi meant it was time to launch me onto the internet dating scene; finding a dating website with a Beatles-themed name, and then both Scott and me enduring a succession of disastrous dates before we finally found each other. It was a route via both hilarious and disastrous events that had brought Scott into my life. You couldn't make it up!

As I felt Scott drift off to sleep beside me I thought about some of the lyrics from "All You Need Is Love", wise words about how there's nowhere you can be that isn't where you are meant to be, and I considered for the first time what that really meant. Was being right here with Scott always meant to be my destiny?

Scott couldn't stay for the whole weekend, unfortunately, as he had too much stuff to do. He'd told me all about his large house on the outskirts of the city; he was having it fully renovated and it sounded like it would be amazing when it was finished, but the builders had called with yet another issue that he needed to be on site to resolve. Obviously his job as a property manager overseeing all those venues meant he had loads of trusted contacts in the building world, but he said you should always keep on top of things yourself. I agreed that made a lot of sense; a renovation on the scale Scott had described was going to be expensive. The last thing he would want would be for his dream home to turn into a money pit. I offered to tag along – I was desperate for a nosy – but he said he wanted me to see it in all its glory when it was finished. That sounded so exciting. He also said we'd have to wear hard hats on site and Bob the Builder wasn't quite the image I was trying to project.

After Scott left it dawned on me I now had time to go and visit Mame. I couldn't put it off any longer and I was overdue a visit anyway, although my poor old mam would have no clue I now had a hidden agenda. I wasn't intending to march in and interrogate her, but I was hoping to steer the conversation around to an area that might yield some fresh information.

As I arrived at Wisteria Grove Care Home I realised, despite my strong suspicions that Scott had unwittingly unearthed a deep family secret, I was the one feeling overwhelmingly guilty. Mame and Tom had been wonderful parents and though we might not have had much, there was always lots of love. It was a well-worn cliché but that didn't make it any less true. I didn't want to do or say anything that might upset Mame, whether she was my mam or my grandma.

Bearing fancy biscuits and a huge bunch of chrysanthemums, I made my way into the Victorian red-brick villa that had been converted into a residential care home. I had to sign in at reception and winced, as I always did, when I had to give Mam's name as Mabel Hopewell. No one who knew her ever called her Mabel; she had always been Mame – even to me – and it suited her well. I had told them at Wisteria Grove many, many times but it seemed impossible for the numerous staff to maintain a switch from the name written down on all of their documents. Sometimes I wondered if constantly being called the wrong name only added to Mame's confusion as well as her irritation.

I found her dozing in a chair by the window in her room. Behind the original Victorian house was a large one-storey extension where residents had ground-floor rooms looking over the well-kept gardens. It was a nice place, which had made me feel a little better when the decision was made for Mame to move in. My small house was far from suitable for an elderly person and she would have been home alone far too much when I was out at work, so Wisteria Grove had been the only sensible solution.

I busied myself finding a vase for the flowers and organising cups of tea to go with the biscuits, and it was only as I placed her teacup on the table that Mame stirred and gave me a weak smile. I thought she looked frailer every time I saw her now, but I suppose that shouldn't have been too much of a surprise given she was well into her nineties.

We sat companionably for a time. I chatted a little about the boys and what they were all up to, she nodded and smiled vaguely and volunteered the odd comment about something she could see in the garden or a remark harking back decades to an event that occurred long ago.

It was hard to watch a woman who was once so vibrant almost evaporate in front of your eyes. The years of living and loving had exhausted all of her reserves and now, although she appeared intact and still with us, her mind had thrown in the towel and Mame was little more than a shell of the woman she once was.

There were occasional flashes of recognition when I mentioned James, Richie and Harry, although I was pretty certain she still pictured them in short trousers or tearing around on their bikes. Thankfully, she clearly knew me well enough, but there was just no curiosity there anymore. She would simply accept any information passively with no question and then be completely distracted by the sight of a robin in the garden.

I tried to turn my conversation to the subject of Deb – we often talked about her, after all – but this time I was trying to look for … what? An expression on Mame's face that indicated a meaning I had never noticed before? A comment that could confirm my new suspicions were not baseless after all? Now I was here I realised how pointless an exercise such a conversation really was. For instance, if I dared to ask an outright question about whether my big sister had really been my mam, I risked creating upset and confusion for poor Mame, and I just couldn't do that. It felt far too cruel.

So I poured more tea, ate more biscuits and chit-chatted about this and that, just like I had done on countless visits before. After a time Mame's eyes started to close and she leaned her head back in her high-backed winged chair.

I sat for a while and watched her, noticing how peaceful she seemed while asleep, a hint of a smile on her lipsticked pink lips. She'd always taken pride in her appearance and the carers here at Wisteria Grove made sure Mame's nails were kept nicely painted and her silver hair was styled. I was so grateful for that. I knew how important things like that would be to her. She had never been one for fancy clothes or following fashion but she'd always liked to dress quite smartly and in good quality fabrics. She would never have dreamed of wearing jogging bottoms to go to the supermarket or going to bed without removing her make-up and applying moisturiser to her hands and face. She certainly had all those old-school ways that smacked a little of a bygone era.

I looked around the room we were in. It was simply decorated; Mame had brought few personal items with her from the home I had been brought up in. A standard lamp with a cream fringed lampshade stood in the corner, and a small Persian rug with an ornate red and gold pattern was at our feet. I remembered sitting cross-legged in the centre of this rug as a child and pretending it was my very own flying carpet. I didn't recognise the small bedside table next to the bed but on its bottom shelf was an object I definitely knew. It was a polished mahogany box that had been kept in my parents' bedroom for as long as I could remember. Over the years I had seen it on her dressing table, on a shelf inside her wardrobe, even under the bed for a while, but although it had moved around it had always, always been kept close by.

I looked at it now and shook my head in wonder that it had never occurred to me to investigate what was kept inside the wooden casket … until now.

Mame was fast asleep, even giving occasional little snores, her eyelids flickering beneath her perfectly drawn pencilled eyebrows, and so I stood and stepped towards the mahogany box.

It was a lockable chest but the cast-iron key had been helpfully left in the keyhole. I carefully lifted the box from the low shelf, placed it on top of the patchwork bedspread and turned the key.

I felt sneaky – I stood quite literally behind Mame's back – as I flicked through the paperwork, photographs and envelopes inside the box, not even knowing what I was looking for. My fingers found a picture and when I pulled it out I gasped to see it was a photograph of me as a baby, being held in the arms of my big sister, Deb. I didn't remember ever seeing this photograph before – was that significant? Was the picture itself significant? Was it any more than a snap of a sister cuddling the latest addition to her family, a late "surprise" baby born to their middle-aged mam?

I examined the picture in detail. It was black and white, of course, and the image not clear and distinct like photographs taken nowadays. Standing against the side wall of our house Deb had a real Sixties vibe, her blonde, shoulder-length hair cut with a thick fringe and her eyes peeping out from beneath made up with heavy black mascara and liner. Her expression was impossible to read. Despite her mini skirt she had a look that made her appear a lot older than I knew she was at that time. I was little more than a bundle in her arms and although she appeared old enough in years to be my mam there was nothing about her at all that made her look like anyone's idea of a mother.

There were a few heartbreaking keepsakes of Deb squirrelled away in the box: one of her hair bands; a small silk scarf I remember she always loved to wear tightly knotted around her neck; lots of photos; a silver bracelet with a letter D charm hanging from it…

I ran the chain of the bracelet through my fingers and gently stroked the tiny silver letter. I couldn't begin to imagine the pain Mame had gone through when Deb died. The thought of anything happening to my boys was too terrible for me to ever dwell on for long. If I thought I had missed out on having Deb in my life for all these years, how much worse must it have been for our mam, having her first-born child ripped away in such horrific circumstances? There and then I resolved to keep anything I found out about my past from poor old Mame. Losing one child was too awful; I couldn't risk her feeling like she was losing me, too. It didn't have to stop me finding out the truth, however, as the question that had been raised in my mind now needed to be answered. I just had to be extremely careful whom I shared that information with, if I shared it with anyone at all.

The silvery chain in my hands made me feel closer to Deb, like she was standing right by my side urging me on. I carefully placed the bracelet back into the box and rummaged around for anything else that might be a clue. I spotted an envelope in Deb's distinctive handwriting, like a smattering of black spiders had cavorted across the page, or a few of her false eyelashes had fallen onto the paper.

It was a letter written to our mam after Deb had moved to London, full of snippets of nothing very newsworthy, but things a normal mother might like to hear about from a daughter so far away. The weather; what she might have later on for her tea; a coat she'd seen in a shop window that she was saving up to buy … all that sort of thing. I scanned the page, turning it over before my eyes spotted the inclusion of my name. *"Give our Bev a big kiss from me and tell her I haven't met a Beatle – yet,"* she'd written. That was all, no other message, no enquiry about how I was doing at school or if I was being a good girl. Although if she was genuinely concerned about those sorts of things and she *was* my mother I figured she probably wouldn't have high-tailed it to London to throw herself into the tail end of the Swinging Sixties and take up an exciting job on a groovy magazine. She would have stayed in Liverpool to raise me instead.

Also in the box were a few birthday cards me and Deb and my dad had given to Mame years ago, some other letters and keepsakes, and a few crumbly pressed flowers in discoloured tissue paper. I think I'd always known this was Mame's box of memories. It was a shame you couldn't keep things in your mind locked up so neatly with a little key. I placed everything back in the mahogany box and sat back down next to Mame, brushing my fingers gently over her hand as it lay in her lap, trying to wake her. As far as Mame was concerned, I remained convinced it was better to keep quiet about my misgivings and say nothing. She would never need to know I had been snooping.

It wasn't until I was driving back home later on that it occurred to me that there was one other person who might just be able to help me find out the truth about whether Mame or Deb was my birth mother … Doreen Duffy!

Doreen had been Deb's best friend and the girl who had briefly dated Ringo Starr when he was in Rory Storm and the Hurricanes. She was also the person who had passed Ringo's well-worn black leather jacket on to Deb when she realised what a massive Beatles fan Deb had turned into. Deb had always made out Doreen was quite sore about the whole Ringo thing and wanted shot of the jacket. I always thought she must have had quite a thing for him, if she gave away his jacket just because the memory of their fleeting affair upset her. Once he was a big star perhaps she found it even more annoying, knowing she could have been part of it all. I couldn't help but wonder if she regretted it in later years. I don't mean shagging Ringo – that would be a pretty daft thing to regret, if you asked me! But if she had realised how valuable Beatles-related items would be, would she have been so keen to pass the jacket on to our Deb?

There was only one way to find out.

If I was going to question Doreen Duffy about whether Deb had been a secret teenage mother, I'd better go armed with her long-lost leather jacket. At least that would give me a legitimate reason for tracking her down.

I was instantly excited about my new plan, and not just because it might be more fruitful than a rummage around in my mam's old memory box. Doreen Duffy might not be in quite the same league as Yoko, Cynthia, Jane Asher or Pattie Boyd, but I was suddenly very keen to meet a genuine Beatles girlfriend.

Chapter Sixteen

Despite the fact that Ringo Starr's erstwhile ex-girlfriend Doreen Duffy was not a famous model, actress or avant-garde artist, she was still pretty elusive. The first issue was that Duffy was obviously her maiden name back when she was my sister's bestie and I had no idea what her current last name might be, if she had married in the meantime – or if she was even still with us. Doreen would be in her early seventies by now, the same as Deb had she lived.

I sent out a few messages to likely Liverpool folk who might be able to help me trace Doreen's current whereabouts, and then I had no choice but to wait and see if any of the enquiries yielded any leads.

Knowing there was little more I could do for now, I decided not to make Scott aware of the fact I was consumed with curiosity because of his chance remark. I didn't have any desire to share my suspicions with him. He'd simply made a throwaway comment, briefly describing a scenario where a teenage pregnancy in the Sixties was covered up by a family. He wasn't seriously suggesting that *was* what had actually happened to me. It wasn't his fault that his comment had hit home so hard it had made me wonder if that could really be the truth of my past. I also didn't want him to think any less of me if it turned out to be true. I know it sounds daft, but it struck to the very heart of who I was and where I came from, and having been on my own for so long after Geoff died I was already feeling like a different person now I was dating Scott. Reinventing Beverley Wilson, not only as a daughter of a teenage rebel but also as the lover of a handsome, successful businessman slash former pop star, was a lot to take on board. I know I'd started out by wanting to shake my life up but I was going to have to be careful I didn't shake it up so much that I completely fell apart.

Trouble was, a certain amount of recklessness had crept into my behaviour by this point. I almost didn't feel like careful, considered Beverley anymore. For instance, I happened to come across the leaflet Detective Constable Levi Collins had handed me when we'd bumped into each other again on Penny Lane. It was stuffed into the pocket of my pink raincoat and when I pulled it out one day on the way to work something stopped me from putting it straight into the bin. I noticed there was an email address included and it asked anyone who was interested in supporting the campaign to save the roundabout shelter to get in touch with their details. Harmless enough, wouldn't you say? I don't know why I did it, really I don't. I wasn't even sure that I would be able to help at all but some little voice in my head told me to go for it, so I did.

I got a response from someone called Helena Ormiston that same afternoon. She said a small group of shelter supporters were having an informal get-together at the old Casbah Coffee Bar in West Derby. The Casbah! I'd heard of the place, of course I had, what Beatles fan hadn't? It was the place John, Paul and George had first played together as a band, way before The Cavern days. I knew it had been opened by Mona Best, mother of the original Beatles drummer Pete Best, and so it really was the birthplace of the band. But it was out of town, not on any of the Beatles tours, and I wasn't sure there would be anything much to see there so I'd never bothered to go and look. Was it even open to the public? I wasn't sure. But here was an invitation to go along and how could I claim to be a self-respecting Beatles fan if I ignored this chance? It barely even occurred to me that DC Levi Collins might also be there. Well, it might have flitted across my mind for a nanosecond, but it had absolutely nothing to do with the fact that I emailed straight back and told Helena I would love to join them the following evening.

———————

I didn't bother telling Scott about it. Nothing suspicious about that, nothing at all, I just didn't think he'd be all that interested, and anyway, he was away working and very busy. I'd tell him about it afterwards if there was something to actually say.

I parked my car on a leafy street in West Derby just after six-thirty the following evening and looked with interest at the enormous houses lining one side of the road. The Victorian villas around there were vast three-storey buildings with bay windows, and some even had turrets or other unusual features. The estate agent in me was trying to work out the value and saleability of the properties behind ornate metal gates as I made my way to the driveway of number eight.

I'd dressed in black jeans and a black leather jacket and I suddenly wondered if subconsciously my outfit referenced the pictures I'd seen of the very early Beatles days when Stu Sutcliffe and Pete Best were in the band. I hoped my blonde hair and pink T-shirt broke up the rockabilly/Hamburg vibe of the boys' dress code in those days. Perhaps I was channelling Astrid Kirchherr, Stu's avant-garde German girlfriend from that time… I could only hope.

There was a metal Coca-Cola sign high up on the wall of the house that said "Casbah Coffee Bar" so I knew I must be in the right place. I made my way around the side and spotted a handwritten note on a bright red door saying *"Shelter Supporters – Come Right In"*, so I did.

Stepping down into the low-ceilinged, windowless basement I wasn't at all sure what I was expecting, but I was simply staggered by what I found. The place clearly hadn't changed a bit since the days when hundreds of teenagers would cram themselves into every available inch of space to hear the new rock 'n' roll music of the day played in one of the tiny rooms down below Mrs Best's front parlour.

I could hear voices coming from further inside so I made my way through a couple of thick stone archways painted in shiny black. The basement wasn't very big but was split into a series of small interconnecting rooms. There were photographs and letters displayed behind clear Perspex on some of the walls and I was desperate to stop and look at it all, like a proper tourist, but I thought it best to make my presence known to the others.

A few people were standing around chatting in front of a stage area where a drumkit and speakers stood in front of a hand-painted spider's web on the wall. They were all very welcoming and a petite woman with jet-black hair introduced herself as Helena Ormiston. She explained the house still belonged to the Best family and they'd allowed the group to meet there as they supported the attempt to preserve another building linked to the Beatles' legacy.

After we'd all said hello I followed them through to the very last room where there were chairs lined along three of the walls, all facing a bar area. I listened as Helena updated everyone as to where they were in the fight to save the shelter. It turned out the empty building had been owned by a local businessman for several years but he didn't seem to be doing anything with it. Now it stood unloved and abandoned in the very spot where tourists flocked to see the place that inspired all the lyrics in "Penny Lane". One of the other women there suggested we should try and put a business plan together to show how viable a well-run coffee shop could be on that site, and I was just thinking of putting in my two-pennorth by suggesting they talk to Tony at the Magical Mystery Tour to ask how much demand he thought there might be from tourists, when we were interrupted by a couple of late arrivals.

Levi and another man came in carrying cardboard trays of take-out teas and coffees. They were greeted warmly and, if I'm completely honest, I was thrilled to see Levi and not just because he was bearing hot drinks… Well, it was pretty chilly down in a basement with no heating!

He plonked himself down in a chair right opposite where I was sitting and gave me a huge grin. I found his presence distracting for the rest of the meeting and consequently I was suddenly too shy to contribute anything much to the conversation, although I did manage to mention tour guide Tony.

After around forty minutes discussing ways to raise the profile of the Penny Lane Shelter the group sort of broke into little groups chatting with each other and going off to look at various interesting things in the basement club. Everyone was finding the space very inspiring. For a moment I felt a bit lost, and wondered if I should make a quick exit, but then suddenly Levi was at my elbow.

"Hi there, Beverley, good to see you," he said. I smiled and said hi, grateful he had made a beeline for me and I wasn't left standing around like a Billy-no-mates. "Here, let me take that," he said then, reaching for the empty cardboard coffee cup still gripped in my hand. My body gave a small, involuntary shiver as his fingers brushed mine as he took the cup from me. "It's chilly in here, isn't it?" he went on, thankfully assuming my shudders were caused by the low temperature, then he added, "I should think the place would have been sweltering back in the day when everyone was rammed in here listening to The Quarrymen."

He asked me then if I'd ever been inside The Casbah before and what I knew about the place. When I admitted I didn't know too much he started telling me about the history, but then stopped and said, "Tell me to shut up, if you like. It's just that I find this place fascinating. It's the real deal, you see, unlike The Cavern, which is only a replica since they destroyed the original place down on Mathew Street." I told him to go on, I knew exactly what he meant. It was amazing to think we were standing in the actual place where musical history had been made. I wanted Levi to tell me everything he knew and I could've happily listened to his stories all night. Mind you, with his deep, sexy voice, if he'd talked about train timetables I would still have hung on his every word.

Levi didn't need to be asked twice. He launched into tour-guide mode and walked me through the rooms pointing out where John, George, Paul, Pete Best, Stu Sutcliffe and even John's girlfriend Cynthia Powell had helped paint the walls and ceilings under the beady eye of Pete's mam, Mona. John's artwork was right above our heads, a ceiling decorated with black on black Aztec patterns. A silhouette figure of Lennon, based on a poster design done by Pete Best, had been painted by Cynthia on a wall in the room where we'd held our meeting. Cynthia would eventually become John's wife. The black ceiling there was decorated in silver stars, a group effort by John, Paul, George, Pete, Cynthia and Stu. It was clear the group of friends had been connected not only by music but also by their artistic flair. It was a real insight into how the friendships had been formed.

George's particular contribution was a stretch of ceiling in the narrowest room, where Levi told me the original stage area had been when the club first opened in 1959. I noticed it was painted an orangey colour, the exact same shade as the robes worn by followers of Hare Krishna, which was incredible given how devoted to the religion George became in much later years.

Before Levi could tell me which ceiling Paul had painted I pointed to the rainbow pattern above the tiny space where the bands used to perform and asked if that was "an original McCartney". Levi laughed and told me I was right. I'd sussed it straightaway as the colours Paul had used and the rainbow theme reminded me so much of the pattern he always used on his upright piano on stage. I was stunned to discover the artwork done by those kids back when they were just sixteen and seventeen had lasted for more than fifty years. It was wonderful to see.

There was also the spider's web painted on the wall behind the larger stage area, an enormous dragon along the wall where the original entrance used to be, and even a beetle by the door to the garden! I couldn't stop myself running my fingers over the cold stone walls and trying to imagine the group of teenagers being bossed about by Mona as she handed out paint pots and brushes to her son and his mates.

Levi told me Mona had a fearsome reputation in Liverpool. "No one said no to Mona," he said, raising an eyebrow. I hadn't realised quite how important Mona Best really was to the Beatles story. She wasn't just mam to their first drummer or someone who let the local kids hang out in her cellar to give them something to do – she had a real vision. Levi told me Mona had seen an item on television about the 2i's Coffee Bar in London's Soho – the first rock 'n' roll café in the country – and she'd asked her son Pete if there was anywhere like it in Liverpool – somewhere young bands could play and kids could listen to the new, exciting music from America. When she discovered there wasn't anywhere like that at all she decided to convert her basement and open her own. She press-ganged Pete and his pals to set to work cleaning the basement, did a deal with Coca-Cola to provide soft drinks alongside the milky coffee and snacks, set up membership and ticket sales and then started finding bands to play. George Harrison was in a band called the Les Stewart Quartet at that time and they agreed to play Mona's opening night, but unluckily for them, they had a fall-out before the big day. Undeterred, Mona asked George if he knew anyone else he could play with instead … and he mentioned a couple of lads called John Lennon and Paul McCartney.

Levi paused for breath as we stood under the low rainbow ceiling in the tiny room and I tried to imagine how it would have felt to be in this underground space with a band playing rock 'n' roll music at full volume. I thought it must have shaken the house to its very foundations.

A large black and white photograph was facing us of a ridiculously young McCartney singing into a stand-up mic, with Lennon seated on one side facing the camera and Harrison with his head turned shyly away towards the wall on his other side. It had been taken on the exact spot where we were standing. This indeed was the absolute birthplace of the group that would become The Beatles, a rock 'n' roll band with a bigger impact and longer legacy than any other band in the history of the whole world.

I realised I had been stood silently for a little while taking all of this in. Levi watched me carefully as if he knew I was processing the information he had given me and how much it all meant.

"Incredible, isn't it?" he said, his low voice rumbling around in the underground hideaway, his passion for the music and history clearly matching my own. I didn't trust myself to speak and simply nodded. He turned and beckoned me towards a narrow corridor where a black dragon breathing red fire was emblazoned across a silvery white wall and told me Mona herself had painted it. I asked Levi then how he knew so much about Mona Best and the history"– and that Roag and his wife Leigh now looked after the historic Casbah and planned to turn the house above it into a Beatles-themed hotel, with six rooms, one named for each Beatle member – John, Paul, George, Ringo, Stu Sutcliffe and Pete Best. I thought that sounded like a brilliant idea.

"Of course Mona herself had *three* sons, but you know that, don't you?" Levi said then.

"What? Three boys? I have three boys, too!" I exclaimed in surprise, feeling an instant connection to Mona the mother, music lover and matriarch of a rock 'n' roll revolution. I decided then and there we should all "be more Mona": follow your passions, live your dreams and just look what can happen as a result! My desire to "shake my life up" had never made more sense. I told Levi as much and he nodded his approval.

I bombarded Levi with more questions as I wanted to know more about Mona Best; she sounded like the most amazing woman. He told me she had been born in India and came to Liverpool on a ship with her husband, John Best, and two sons, Pete and Rory, in the 1940s. Roag, her third son, was born much later and his dad was Neil Aspinall, another key figure in Beatles history.

According to Levi, the story went that Mona was able to afford the huge house in Hayman's Green, West Derby, owing to her gambling winnings on a horse called Never Say Die ridden by a young jockey called Lester Piggott.

"Blimey," I said, "Mona was a bit ahead of her time, wasn't she?"

"Well, if you think about it," Levi said as we looked at a display showing how The Casbah had been twinned in recent years with its American equivalent, Sun Studio in Memphis, "with the work Mona did finding and helping bands to get gigs in and around the city, she wasn't just the first female rock promoter in Liverpool, she was first female rock promoter in the *world*! She was the original Sharon Osbourne!"

Good grief… Go, Mona! I realised Levi was right. What an amazing achievement and by a woman at a time when women were supposed to stay home and look after the kids and put tea on the table for their husbands. Instead, Mona Best had ripped up the housewife rulebook and allowed herself to follow her love of music wherever it led her – and just look what had happened! I found myself completely inspired by Mona's story, her power and influence clear to me as I stood in her basement that day. By sheer bloody-mindedness and with amazing foresight she had created somewhere equal in importance to the famous Sun Studio, the one-room recording studio in downtown Memphis where Elvis Presley was discovered by Sam Phillips in the 1950s. Both were tiny places where the walls still vibrated with the musical explosions they had experienced so long ago. I could hear the echoes for myself! In my whole life I'd never felt so connected to a moment in history.

"Wow" was the only thing I was able to say as Levi and I carried on looking around The Casbah and soaking up the atmosphere until I could almost imagine it really was 1959 and we were excited teenagers waiting for the music to start.

It was when I suddenly realised I really needed a wee that I was brought sharply back to the present day. Not because I was directed to The Casbah outdoor lavatories – they were basic and breezy but perfectly acceptable – but as I wriggled out of my jeans my mobile phone started to ping repeatedly. The basement rooms had obviously blocked my phone reception but now messages were flooding in. Who on earth was so desperate to reach me?

Scott! With a lurch in my tummy I realised I hadn't given him a thought for the last couple of hours. He didn't know I was out so probably expected me to be at home, watching TV on my own, like I did most nights he was away. There were dozens of missed calls, text messages and a couple of voicemails. Was everything okay? The messages didn't indicate he was in any sort of difficulty. Where was the fire? I should have been flattered he was so keen to reach me but in fact I found it pretty irritating. Wasn't I allowed to go anywhere without clearing it with him first? I'd only just got used to being able to make my own arrangements without factoring in the needs of three small boys; now it seemed I had another person to answer to. But then I thought about how cosy I'd been getting with lovely Levi, how his deep, sexy voice had been making me feel all evening, and I had a pang of painful guilt. I stepped out of the outdoor cubicle and immediately tried to return Scott's many calls, but he didn't pick up.

I went back into The Casbah but the spell had been broken. I felt anxious and alarmed at my own behaviour. What did I think I was playing at, flirting with Levi when I knew all along that I was involved with another man? It wasn't fair on either of them, and if a man ever did that to me I knew exactly what names I would call him! I had known very well that Levi could be at the meeting. In fact, it *was* the main reason I had gone along – I felt there was an attraction between us and I had wanted to see him again. There, I had finally admitted it to myself and therefore left myself no option but to come clean and get myself the hell out of there before I got myself into any more trouble.

I wasn't sure how to read the expression on Levi's face when I abruptly announced I had to go and then muttered something about "my boyfriend". He looked surprised, for sure, but was he also disappointed … or annoyed? I didn't know him well enough to be able to tell and now I knew I never would.

As I drove away my heart sank and my stomach was in knots. Being this new and brave version of Beverley wasn't that easy after all. I wasn't a formidable woman-to-be-reckoned-with like Mona Best, I was just me, Beverley Wilson, part-time estate agent, full-time Beatles fan, mum of three, and clearly completely terrible at romantic relationships.

I decided that if I was going to hang on to Scott, I'd better sort myself out and try an awful lot harder before he came to his senses and dumped me.

Chapter Seventeen

By the time I got home I was rather relieved that Scott hadn't answered my call from The Casbah khazi. I hadn't had to tell him where I was and what I was doing while I was standing just a few feet away from Levi. I was going to tell him the truth, of course – or at least *most* of the truth – and I felt it would be less stressful to talk about once I was home and in my pyjamas, curled on the sofa with a cocoa.

It didn't go quite the way I hoped however... Why was I surprised? He didn't answer when I tried him again or respond to my texts or messages. Giving me a taste of my own medicine, no doubt... Could I really blame him? It jangled my nerves to find I couldn't get hold of him. Did he somehow know what had been in my mind when I was lapping up all of Levi's attention? Was he furious? Was it all over between us? My mind was whirling way ahead of what could actually be happening and I had to force myself to stop trying to reach him. I didn't want to behave like a silly teenager but that seemed to be an unforeseen consequence of signing up to a damn dating app.

I was just getting into bed when Scott finally called me back. It was a little awkward at first. I didn't want to demand to know where he had been or ask what he'd been doing in case he was about to do the very same to me. The conversation was stilted and sort of business-like.

"It's been a very busy day today," he said, not offering any more detail on what had been keeping him occupied.

"Oh, same here," I said, seizing the chance to make out I'd been up to my eyes.

Neither of us appeared keen to volunteer too much more information so I took the plunge and told him that I'd been to visit The Casbah and how amazing it was, how well preserved the place had been and how much I'd learned about Mona Best and the very beginning of the Beatles' story. I enthused about how inspiring it all was to the group who wanted to save the shelter on Penny Lane.

Scott let me rattle on for a good while before he spoke slowly and clearly into my ear. "So, tonight was organised by that Black guy pushing leaflets on people in Penny Lane? I thought you said you didn't know him?"

I sensed hostility in his tone. Why had he even mentioned Levi's skin colour? I stuttered and stumbled over my reply but eventually managed an explanation that didn't make it sound like Levi was the reason I had gone along to The Casbah.

It was all very confusing. Was Scott angry? Jealous? I was already keeping secrets from him since deciding not to tell him about my suspicion that he might have been right about my sister being my real mam. Now I was sort of hiding something else, it was no wonder he was picking up weird signals. I tried to move the conversation onto safer ground, telling him how much I missed him, and asking when we would see each other again. He was vague and said he had a lot of work on but would call me soon. I didn't sleep at all well that night.

The very next day, however, he called at lunchtime and sounded back to his usual, lovely, jokey self and told me he'd see me the following night. Phew.

I decided to keep my inner turmoil to myself. The last thing I thought Scott would be interested in would be a mixed-up middle-aged woman with a complicated past, and the very less said about Levi then clearly the better.

It was a hiccup, that was all. Every relationship had them. This was all very new territory for me and I didn't have a road map – it was no wonder I'd taken a couple of wrong turns – but I was determined to get everything right back on track.

My thriving relationship with Scott had boosted my confidence and what is it they say about pride? Yep … it comes before a fall! Luckily I'd managed to pull myself back from the brink of doing anything too catastrophic, but my inflated ego had allowed me to flirt not only with Levi, but also with danger. I felt more attractive than I had in years just because one man found me sexy, and I had been tempted to test my new-found powers on Levi. I gave myself a stern talking to – men were not like buses, you didn't have to jump on any available one that happened to come along. One man was more than enough for me and I resolved to double down on my efforts to keep Scott satisfied otherwise I'd be back to standing at the bus stop all alone.

I shouldn't have worried as Scott also seemed keener than ever from then on. He began to pull out all the stops, wining and dining me as though his life depended on it. We were going out more than ever and to some seriously fancy places. Maybe sensing there could be a rival for my affections had worked to my advantage after all. I had no idea men like Scott really existed outside of the movies or the pages of a romantic novel.

The longer we were together the more I realised just what an amazing catch Mr Scott Smith really was. Not only was he great-looking and good company, he also clearly had money to spend and had no hesitation in spending it on me. When we first met I didn't notice how nice his clothes were or how expensive his watch was. Things like that don't matter a jot to me. In fact, thinking about it, I wondered if Scott had played certain things about himself and his lifestyle down at first so that he didn't end up with some sort of gold-digger. Smart move.

As a former pop star, he'd probably come across a lot of women who were happy to throw themselves at him just because he was in a band. Maybe Scott Smith and the Silhouettes even attracted groupies? That might be fun for a while, but at our age surely you needed to know someone wanted to be with you for yourself and your personality, not just because they wanted a fleeting brush with fame or were after what your money could buy. In my mind, it just went to prove the point The Beatles had so eloquently made when they said, "Money can't buy me love".

I realised it was also probably down to his background in the music business that Scott had developed a liking for the good things in life, such as lovely food and swish hotels. I was more than happy in Beppi's Bistro with a plate of pasta I hadn't had to cook myself, but we started trying some of the more expensive places in the city where Scott tucked into steak and encouraged me to try lobster for the very first time. It was a bit like crab, I thought, but not quite as tasty. Scott laughed and jokingly called me a "cheap date". I didn't mind; anything was better than him thinking I was a money-grabbing minx.

When he first suggested a weekend away in a spa hotel in Cheshire I couldn't wait to tell Jools. Then I remembered that things were still a bit dicey between her and Mickey so I made sure not to sound like I was bragging too much.

"Oh My God," Jools said, despite the fact I'd tried to sound très casual when I dropped in the conversation that we were having a couple of nights away. "Is there a hot tub? Will you drink champagne in the bath? Will you be able to see herds of deer from your bedroom window? Will there be rose petals on the bedspread and a chocolate mint on your pillow? Is it *that* posh?" I told her I had no idea but it turned out she was right on the money and that was *exactly* what it was like, and we ended up experiencing *all* those things and even a few more.

It wasn't those things that made me start to fall in love with Scott, mind you. You can't blame a girl for lapping up all that luxury but I'm really not that shallow. It was the more mundane, ordinary things he did that made me realise how much I had missed having a man about the house and how wonderful it was to have someone to help out sometimes.

Take the night we heard weird noises coming from my attic. Well, I wasn't sure what I heard but Scott woke me up saying he was sure he could hear some scratching just above where we were lying in bed. He got up and stood out on the landing, listening under the loft hatch door and then paced from room to room to see if he could work out what it was. Harry was away that weekend – he'd gone down to stay with James at his uni digs in Birmingham for a few days – so Scott was able to go into all the upstairs rooms to do a thorough check.

He said he'd have to go up into the loft the next morning to see what he could find. That night I barely slept, lying there after Scott had gone back to sleep and freaking out at every creak and squeak my old house made around me.

Scott was as good as his word as soon as we'd had our breakfast the next day, and when he came back down from his intrepid loft investigation he confirmed my very worst fears. I'd got mice! I clamped my hand over my mouth in horror and tried not to scream but straightway Scott did his best to calm me down.

"An old house like this is bound to get mice from time to time," he said reasonably. How could he just take an infestation of disease-ridden rodents in his stride? "They could do quite a bit of damage if we just leave them to it though," he added. "They could chew through cables or start to eat anything you've got stored up there ... as well as make nests and have more babies, of course." I thought I was going to be sick.

He said we needed to lay some traps, and while the thought of catching and killing mice in vicious spring-loaded metal devices completely appalled my animal-loving, almost vegetarian soul, I just wanted the little beasts gone. Scott could see I didn't have the stomach to deal with it myself so he took care of buying the traps from the local hardware store and then went up into the loft to lay them down in strategic places.

"You can see by the droppings where the regular runs are," he told me. Was the guy a bona fide wildlife expert? How did he know all this sort of stuff? Could he wrestle crocodiles, too? He even knew that peanut butter or chocolate was better bait for trapping mice than cheese! I just nodded and left him to it.

He made a point of checking the traps regularly whenever he stayed over and would come down with the little bodies in a black bin bag before taking them out to dispose of them on the waste land at the end of the road.

"That'll be a tasty little treat for the owls and foxes," he said, which did make me feel better about it all. It was the natural circle of life, and foxes and owls did have to eat, I supposed.

He only tried to get me to look at a dead mouse once.

"This is the biggest one yet!" he said with a satisfied gleam in his eye when he came down to the kitchen where I was hoping he was going to say we'd won the mouse war and they were all gone. As he came towards me opening the bag for me to take a look I backed away, terrified, and almost burst into tears. He quickly tied the bag up and told me not to worry, he'd deal with it all and they would soon be gone. It couldn't happen quick enough for me.

The nights Scott was away working and I was home alone I fretted and fussed over every tiny noise I could hear, although the noises were never that loud so I knew Scott's plan must be working. I was so grateful I could kiss him. So I did.

If only we could have stayed at his house occasionally but the renovation work was dragging on and on, as these things always tend to do. He often showed me pictures on his phone of the latest bit of progress, some new flooring here, a section of bathroom tiling there, but it did look like the place was in far too much upheaval for anyone to stay there.

When he wasn't at mine he stayed in a B&B in town where the landlady was apparently a dragon who had very strict rules against "overnight visitors".

"It is a bit like something out of the dark ages," he said with a laugh when he explained why it wouldn't be a good idea for me to go back there. "But when I'm on the road the company put me up in pretty decent hotels, so it's not worth paying out for anything fancy back here as I just need somewhere to rest my head and keep a change of clothes until the house is done." It made sense and I was just glad I was able to offer him some home comforts occasionally when he was back in Liverpool. He was always working so hard.

Jools had started nagging me to arrange a double date with her and Mickey so she could finally meet Scott and give him the full Julia Gillespie once-over. I think I was probably more nervous about that than Scott; after all, he didn't know her and her capacity for forensic questioning. I put off even mentioning the possibility to him for several weeks; I was desperate not to do anything to scare him away. Harry was helping me out by arranging sleepovers at his mates' every time we knew Scott was going to be around. I was truly grateful for the space he was giving me. It saved both of our blushes in many ways. I also felt more comfortable not making Harry feel he suddenly had an instant "new dad". I knew he wasn't a toddler who would get confused by Mummy's "new special friend" but I didn't want to force the two of them together too soon. If Scott was going to end up being a member of our family it all needed to be handled with a great deal of care, and if, for some reason, it wasn't going to last, then I didn't want any of my boys to have grown attached to a man who might suddenly disappear from their lives. Dating when you've got kids, no matter how old they are, is an absolute minefield.

Eventually, though, I could no longer avoid Julia's repeated requests for a meet-and-greet with Scott, so I chose my moment to mention it to him with extreme care. We were snuggled up on my sofa watching a movie and drinking wine. I hadn't expected to see Scott at all that night as he had been at a conference in Swindon or Slough, or somewhere like that. The kind of place businesspeople always moan about having to go to. Anyway, I knew he would be busy there for a few days so I'd planned a quiet night in – a catch-up on the soaps, long hot bubble bath, that kinda thing. I'd just towel-dried my hair, slathered on my favourite amber and vanilla moisturiser and wrapped myself in the super soft velvety robe Scott had treated me to after I said how much I liked it at the fancy spa hotel, but then suddenly the doorbell had rung.

You could have knocked me down with a feather when I discovered Scott standing on my doorstep. He'd looked at me with a mischievous expression on his face, delighted to have caught me unawares and even more delighted to find me in a state of undress.

"Special delivery," he said, swinging a fancy yellow carrier bag out from behind his overnight bag. His conference had finished early and he'd picked up some delicious take-out tapas and wine from Selfridges and headed straight up to Liverpool to surprise me. I honestly went quite weak at the knees.

After we'd eaten and made out on the sofa like a couple of teenagers … or was it the other way round? Well, after all that, Scott picked out an action movie and we settled back all cosy and content. I knew it was a risk bringing up the subject of a meal out with a couple of my oldest friends. If he felt I was rushing things or trying to manoeuvre him into something too "coupley" it could really ruin the mood. Men can be so funny about those sorts of things, can't they? But not for the first time that night, Scott surprised me.

"Yeah, sure, great idea, I'd love to," he said.

"Really?" My gast was flabbered. Scott really was the sort of guy who could take almost anything on the chin; it felt amazing to be with someone so happy to be spontaneous. I couldn't remember what I had been so panicky about in the first place, I decided there and then I needed to relax more and give Scott a lot more credit.

He scrolled through his diary on his phone and gave me a couple of possible dates and I texted Jools immediately. Within half an hour we had a date all set and Jools was going to call a new Japanese teriyaki restaurant down in Liverpool One to book us a table.

Social engagement arranged, we settled back to watch the rest of the movie, although by now we'd lost the thread of the plot so Scott suggested we go upstairs instead and engage in another sort of action. Things were definitely improving in that department, too, and I remember thinking this guy was so good he could be made of chocolate. Either way, I just wanted to eat him up.

The double date with Jools and Mickey came around super-fast, but then my entire life seemed to be set to fast forward at that point. On the night we'd arranged to meet I checked out my reflection in my full-length wardrobe mirror as I tried to ignore the butterflies in my tummy at the thought of Scott coming face-to-face with Jools. I reflected on two things as I studied my own reflection. The first was that being with Scott had given me a glow I didn't remember having before. My eyes were bright, my hair bouncy and shiny… In short – despite making myself sound like a finalist at Crufts – I looked better than I had for years. The second was that the outfit I'd selected for our Japanese meal foursome was flattering but maybe a little too business-like. A white silk shirt tucked into high-waisted black pants and nude patent heels made me look like I was about to present my case to the judge in high court. I briefly wondered if my subconscious had again decided to dress me, this time in a way that would help me present the defence for Scott if Jools decided to launch too strong an inquisition. That was ridiculous, of course. Jools was my best friend, she wouldn't behave in that way, and Scott wasn't the defendant, he was my boyfriend. There, I'd said it. I looked myself straight in the eye and said it out loud for the very first time. "Scott Smith is my boyfriend."

The butterflies swooped and swirled but now for a different reason. I fluffed my hair and grabbed a silk scarf with a pink and purple abstract pattern to soften my look. I felt great, I looked good, and I was about to head out to one of the best restaurants in town to meet up with my best mates and my *boyfriend*. Does life get much better than that?

———

Unfortunately, the evening didn't stick to the good vibe script. Jools and Mickey were already at the table when I arrived, waving me over wearing goofy grins and looking over my shoulder expectantly as I walked towards them.

"Scott's not with me. He's on his way here straight from work; he's been somewhere in North Wales today," I explained as I approached the table, only to be rewarded with the grins being instantly replaced by grimaces. You'd think I'd just cancelled Christmas. "He'll be here soon, I'm sure," I added, rolling my eyes at their obvious impatience. Were they really so starved of excitement in their own lives that meeting my new fella was a such a highlight?

Jools looked like she'd put a real effort into her

appearance, I hoped it was just as much for Mickey as it was to make a good impression with Scott. She wore a vivid green chiffon blouse that really complimented her bright red hair. She'd styled her hair slicked back at the sides and high and spiky on top which looked really cool. Mickey just loved a flowery shirt, we were always teasing him about them, but on closer inspection the one he wore that night had an unusually high collar that almost met his newly grown extra-long sideburns. I could see what Jools had meant; it all had a definite whiff of Elvis worship.

We ordered drinks and sat chatting while we watched the Japanese chefs expertly cooking steak, fish and assorted vegetables on a sizzling hot plate close to our table. It was mesmerising and also made us increasingly hungry.

I tried not to be too obvious checking my watch but Scott was clearly running late. I put off looking at my phone for as long as possible, too, but eventually I excused myself to go to the loo. I was standing just outside the ladies' room when I read the text that made my heart sink right to the soles of my slightly too tight shoes.

Bev soooo sorry, car broken down just outside Chester. Waiting for AA man now

The message had been sent about twenty minutes ago. I quickly typed a reply.

OH NO What happened? Is AA man there yet?

I stood shifting my weight from foot to foot, thinking I

should have worn these shoes in more before wearing them outside – put them on to do the ironing, or hoovered the house from top to bottom maybe. I read somewhere that was a good way to wear in new shoes.

My phone pinged with a reply.

Not yet. Could be 2 hours wait. Sooooooo sorry. Apologise to Julia and Mickey for me XX

So that was that.

Jools and Mickey actually put a pretty brave face on it, which I'm sure was for my benefit. They were disappointed but they didn't want me to feel embarrassed, like my boyfriend had stood me up or something. They were such good friends.

I couldn't help keeping an eye on the door and hoping my phone would vibrate in my bag telling me Scott was on his way after all though. Chester wasn't so very far away; surely it would be better for him to arrive late than never? But it wasn't to be. We ate our meals, ordered several rounds of drinks and did everything we could to make the best of the evening.

Jools and Mickey were good company, as always, and it was a relief to see them looking happy and relaxed together, though when Mickey was in the loo Jools was vague and just shrugged when I asked her how things were going. He'd mentioned that he had a lot of party bookings coming up for his DJ sets; that meant more time away working, of course, but it also meant an increase in money coming in so I was pleased for him. I understood how difficult it was to be in a relationship with someone who had to be pulled away by work – look at what had happened tonight – but that was the price you paid for being with a hard-working, successful man. It had to be better than having a useless, work-shy no-mark hanging around the place, scrounging off you all the time. I felt both Jools and I were lucky not to have to worry on that score.

Eventually my bag did judder with a message arriving on my phone. Just as we were asking for the bill Scott let me know the AA man's verdict was that his *"Big end had gone"* – after several hours swigging saki, Jools couldn't help but make a few choice remarks about that – but the sharp disappointment inside me prevented more than a wry smile from me in response to her banter.

Mickey insisted on us all sharing a taxi and they went out of their way to drop me off first before heading home, leaving me to let myself in to Western Avenue. It wasn't an empty house as Harry was home, sprawled across the sofa playing video games when I came in, but I felt a little empty myself. I'd been planning to call Scott to tell him to come over no matter how late it was, but he'd pre-empted my request by sending a message saying the breakdown recovery would be dropping him back at his own digs and he'd be staying the night there as he had another early start in the morning.

It was close to one a.m. and I was tucked up in bed just dozing off when suddenly my mobile rang. I grabbed it off the bedside table. "Scott?"

"Oh Bev, I'm so sorry… What a bloody nightmare!"

"Don't worry, love, we'll do it another time. Are you okay?"

He said he was fine but exhausted and he certainly sounded very tired.

I told him I was sorry about his car, which sounded like it was completely done for. He wasn't nearly so worried about that, however. I hadn't realised but it had been a company car and he said they would be sending another one round in the morning. Even better, it would be an upgraded, new and improved model. Every cloud.

I was pleased for him but joked that he better not get any ideas about trading *me* in for something similar anytime soon.

He gave a throaty laugh at that. I loved making him laugh. His voice came through the phone low and husky with a seductive edge to his words. "Baby, you can drive my car," he whispered.

The disastrous night ended on a high after all... Beep, beep, beep, Yeah!

Chapter Eighteen

A couple of days after the Japanese restaurant fiasco my luck changed and I got a message from someone I knew who worked at The Beatles Story, the exhibition dedicated to the band down on the dock. They'd heard I was on the hunt for Ringo's ex-girlfriend Doreen Duffy, and said they might have some information that could help me.

I knew Linda, who worked in the ticket office, from the brief but eventful time I had worked there myself as a tour guide, so I decided to pop over to see her in my lunch break. It would be good to catch up and I never needed much of an excuse to revisit the museum. It was such a great, atmospheric place and there always seemed to be something new there to see.

The museum is all below ground and the subterranean sense it lends always feels welcoming and womb-like to me. It particularly suits the recreated Cavern Club it houses where the low arched ceilings and black painted walls are made to look like they are shimmering with sweat. Beatles music pumps out from the speakers in each of the sections, something suitable for the timeline each exhibit is illustrating, from "Twist and Shout" in the gloomy Cavern space to "Imagine", where a white piano in a light-filled room has a pair of Lennon's round-framed glasses placed poignantly on its lid.

There are colourful illustrations of the *Sergeant Pepper's Lonely Hearts Club Band* period alongside replicas of the band's satin military-style costumes, and mad psychedelic pop art showing cartoon Yellow Submarines and Blue Meanies. I particularly enjoy spending time in the recreated Nems Music Store. I like to imagine what it must have been like back in the Sixties, to be able to go in and hear a Beatles record for the very first time in a little booth, sharing a set of headphones with your mate.

I was sad that I had to stop working at the popular attraction. It had suited me down to the ground, being able to share my extensive Beatles knowledge with tourists and locals alike, but after the incident on my maiden voyage as driver of the amphibious duckmarine bus my presence had no longer been required. I enjoy being a part-time estate agent now anyway, and at least all my work is on dry land.

I stopped to study the four waxwork models of John, Paul, George and Ringo positioned behind glass as though midway through a recording session at Abbey Road Studios. The suited figures were all matched with their well-known instruments – Lennon with a short-scale Rickenbacker, Harrison playing lead guitar, McCartney on bass, and Starr with his mop of shaggy hair and drumsticks aloft behind the kit with the world famous black and white Beatles logo on the drum skin.

Ringo! That reminded me why I was here in my lunch hour: not to walk down Beatles memory lane yet again, but to find out if I had a chance of locating Doreen Duffy in my quest to discover the truth about who my mam really was.

Linda grabbed us a couple of coffees and we quickly caught up with each other before she eventually slid a piece of paper across the Formica table between us.

"She's called Doreen Jordan now," she said, the r's in the name catching in her throat owing to her pronounced Scouse accent.

Linda said a friend of a friend had given her the intel. Liverpudlians are like the Mafia; everyone knows someone and they feed on intrigue and passing information. It's a wonder secret services like MI5 and MI6 aren't completely made up of Scousers. Maybe it's because the accent would give us away? I've always said if you want to find something out, ask a Liverpudlian, and God forbid you should ever cross one, the whole city will come out to fight your case, quick as you could say, *"Do one, soft lad!"*

I had to throw Linda off the scent regarding what I really wanted to speak to Doreen about. The last thing I needed was word getting out that "Beatles Bev" suspected her sister was really her mam. If that hit the local jungle drums it would be bound to lead to rumours my big sister had been shagging a Beatle, which would in turn immediately brand me an unclaimed child of one of the Fab Four to boot.

So, I stuck to the story that I'd realised something in my memorabilia collection may once have belonged to Doreen and I wanted an opportunity to return it. It drove Linda mad that I wouldn't even tell her what it was.

"If the daft cow hasn't come lookin' for it, why go to all the bother?" she queried dismissively, clearly rattled she had no clue as to what the lost Beatles treasure might be.

I reassured Linda I knew what I was doing and extricated myself from further questioning by telling her I had to get back to work. It wasn't a lie. I had to get a shift on to make it to a viewing I'd got lined up at a loft apartment in the old Tobacco Warehouse. I'd cannily booked the appointment knowing it was just around the corner from the museum.

———————

I was only able to sit on the information contained on the scrap of paper Linda had given me for a few hours. By the next day I was itching to go round to the address in Norris Green and see what I could get out of Doreen Jordan née Duffy.

I considered taking Ringo's leather jacket with me as an ice-breaker but that would involve braving the mice-infested attic. I thought I'd rather put that off as long as possible and anyway, she might not even want it. I hadn't heard any sounds coming from above my bedroom ceiling for a while, but every time Scott went up to check he came down with yet another rodent cadaver. I would have to make a lot of noise and flash the lights on and off when I eventually went up there myself, to make sure the little beasts were more scared of me than I was of them. I didn't want to ask Scott to do it for me although I was sure he would do it in a heartbeat. I knew what I was looking for and anyway, I was hatching a plan to retrieve a couple of other items while I was up there. Scott had been so good to me, buying me stuff, treating us to meals out and nights away, I wanted to be able to treat *him* to something for a change. I reckoned if I could sell the little Olive Adair Beatles perfume bottle I had – it was mint condition and still full of scent – I might be able to afford to pay for a little holiday for the two of us. I knew it could easily fetch over a grand. The thought of that would be enough to make me overcome my mice fears. Fingers crossed.

I was fantasising about surprising Scott with plans for a foreign holiday while I drove towards Doreen Jordan's house. I was thinking Italy – Tuscany, perhaps? The romance of a boutique hotel with rustic charm, warm evenings sipping red wine under the stars, walking hand in hand through charming cobbled streets then stopping to kiss by a tinkling fountain, was all bound to create the mood for luuurve. Maybe in that sort of setting I would be able to fully relax and let myself go. Sex with a new man had been an unsettling experience for me. I mean, don't get me wrong, after such a long drought this sex was much better than no sex but it still wasn't quite ringing all my bells … yet … if you know what I mean. A little Italian getaway might just be my ticket to paradise!

It was a shame Scott hadn't yet met Jools and Mickey. They were still keen as mustard to arrange another meal out but Scott hadn't yet been able to find a suitable date. He'd also confessed, the last time I asked him about it, that he was guilty of wanting to keep me to himself a bit longer.

"I've got nothing against meeting your friends, honestly," he'd said, looking a little bit sheepish. "But when I've been working away I'm not always in the mood for making small talk with strangers, not when I've got the chance to be alone with you." He'd pulled me towards him then, nuzzled my neck and carried on, making a rather convincing argument why we should not rush into double dating with Jools and Mickey anytime soon.

Before I knew it, I was standing outside Doreen Jordan's front door and having to quickly get my head around what I was going to say if she answered. I'd decided to try my luck on my way home from work as teatime seemed the most likely time to catch somebody at home.

I wasn't wrong. Just as soon as I rang the doorbell I could see a figure through the bevelled glass panels of the front door making its way down the hallway towards me.

I quickly explained who I was as I took in Doreen's appearance and she appeared to give me the once-over in return. She was a stout woman with dyed jet-black hair piled on top of her head in something that only just stopped short of a beehive. She wore a fluffy leopard-print jumper over stretchy black leggings, which were tucked into patterned socks, and to complete the ensemble she had a pair of pink furry slippers on her feet. She was dressed far younger than her age but her careworn face told the truth of her seventy-plus years. I found myself shocked to register again that if Deb had lived she wouldn't be far off the same age as the woman before me.

"You're little Beverley Hopewell?" Doreen said, giving me a searching stare as though looking for further evidence. She seemed as bewildered as I was at how fast the years had flown.

I held my nerve and convinced her I was Beverley Hopewell all grown up, and she immediately softened and invited me in. We went straight through to her kitchen where I perched on a stool at a tiny breakfast bar while she leaned back against the washing machine, with her arms folded over her bosom and her head on one side.

She let me deliver my stuttering account of finding Ringo Starr's leather jacket in my attic and remembering my big sister Deb had said it had once belonged to her friend Doreen. I stopped short of mentioning the detail about her being Ringo's girlfriend or the fact that once he'd dumped her, she'd given the jacket away. If those facts were true she wouldn't need me to explain them to her, and if they weren't, I risked causing major offence.

I needn't have worried. Doreen didn't hesitate in confirming the story.

"'Course I knew 'im as Richie," she said, going a little misty-eyed at her memories of the young Richard Starkey, yet to be Ringo Starr. "We used to 'ave such a laff; 'e was a right one," she said, her face breaking into a huge smile. I could suddenly see the pretty girl she used to be, with bright blue eyes and dark, shining hair. She had a heart-shaped face and a petite frame under the layers of middle-aged spread and leopard-print knitwear.

She talked for a while about her days running around

town with Ringo and how exciting it was to date the drummer in a band.

"This was before 'e was in The Beatles, o'course," she said, as if I didn't know. "I suppose I knew even then that it couldn't last," she carried on. "There was something in the air, y'know, like we all knew something was gonna happen but not exactly what it was gonna be. Those of us who followed the Liverpool music scene weren't too shocked when the Mersey bands started to make it big. We always knew 'ow great they were. It was just the rest of the world takin' its time to catch on."

I remembered hearing Deb say something very much on the same lines way back in time.

Doreen suddenly seemed to remember I was still there when she asked, "You say you've still got 'is jacket?"

I nodded. It was obvious she was going to want it back – it was written all over her face – but then she said something that gave me a glimpse into the heart of this very ordinary Liverpool housewife, currently living a very ordinary Liverpool life.

"I've regretted giving that jacket away for years," she said. "I suppose I wanted it back as soon as I'd let it go but I was just too proud to say so. Then, when they got famous, I was kickin' myself and over the years every single time I saw them on the telly or 'eard one of their songs I would think about that leather jacket and about … about how things might have been."

My heart broke a little for Doreen in that moment. Did she really think her life could have turned out so very differently? Instead of standing in a poky kitchen wearing worn leggings could she imagine herself in an LA mansion or flying around the world in a private jet? But it seemed it wasn't just the rockstar lifestyle she hankered after as she added, "I could keep it in me wardrobe. Jim wouldn't need to know – 'e never looks in there anyway – and I could take it out now and again and slip it on. It would be like having Richie's arms around me again, just like when we were young."

The longing in the woman's face at that moment was proof positive that age was no barrier to wanting to feel loved and adored. The older I get the more I realise that youth has no monopoly on desire. The only difference is the more world-weary of us get better at hiding it. I'd awakened emotions in Doreen that she clearly hadn't allowed to surface in a long time. Obviously, I promised I would get the jacket to her as soon as I could.

I'd been waiting patiently for an opportunity to also ask if Doreen knew anything about the circumstances of my birth. Had Deb got pregnant during their forays into the murky world of musicians and music clubs? Had Doreen known anything about it? But just as I was about to form my thoughts into a question Doreen practically slapped her forehead and blurted that her husband would soon be home and she'd not even started his tea. She then announced something that clearly alarmed her even more.

"My Jim knows nothing about the … 'Ringo business'." She practically mouthed the last two words, as though Jim might be able to hear from wherever he currently was. I promised to say nothing but I found it hard to believe that Jim Jordan wouldn't have come across the rumours of his wife and a Beatle at some point in their marriage. If I knew about it some scally down the pub was bound to have filled him in. After all, it's virtually impossible to keep a secret in Liverpool ... or so I thought.

Doreen began wrenching open the fridge and crashing about the tiny kitchen, slapping a couple of potatoes and a carton of eggs onto the counter.

"He won't be 'appy. I promised 'im a chicken pie and he's gonna end up with chips and egg, 'ow very Shirley Valentine," she said with a knowing roll of her eyes.

It was literally like being stuck in a kitchen-sink drama as I watched Doreen begin to expertly peel potatoes for the husband she characterised as a man who hailed from an era when husbands expected wives to have tea on the table and never, ever mention previous boyfriends. I thought about Mona Best and what she would have made of Doreen's panic to stick to a timetable dictated by her husband's shift pattern. If Mona had worried about keeping her man happy and fed there would never have been a Casbah Coffee Bar and therefore no Beatles, I'd learned that much. It made me wonder, How many other amazing events simply never happened because women were too busy keeping everyone else happy? It wasn't quite the right time to debate the course of feminism or challenge Doreen's way of life, however, so I kept my musings on Mona and a woman's lot in life to myself.

I was also in no position to mock Doreen's continuing affection for Ringo considering my long-term love for Paul, but I thanked my lucky stars all over again that day for the stroke of fortune that had brought Scott to me. Not only was he a modern, happy to help, thoughtful man, his arrival in my life also meant I didn't have to spend *my* days dreaming about someone famous who would always be out of my reach.

Doreen was distracted, bustling back and forth, but I was still focused on the real reason for my visit and I was worried I might have to leave before I was able to find out what I was there to discover. Eventually I couldn't wait any longer and so blurted my question.

"Doreen, was Deb my real mother?"

"How did you find out?"

Her answer was an automatic as she turned to face me before she'd had the chance to realise what she'd said. She clapped her hand over her mouth when she saw the expression on my face but it was too late, the cat was out of the bag.

Doreen came over and took my hand then, her blue eyes kind and full of sympathy. She listened when I told her that it was just a chance remark by someone that had set me thinking it could be true. Perceptively she observed that at some level I must have already suspected it to be the case if such a small thing had triggered my journey to her door.

She told me Mame and Tom were "salts of the earth", loving parents who wanted only the best for Deb, their gorgeous, clever daughter. Doreen reckoned everyone knew Deb was destined for great things. She was bright with a real talent for writing, she said, someone who could make a success of life on her own terms. The way she told it, Tom and Mame didn't want her to throw that all away and a baby would have surely clipped her wings. Deb promised to make the most of the chance they gave her; she worked hard and got herself a big break in London … but then she was killed and it was too late to own up to the deception.

"But what about me?" I asked, my voice hoarse thanks to the immense pressure in my chest.

"She loved you, Beverley, you must have known that." Doreen was trying so hard to be kind.

"But as a sister, not a mother," I said mournfully, my mind doing backflips trying to compute this new information.

"Love is love," Doreen said simply. I nodded and tried to accept the point she made.

She also told me she'd attended Deb's funeral and spoke briefly to Mame, who had told her they intended to carry on bringing me up as their own daughter. No one else but Doreen had known about Deb being my real birth mother, and so it was easier for them to carry on the lie than to admit the truth.

"I suppose it was for their sake as well as yours," Doreen said. "It was hard to blame them, after losing their girl like that. Having you brought them some comfort and they couldn't bear the thought of giving you more pain than you had already experienced losing Deb."

It was a solid enough argument, but it didn't stop it hurting like hell to find out my whole life had been based upon a lie. But none of that was Doreen's fault and I could see it wasn't her place to hunt me down in later years and reveal what she knew.

She seemed more upset than me by that point and I felt guilty then, for turning up unannounced, stirring up a whole host of emotions and secrets, as well spoiling her husband's tea. She gave me her mobile number and I promised to reunite her with Ringo's jacket.

I wanted her to have the treasured piece of clothing, and it felt like the right thing to do, so I made her a promise. It might not be the same for everyone else in the world, but when I make a promise, I keep it.

Chapter Nineteen

I expected the revelation about Deb being my mam to make me feel like a completely different person, but that's not quite the way it worked. I was still me, Beverley, widow of Geoff, mother of three and Beatles fan, but the world around me now felt like it had shifted into a strange new shape. That was pretty disconcerting in itself. I was the same person, looked the same, sounded the same. No one was looking at me any differently than they always had. It was the way I saw the rest of the world that had changed.

Everything felt like it was on shaky ground, as though I was walking along a fault line that could rip apart in a massive earthquake beneath my feet at any moment. There were no hard or straight edges anymore, everything appeared to have a wobbly outline and a precarious existence. I knew I couldn't rely on anything, only myself. It was strange how solid and real I felt in the middle of a new world where everything now felt ephemeral.

I wasn't angry, I wasn't tearful. The decisions Deb and

my grandparents had taken decades before were rooted in a logic that I could understand. I could even go along with the theory that if Deb had not died so tragically young it might not have stayed a secret. There might have been a day where I was asked to sit down, probably in the front room rather than the kitchen, and Mame and Deb would have done their best to explain the truth of my birth and why things had been handled the way they had. I couldn't imagine Tom being part of the conversation; he would no doubt have found something vitally important to attend to in the garden or the shed until it was all over.

That was what was so bizarre, I knew these people so well – Deb, Tom and Mame – and yet I'd just discovered I didn't really know them at all.

I didn't want to talk to anyone about it, not yet. I wasn't ready for the questions and I didn't have any answers anyway. It wasn't until the day after meeting Doreen that I realised I hadn't even asked if she knew who my dad was. That was another can of worms I wasn't quite ready to open. One thing at a time. I just needed to live with the news I did now know about a while longer. I definitely didn't want head-tilting sympathy or looks that would make me feel like a total sad sack. I thought it would be best to give myself chance to recalibrate, see if my surroundings took on a more solid quality as I got used to the idea. I hoped to God the feeling that I was walking on dangerously thin ice wasn't one I was going to have to live with for ever.

It was on that basis that I also decided not to share the news with my boys just yet. Thinking about how to approach that part of the equation actually made me have a little more sympathy for the dilemma that had faced Tom and Mame after Deb died. It's a fact of life that you will do *anything* to protect your kids if you can; it was an instinct I couldn't argue with.

The next couple of days I simply went through the motions, acting out the part of Bev at work, at home, on the phone with Scott. I wasn't daft enough to meet face-to-face with Jools as she was likely to sense something was up and I wouldn't be able to bat her away once she sniffed blood. I promised to catch up with her at the weekend, buying myself just a little more time.

Tony, the Magical Mystery Tour guide, called up on one of those days I just didn't want to see anyone at all. It was terrible timing. He'd been once before with a couple of tourist groups and it had been loads of fun. They were mainly Chinese and spent most of the visit snapping away with their cameras, capturing images of the outside of my rather ordinary-looking house. A few of them wanted to ask questions about me being a lifelong Beatles fan, and they even asked to have their pictures taken with me! I'm not sure if some of them thought I was related to a Beatle in some way but I never claimed any personal connection. I wore my jacket covered in Beatles badges and black corduroy Lennon cap and brought out trays of tea in Beatles mugs and they seemed delighted by it all. But I couldn't face another visit the way I was feeling so I put Tony off and told him I was suffering with a migraine. I felt even more terrible about it when he was so sympathetic, but I felt I had no choice.

The one thing I did feel up to doing was honouring my

promise to Doreen Duffy. I wasn't looking forward to going up into the attic but I reckoned the sooner it was done the better, a bit like ripping off a plaster. I was also still hoping to sell the Olive Adair perfume bottle to raise funds for a romantic Italian holiday. In fact, it was only the thought of getting away from it all with Scott that was keeping me going.

In what I thought was a stroke of complete genius I managed to locate a headlamp from a box under the spare bed. I'd remembered James buying it to take to a festival a few years back, so he could find his way from his tent to the toilets in the middle of the night. A quick change of batteries and I was good to go. Watch out, Mickey and Minnie, I thought, I'm coming up.

I opened the hatch to the loft with the long metal pole, hooking it into the catch that pulled the loft ladder down towards me. So far so good. I climbed the ladder towards the black hole above me, dreading having to put my hand out to find the light switch that was on the floorboards to one side.

As my head poked up through the opening, the beam of light from my head torch swung back and forth through the gloom. Suddenly I saw something far more terrifying than a little mouse. A face – a man's face – was looking straight at me… Wait … not just one man … there was another man standing right next to him!

I screamed, teetered precariously on the flimsy ladder and had to throw my arms out to stop myself from plunging to my death. Why are loft hatches positioned so close to the top of the stairs? Such a dangerous design.

The noise of my ear-splitting shriek reverberated around the rafters of the house but there were no corresponding screams or shouts from the men I had disturbed hiding in my attic space. In fact, there was no noise from their direction at all. No shuffling of feet or creaks on the floorboards as they backed away. Not even any heavy breathing as they froze on the spot, their hiding place discovered.

With a strength I didn't even know I possessed I dragged my eyes back to the place where I'd seen the frightening figures looming ominously over me. I gasped again as their blank faces looked straight back at me but then realisation slowly began to dawn. There wasn't just one man standing there, filling the space where the apex of the roof was at its highest. There weren't even two of them, partners in crime. There were four and their faces were weirdly familiar.

How had I forgotten about my life-size cardboard cut-outs of John, Paul, George and Ringo? The four of them propped up together appeared to be in a huddle just waiting to cause trouble. Well, they'd certainly managed that. I blew out my cheeks and tried to regulate my breathing, which was tricky as I didn't know whether to laugh or cry. At least it had taken my mind off the mice a little. I gingerly clambered into the loft, feeling somewhat embarrassed about all my huffing and puffing as the Fab Four continued to look down on me.

"I wish Scott had mentioned bumping into you lot," I said as I got to my feet and brushed the dust off my jeans. "I suppose he was too busy dealing with the mice. I hope they haven't been nibbling at your toes?"

The guys stared back at me. I couldn't really blame them. I was babbling away to men made out of cardboard, but so long as it kept the mice away, I would have happily done a song and dance routine. Talking out loud was helping to keep me calm. I've always been a talker; find me a conversation gap and I'll fill it. Silence has never been golden in my book as I much prefer a non-stop stream of consciousness.

You may, perhaps, have noticed?

"I'd forgotten you lot were even up here," I chuntered on, looking around the storage space and trying to get my bearings. It had been so long since I'd ventured up there it all looked different to how I remembered. "Sorry I stuck you up here in the dark. At the old house I always kept you laid flat under the bed, do you remember?" I rolled my eyes at myself. Was I really now asking the cardboard men questions? Actually, I was quite enjoying not being interrupted. "Geoff would have done his nut if I'd had you all out on display." I moved towards them as I spoke, lifting them up and checking for any signs of nibbling around their edges. "Daft sod would have been proper jealous if you lot had been hanging around all the time." I couldn't see any signs of damage to their extremities so I carefully stood them back into their line-up.

There was an old upturned teachest to one side of the figures so I plonked myself on it and tried to work out where to begin my search. It was too quiet when I stopped talking though, so I started again, chatting away whilst I pulled a large bin bag towards me.

"So, you've met my Scott then," I said brightly. "He's not like Geoff though; he doesn't feel threatened by you lot. Mind you, that might be coz he's a musician too, y'know?" I nodded towards Paul and George, the nearest figures to me. "Oh, I know he's not in your league, lads, but they were pretty big back in the day. It was Adam and the Ants versus Scott Smith and the Silhouettes, and it could have gone either way. If it hadn't been for that incident backstage with A Flock Of Seagulls, who knows how successful they would have been?" I could have sworn Lennon had a sneer on his face as I filled them in on the historical struggles of Eighties bands, but that could just have been his usual expression.

As I had been talking I'd pulled the contents of the bin bag out and discovered it was my old yellow submarine costume. I'd decided I didn't want it on top of my wardrobe anymore so I'd stuffed it into a bag and asked Scott to stash it up here. I hadn't told him what it was and thankfully, he hadn't asked.

"How about this then, lads," I called out, proffering the padded blue and yellow outfit towards them. "D'you think I should try this on one night to give Scott a laugh? Love me, love my Beatles, eh?"

I carefully folded the costume back into the bag and moved across to the couple of large boxes I recognised from the night Scott had first come round to visit. I'd got Harry to bring them down for me and Scott had put them back up so no wonder everything seemed to be all over the place.

They'd obviously just dumped stuff wherever was easiest. Typical blokes!

I bent my knees to lift the box onto the top of the tea chest so I'd be able to look through it more easily, and I rocked back on my heels when it wasn't as heavy as I expected. I was shocked that it weighed so little. Maybe that Davina exercise DVD was working miracles with my muscle tone?

Once the box was open it was clear why it had been so light. It was practically empty. That was irritating. It was one thing for Scott to suggest I should keep this stuff more organised but it was quite another for him to take it upon himself to start moving things around. How was I going to be able to find anything now? I presumed he must have come up with some sort of system, grouping the items into particular collections or something like that.

I pulled another box towards me. This one was incredibly light, too, and it didn't drag along the floor the way I expected it to. I looked inside but save for a couple of old flyers and a few bits of paper it was empty.

Time and again I reached for a box and tore open the top only to find it had none of the treasures I was expecting to find.

"What's he bloody playing at? Where's everything gone?" I wasn't asking the cardboard Beatles the question this time, I was asking myself.

It was maddening that everything seemed turned upside down but I knew there must be a rational explanation. I pulled my mobile from the back pocket of my jeans and punched in Scott's number. Just wait until I got hold of him!

Annoyingly, the call went to voicemail. As I couldn't tear into him the way I would have done if he'd answered, I tried to keep my voice reasonable. I was sure he would be able to tell I was rattled though.

"Scott, it's me, Bev. I'm just... It's just... I know you're probably trying to help but I'm looking through me Beatles boxes in the attic and the stuff is ... well, it's all over the place and I can't find hardly any of it. Have you moved it? Why would you move it? Can you give me a call when you get this? Please?"

I was wound up now and I didn't like the creeping sensation that was spreading up from my gut. I tore into box after box, I scoured every corner of the loft. I could only find a handful of my precious Beatles items and there was no sign of Ringo's leather jacket.

I redialled Scott's number. This time his voicemail did not answer. Instead, a recorded message played, sending an icy chill down my backbone that froze the blood in my veins.

"The number you have dialled has not been recognised. The number you have dialled has not been recognised."

My knees gave way then and I sank to the floor, stifling sobs.

"No. No, no, no, no..."

I wasn't worried about the mice anymore because now I knew there were no mice. There had never been any mice. All those trips up to the attic and those bags Scott brought down containing "the bodies"… He'd stolen practically my entire Beatles collection from right under my nose.

There was me thinking I'd bagged a handsome guy who just loved to spend his money on me. But it wasn't *his* money, was it? By the looks of the state of my attic it was *my* money he had been spending all along, on fancy restaurants and weekend breaks, on treats and gifts that I'd thought meant he loved me. His smart new clothes, that expensive watch … his new upgraded "company" car…

I stayed on my knees for a long time, rocking back and forth and trying to process what I had discovered in that dimly lit, dusty loft space. My nails were broken from ripping open boxes, my hair was full of cobwebs and I was covered in a layer of grime. Grime and shame. I was ashamed of how foolish I had been, how easy I had been to trick and how quickly I had fallen for someone willing to pay me just a little bit of attention. Mame and Tom and Deb would all be thoroughly ashamed of me. And my boys… My heart twisted in pain even more as I thought of how I would never be able to face my sons.

As the sky grew dark outside and the temperature dropped, I sat there shivering and snivelling like a little girl who had strayed too far away from the familiar path. I felt so lost and there was no one there to help me, only the four members of the band I had loved for so long, watching me silently from the shadows. There was nothing they could do to help me now.

Chapter Twenty

I was still in a complete state of shock when I called the police. I can't really remember what I said, something about being conned and my priceless collection of Beatles memorabilia having been plundered, I think. I didn't mention my broken heart or the theft of my faith in human decency, but I still doubt I made much sense to the poor woman on the other end of the phone who tried to take down all the details. She said they would be sending someone round to take a statement but I didn't hold out much hope. Hope wasn't a feeling I expected to experience ever again in my lifetime.

Despite reeling from the shock of uncovering Scott's deception, it turned out I still had some capacity to be surprised. First of all, that the local constabulary did indeed take my crime report seriously and promised to send a copper out to Western Avenue within twenty-four hours of my call. My surprise then turned into open-mouthed amazement when I opened my front door to find DC Levi

Collins standing there. Of all the policeman in all the world, or at least Liverpool, why did it have to be him?

I shuffled in my slippers towards the kitchen, pulling my baggy old grey cardigan around the stained T-shirt I'd worn for the last two days straight. I didn't ask DC Collins if he wanted a cup of tea, I just did it on auto pilot. Putting the kettle on is what we British do in a crisis, isn't it? In other parts of the world you see people weeping and wailing in the street, joining paramilitary forces, taking up arms and storming seats of power. Faced with a disaster in this country we don't blow up, we brew up. As if a strong pot of tea is the answer to it all.

I carried the tea tray through to the lounge to find DC Collins standing awkwardly by the sofa looking down at the Beatles-themed cushions scattered across it. They'd been a present from the boys last Christmas, a selection of coloured covers each with a different album sleeve printed on it. I'd loved them but now I felt my Beatles-themed home decorations made me look even more like a demented fool.

"I haven't got any biscuits, sorry…" My voice was croaky. That's what you get for crying non-stop for hours. "I thought I had some hidden in the back of the cupboard but I can't seem to find them…" My voice cracked completely at that. How ridiculous. Just because I couldn't find my secret stash of custard creams I was actually going to burst into tears.

DC Collins gently took the tea tray from my shaking hands. He seemed to think I was on the verge of collapse.

"Don't worry about all that, Mrs Wilson." He was being

very polite and professional, almost as though we hadn't already met before. I suppose that's how they are trained in the force. Then he added, "Now, have you made a list of the items that are missing? Not including the biscuits."

I completely exploded at that. Had he just come around to mock me? That was the last thing I needed. "You think this is all a bloody joke, don't you?" I snapped angrily. "I don't even know why I bothered callin' you lot." I was about to tell him to get the hell out but then I saw the sheepish expression on his face and realised he was probably just trying to break the ice.

"You did the right thing calling us, Mrs Wilson … Bev," he said, sounding like he was already regretting his attempt at humour. "I'm sorry, I was just trying to lighten the mood. I should know by now that's never a good idea. Let's just stick to the facts, shall we?"

I told him then the simple fact of the matter was that I was a gullible goose of a woman who had got everything she deserved. I rattled through the detail of how a man I had met on the internet had managed to con me out of the only things I had ever owned that had been worth anything at all. He presumed I meant financially, and I did of course, but my collection's sentimental value was something I would never be able to calculate.

DC Collins listened patiently but took issue with my self-flagellation. "No one deserves to be conned, Mrs Wilson … Beverley."

I was utterly unprepared for what DC Collins said next. He proceeded to give a detailed explanation of how a conman like Scott might operate. He seemed to be suggesting that at first Scott wouldn't have known I had a treasure trove of stuff he could steal, but a widow who owned her own home would be interesting enough to a man like him. There was me thinking my "Penny4" nickname afforded protection, but DC Collins reckoned Scott would have soon been able to figure out who I was. The fact that I'd appeared in the local newspaper when I bought my house, how the headline had read "Beatles Bev" and mentioned I loved collecting memorabilia, were all factors the detective said Scott would have been able to discover right from the start. Once he knew all that he would have been determined to pursue me; nothing to do with my stunning good looks and vibrant personality then? Ha! When I thought about it, the detective's explanation did make a lot more sense.

My head was spinning to think that it could all have been so calculated right from the start. Surely not?

"These people are very clever, and they choose their targets very carefully," DC Collins said sagely.

"TARGETS!" I practically spat the word out. "Is that all I was to him? What do they call people who get hustled? A 'mark'?"

"We'd call you a victim," DC Collins said, instantly making me feel even worse.

"Well, don't!" I just couldn't seem to stop snapping at the well-meaning detective. "I don't want to be a bloody 'victim'. I don't want to be..." I sank onto the sofa then, my anger dissipating to leave me feeling wrung out and wretched. "All I wanted was someone who gets me," I lamented. "What I ended up with was someone out to get me."

"Mrs Wilson, Bev… May I sit down?" I nodded silently in reply and DC Collins pulled out a chair from the dining table and sat across from me on the sofa where I was trying to compose myself. He busied himself getting out a notebook and pencil while I wiped my eyes and blew my nose. I stuffed the tissue back into the pocket of my cardigan and raised my eyes to find him looking at me, waiting.

"Okay, can you tell me when you realised this Scott Smith had been stealing from you?"

I started to try and explain how the penny had dropped when I couldn't get through to his mobile after leaving him that voicemail, when I suddenly realised that was the only number I had for him, and that I didn't know his home address. It was only when I said it out loud and heard myself that I realised just how incredibly stupid I must sound. His important job at the event company; the big house he was renovating on the edge of the city; his poor, dead wife Meg… I didn't have a shred of evidence that any of those things ever existed. Now I had finally realised how much of a con trick Scott Smith had pulled on me I knew I couldn't trust a single, solitary thing he had ever said or done. The only thing I knew for sure was that I had been a complete idiot.

Detective Collins was very good at his job and keeping his expression neutral but clearly thought I was dumber than dumb as he then questioned me very slowly. "You knew he had been stealing because you couldn't reach him?"

Christ, I was coming across as a complete mad woman. I should be locked in my ransacked attic and left there to rot. I tried again to explain things better. "No, what happened was, I went looking for a bottle of perfume, a bottle of *Beatles* perfume by Olive Adair of Liverpool. It's from 1963 and collectors will pay hundreds, even for just an empty bottle. Mine was in mint condition, you can't get them anywhere. But, you see, I couldn't find it. I went through a couple of boxes thinking Scott had just been moving things around, or I was going mad."

I stopped then, wishing with all my heart that either of those two options were true. How desperately I'd clung to that vain hope that Scott had just taken it upon himself to reorganise stuff – until the evidence was too overwhelming to ignore. Rather than face that horrific truth, I thought I would really rather be found certifiably insane and have imagined the whole Scott affair from beginning to end.

Taking a deep breath, I told him how there was hardly anything left in any of the boxes I had kept safe for all those years. I also described how Scott had been able to access the attic regularly on the pretext of a mice infestation. I was sure a look of disdain flashed across the detective's face at that point, as though he was disgusted by the duplicitous convolutions of Scott's betrayal.

DC Collins rose from his chair then and I wondered if that was it, whether he'd heard enough and decided to leave as there was nothing he could do to help me, but instead he said, "Do you want to show me where you kept all this stuff?"

I was confused. "You mean go up into the attic?"

DC Collins nodded and answered, "If you wouldn't mind?"

I did mind really. I had no desire to clamber up that stepladder and view the scene of the crime ever again but I just shrugged and headed towards the stairs, saying rather sulkily, "You can if you want but I don't see what good it'll do. After all, you can't see what *isn't* there, can you?"

DC Collins followed me, saying quietly, "I don't suppose you can, Mrs Wilson. All the same…"

He was only able to stand to his full height in the very centre of the loft space, as he was easily over six foot tall. I slumped down onto the upturned chest and regarded the debris scattered all around. I'd made a right mess trying to find a box that hadn't been ransacked. Being in the midst of it all again, the memories came flooding back of how my life had so quickly unravelled.

"So, like I said, I called Scott and he didn't answer," I began. "I left a message on his voicemail, of course, but I keep wonderin', if he'd actually answered the phone, what he would have said. How he would have explained what I'd discovered. But of course he never even had to try and do that. Once he'd heard my message he must've realised the game was up so he never had to face me." Every time I went over it in my mind I kicked myself for showing my hand so early. "I couldn't have played it worse," I muttered, more to myself than to DC Collins. "I don't know who to despise more – him … or me."

The officer had his back to me, peering into the empty boxes and looking into dark corners under the eaves. "So after that call he just disappeared?" he asked over his shoulder.

"Well, he wasn't daft enough to come round for his tea!" It wasn't right to take out my frustration on a policeman, but God he did ask some bloody stupid questions!

He whipped his head around to look at me at that but then he swallowed and asked conversationally, "How much do you think the stolen items were worth in total?"

Oh Christ, I didn't think I could take much more. Through gritted teeth I told him, "They were *bloody priceless!*"

He just stood there then, looking at me gormlessly, obviously expecting a more helpful answer. I tried to fight the bubble of anger that was welling up inside of me but the more I spoke the more it seemed to build.

"Some of it probably looked like tat, if you didn't know much about it, but even the hair brushes and the talc could fetch loads 'cause it was all in the original, branded, Beatles packaging. I mean *thousands* of pounds for each thing. Then there were all the autographed pictures and things like that. Beatles collectors know their stuff and they can spot the genuine signatures a mile off and mine were the real deal."

"I can see you're a bit of an expert," he said. "Did you share all of this information with Scott Smith?"

"Oh yeah," I snapped again. "I told him pretty much everythin' he'd need to know. We even went to a collectors' fair together and met all the likely-lookin' characters who'd be dyin' to get their paws on it and pay him cash in hand. He must've thought he'd won the bloody jackpot!"

A sudden thought hit me as though the roof had fallen in on my silly head. "Oh God ... I bet he didn't even like the Beatles."

DC Collins grimaced but didn't answer that, he just swept his eyes across the four cardboard cut-out figures of John, Paul, George and Ringo standing just behind him. "I think it's fair to say you certainly wear your heart on your sleeve about how much *you* love them." He paused and pulled a comical face. "It's kinda like their eyes follow you around the room," he said, and I couldn't help but give him a small smile in return. He was trying to lighten the mood again, and I gave him credit for the effort, even if it wasn't making me feel any better.

He said he wanted to take a few photos and suggested I go back down and make a fresh pot of tea while he finished off up there. I didn't hesitate to follow his request; I couldn't get out of there fast enough.

When he came into the living room I gestured to the fresh mug of tea I'd poured for him on the dining table but he didn't sit down straight away on the chair he'd pulled out earlier. He was standing over me before I realised he had something in his hand.

"Um, I don't know if this is much consolation, considering all you've lost, but" – he held out what looked like a bundle of papers towards me – "I found this under the eaves. Looks like it's been tossed aside at some point..." He tailed off as I took the dog-eared scrapbook from his hands. It was Deb's original collection of Beatles pictures and cuttings, some ticket stubs and flyers and loads of other bits and pieces all stuffed haphazardly between the bulging pages. It was so over-filled it had long ago been tied up with a long piece of silky blue ribbon. It was all discoloured and tatty now but the sight of it made my eyes fill with tears. I could only manage to whisper, "Thank you."

While I nursed the scrapbook on my knee and he drank his tea, DC Collins asked me a few more questions and told me to call him Levi. Despite his questionable attempts at humour, he was being very kind.

He listened, occasionally taking down notes, as I explained what had originally motivated me to go looking for the valuable Beatles perfume bottle. "Scott had been so good to me, y'see, takin' me out, treatin' me like I was a proper queen. I just wanted to treat *him* to something for a change. I've never been tempted to sell any of it before. I've always been so careful because I thought if I kept it all safe and in good condition it would make a nice little nest-egg for my boys. If it was worth such a lot now, just think what it would have been worth in the future." Levi kept his head bent over his notebook as my tears threatened to flow yet again. I caught myself in time and changed my tone to sarcasm as I added, "It's ironic, isn't it? I was going to *share* it with him, he didn't even need to steal it!"

Levi asked if I had a list of all the things I thought were missing and I handed him the crumpled sheet of paper I'd been keeping in my cardigan pocket. I'd jotted it down after calling the police. "I'll never get any of it back, will I?" I asked forlornly as he took the paper from my fingers.

He looked like he wanted to hold my hand at that point

but he folded the page into his notebook and told me it was unlikely but that I should talk to my insurance company once he'd issued a crime number.

I answered that I didn't think I was insured for acts of complete stupidity.

"It's a shame you don't have more information on where we could find him," Levi said. "He certainly managed to play his cards close to his chest."

It was so hard to get my head around how I had allowed this to happen. Surely Scott wouldn't be able to get away with it that easily? "But you know his name," I said, "and I met him through the Lonely Hearts Club dating website."

"I doubt very much Scott Smith is his real name," Levi told me gently. "Men ... people ... often use aliases in these sorts of cases."

I suddenly remembered a vital piece of information that I had so far failed to give. "Oh but that can't be right ... he was Scott Smith of Scott Smith and the Silhouettes!" I was practically triumphant in that moment. Of course they could trace a former pop star, there was bound to be a trail to follow in Scott's case.

Levi looked blank and then a bit embarrassed. "Sorry, who?"

Now it was my turn to be embarrassed and a hot flush of shame consumed me as the final penny dropped. "Scott Smith and the Silhouettes" indeed. I'd wanted to bag my very own rock star so much I'd even convinced myself I'd heard of them!

I realised I had to get DC Levi Collins out of the house as quickly as possible. To think that at our first meeting I'd deluded myself into thinking he might have actually fancied me. How completely ridiculous! He was a handsome, accomplished professional, not a feckless fly-by-night, which was obviously the only kind of man who would be interested in me. DC Levi Collins had originally thought I was a daft old biddy living in a house of creepy dolls, but now he'd gathered enough evidence to prove I really was a mad old bat. Instead of dolls I'd surrounded myself with Beatles keepsakes and cardboard cut-outs and I was so stupid conmen sought me out as easy prey.

I stood and tried to sound business-like as I told him I didn't want to keep him any longer and I was sure he had much more important things to be getting on with. "Just file me under G for 'Gullible Goose'," I said, attempting my own stab at gallows humour. "You can get on now with solving a real crime."

Levi looked a bit surprised by my change of tack but stood slowly. "Mrs Wilson ... Bev, this *is* a very real crime," he said in a very serious tone. "It might be better if you decided to take out some of your anger on Scott Smith, or whatever his name is, rather than yourself."

I appreciated his professional attitude but I was also pretty sure he'd be laughing about me behind my back once he got back to the station, joking about the daft cow who thought she'd seduced a faded pop star and got her just deserts when he robbed her blind.

Levi was still playing the concerned copper as I ushered him towards the door. "You're not the first woman to fall for a smooth-talking conman, but unless you stand up for yourself and get your story out there you won't be the last either."

I was running out of patience with Levi Collins. "What d'you want me to do, shout it from the rooftops?" I asked him, opening the front door wide.

He turned to face me then as he stood on my doorstep. "I'm sure you wouldn't want this to happen to anyone else if you could help it," he said earnestly, looking at me so intently I felt even more raw and exposed. "Think about it, Bev. If there's any way of warning other women like you about Scott Smith... Like I say ... think about it."

After giving me one last searching look he turned and headed down the path. I mustered all my strength to call after him brightly, "Thanks very much but don't you worry about me, y'hear? Tough as old boots I am, it'll take more than a smooth talkin' conman to bring me down!" I even gave a cheery wave before I closed the door, so desperate was I to change DC Collins's perception of me as a pathetic victim.

He looked rather unconvinced as he raised his hand to say goodbye before getting into his car.

I heard him start the engine as I stood with my back pressed against the door, my forced jollity immediately abandoned as my mood plummeted and I muttered darkly to myself, "Bloody hell, Beverley, you're not even kiddin' yourself."

Chapter Twenty-One

I kept the door closed on the world for a couple of days after DC Collins's visit. I called in sick at work and just answered the boys on text when they called. Harry came in late one night after I'd gone to bed and then slept most of the day while I sat staring into space for hours. When he headed into the kitchen to grab something to eat before heading out again I flicked on the TV and pretended to be engrossed in daytime tele. If he noticed I'd sunk into a pit of despair and wasn't my usually chatty, cheery self, he didn't mention it. Sometimes the monosyllabic, self-absorbed nature of a teenager can be a blessing, I suppose.

Levi's words kept on reverberating in my mind. What was it he had said, something about *"other women like you"*? Were there other women like me? I couldn't imagine there was anyone quite as stupid and naive and it wasn't very likely that there would be anyone else out there who had hoarded priceless musical memorabilia and was just waiting to invite a conman in to take their pick of it. But the detective had got me thinking. What if there was someone full of hope and anticipation exchanging messages with Scott – or a nasty piece of work just like him – right at that very moment? What if they were about to welcome said evil person into their life, their home, their bed? I shuddered at the thought of how terrible it would be for them to go through what I was going through right now. Was Levi right? Did I owe it to other women to try and warn them about Scott and his type? I certainly hated the idea of him being able to repeat this crime again and again and just get away with it "Scott-free", so to speak!

So that explains how, that same afternoon, I found myself high above the Liverpool skyline on the roof of the city's most iconic building. I was, quite literally, a woman on the edge.

Getting inside the Liver Building wasn't as difficult as I thought it might be. I simply breezed into reception and told the security officer on the desk I was taking part in a charity event before heading to the lift and going as high as it would take me. It was as though the trauma of Scott's deception, not to mention my recent discovery about Deb being my real mother, had stripped away any last vestige of my previous timid and careful self. I just didn't give a shiny shit anymore. It was a bit like having a superpower where you felt you could do absolutely anything. So what if I told a lie? So what if I even did something illegal? Other people just did whatever they wanted and hang the consequences, so why shouldn't I? My total self-belief clearly convinced the security guard I was kosher. That's the way to do it, I told myself, just act like you own the place and people get the hell out of your way.

It probably had helped my case that I gave the guard a flash of the yellow submarine costume I had stuffed in a Marks & Spencer's bag for life. Why else would a middle-aged woman be heading to the top of the Royal Liver Building with a ridiculous fancy-dress costume if not to raise funds for a worthy charity? You couldn't blame the guy for not guessing what I was actually about to do.

I found the stairwell and climbed up several more floors above where the lift had taken me. I don't remember how many flights there were, but the way the adrenaline was pumping in my veins I wasn't even out of breath when I eventually got to the fire door right at the top.

Once I'd shoved the heavy door open the sight before me did make me gasp for a moment. I was so high. The wind was strong up there and seagulls screeched and called as they whirled in the air around me. I closed the door for a moment, stepping back into the stairwell and clambering into the cumbersome submarine costume. I'd come this far. There was no going back now.

I'd never realised quite how big the famous Liver Birds actually were. Anyone who has ever been to Liverpool has seen the two sculpted green metal birds with their outstretched wings sitting on top of the Liver Building. One bird faces inwards towards the city, the other out towards sea, and legend has it that the birds are a male and female pair. Bella the female looks out to sea, waiting for sailors to safely return home. Bertie the male looks inwards towards land, watching over the seamen's families while they are away, so they say.

From down on the ground the birds didn't look very big at all, but now I was in the presence of Bella I could see she was almost twenty foot tall and her wingspan was even bigger. I'd had the crazy idea of scaling the statue and straddling the majestic bird, but now I was actually at the top of the clock tower I realised I would never be able to get a grip on the dome the bird stood on without specialist equipment.

I was safe enough where I stood under the dome and behind the ornate walls of the clock tower. But safe wasn't going to cut it, and my yellow submarine costume was completely wasted if I was going to stay partially hidden by the carved stone balustrades. I fished a rock-climbing rope from my bag and began to wind it around my middle, praising the heavens for giving me three sons with such diverse hobbies and interests.

While Bella the enormous metal cormorant watched me with her beady eye, I lashed myself to a stone pillar and climbed over the wall so I could teeter in all my yellow submarine glory on a small plinth that jutted out just above the clock face itself.

Far below me the Mersey's waters swirled around the boats using the busy waterway and there were lots of people milling around on the dock in the early afternoon sunshine. I paused for a moment, impressed with both myself and the majestic view from my incredible vantage point. I was too focused on my mission to be scared or worry about health and safety issues. However, I hadn't gone all that way just to admire the scenery, I fished the rest of my "equipment" from the bottom of my Marks bag – a batch of homemade flyers and a megaphone.

"ROLL UP, ROLL UP, come and hear all about it! This is one Liver Bird who's gonna be heard right across the Mersey." My amplified voice rang out and heads began to turn this way and that down below as some of the passersby looked for the source. I repeated my rousing call a couple more times and once someone had spotted my luminous bright yellow form high above their heads, people began pointing and gesticulating, and to my immense satisfaction an actual crowd began to form.

Once I had their attention, I launched a handful of flyers into the air and let the wind take them, hoping a few would fall into the hands of those watching, but also hoping they would fly much further afield. The more I could spread the word about shady "Scott Smith", the better.

For now though, my public awaited. I lifted the megaphone to address them. "I'm Beatles Bev," I told them, "a middle-aged housewife robbed by a conman she met looking for love on the internet. I'll even write you tomorrow's headline: 'Beatles Bev Begged Love Me Do'. Have you ever heard of a more ridiculous cliché? I'm a ridiculous cliché!"

The crowd below was building nicely as I bared my soul. I literally felt on top of the world as I vented my anger from my elevated position. I had a lot to get off my chest. My fury at Scott was compounded by the fact that I had *tried* to protect myself as much as possible when I first signed up to the dating website. I'd used a nickname, only agreed to first dates in public places, told someone when I was out meeting a man for the first time… I'd done everything the way you were supposed to. I'd even tried to make sure I matched myself with exactly the right sort of date, back when I thought an "unsuitable" or "boring" man was the most important thing to avoid. All that time I spent creating my profile and vetting the candidates. God help me, I thought I had it covered. A few harmless dates in a coffee shop and I thought I'd be able to tell if he was a saddo or a psycho! Turned out I'd have been better off with a Morris Dancing Chubby Brown fanatic … well, maybe not.

I picked up the megaphone again to proclaim my anguish. "I've been ripped off, me heart ripped out, me life ripped apart… Me! Careful. Boring. Beverley."

Scott had stolen more than a few Beatles mementos from me. He'd taken away the one constant thing I had ever had in my life. My love for the band linked me back to Deb. Just as I had learned my beautiful, brilliant big sister was *not* my sister but my mother, he'd sabotaged the only connection between us. That's what tortured me more than the amount of money I'd lost or even that our entire affair had been fake. I wasn't sure I would ever be able to hear a Beatles song ever again. Just the sound of the opening bars of any of their music would cut me like a knife, I was sure of it. So there was no point keeping anything that reminded me of them anymore. John, Paul, George and Ringo had to go.

The four of them watched me as I stood there, being buffeted by the wind. I'd folded each cardboard cut-out to get them into my bag and I'd got them out and lined them up along the watchtower wall before I'd climbed over to stand on the plinth.

I leaned back over the wall, grabbed hold of George, and held him aloft. "You wanna take my Beatles from me?" I yelled. "Well you can have 'em. Have the whole bloody lot of 'em." I flung George away from me and towards the river. The wind really got hold of him and I thought I heard a woman scream as his cardboard body plummeted. I was definitely drawing a crowd now. Good.

I got hold of Ringo next. "C'mon, Ringo," I said, "your turn next. Look out for yellow submarines!" As I released him into the air a riverboat honked loudly from down on the Mersey. My actions seemed to be attracting Liverpool's attention. I threw more leaflets out after the flying Beatle members. I know social media is all the rage now and that would perhaps have been a far less exposing way to make my point, but I hadn't got a bloody clue how to make something "go viral". Instead, I'd used a tried and tested old-school method. I'd taken the only decent photo I had of "Scott Smith" – no wonder he was always so camera-shy – and gone mad with a photocopier. The waiter at Beppi's Bistro had taken a shot of the two of us one night before Scott could object. Scott had spaghetti sauce on his chin and a rather surprised look on his face but it suited my purposes perfectly. I'd basically created an "UNWANTED" poster featuring the picture of Scott in the centre, detailing his crimes and warning women to avoid him at all costs.

"Just try and do this again, you sleazeball!" I shouted as the flyers fell like confetti on the ground all around the Liver Building. "Go on, try! I was such a fool, I shoulda known better. If something seems too good to be true, it usually is."

I wanted the whole of Liverpool to hear me. No, I wanted the whole *world* to hear me because I was sure that if it could happen to me it could happen to anyone. I might have been dressed like a yellow submarine but that was just to get some attention. I wanted my message to be taken very seriously and I spoke directly to other women, those other women who might be just like me. "It could happen to you," I warned. "I bet it's happening to someone else right now, it's bound to be. There are loads of us out there, ready to fall for the first flatterin' line we've heard in years. It's all those bloody adverts tellin' us, 'Because You're Worth It!'. Well, it's time to grow up, girls. Prince Charming is *not* on his way, we don't *deserve* a fairy-tale ending. If you want to find a light at the end of the tunnel you have to bloody well grope your way down there in the dark and switch it on your bleedin' self, coz no man is gonna do it for you!"

I was desperate for my message to be heard loud and clear but I got a bit carried away with my leaflet throwing then, and with one energetic fling of my arm I lost my balance and my foot slipped off the small plinth where I was precariously balanced.

There was a collective gasp from the crowd down below and then a voice much closer to me suddenly shouted, "BEV! Don't do anything stupid!"

As I grabbed hold of the balustrade and stabilised myself, I remember thinking that was a rather ironic instruction. "It's a bit bloody late for that, I'm afraid," I said, looking over my shoulder to see where the comment had come from. Out of the corner of my eye I spotted a young woman in a navy raincoat edging along the balustrade toward me. She looked completely terrified.

"Bev, Beverley … Mrs Wilson, please don't do this."

I remember thinking it was odd how she'd addressed me, almost as if we'd met before. I just couldn't place her. "Do I know you?" I asked and she looked at me incredulously. At the time I thought it was because she expected me to recognise her, but later on I realised it was because I was just chatting like we were standing at a bus stop and she was terrified we were about to plummet to our deaths.

"It's Tanya, from the *Echo*," she told me in a quivering voice. "I interviewed you a few years ago when you bought Paul McCartney's house at that auction."

Ahhh, yes, that jogged my memory, I knew I'd recognised her face. She really didn't look like she was enjoying the experience of being on top of the Liver Building all that much. "Hello, Tanya, what are you doin' up here, love?" I asked.

Bless her, she took my teasing on the chin and came back with a quick retort. "Oh … I just thought you might fancy a chat," she quipped before having to lean back and close her eyes after catching sight of how high up we both were. She'd gone quite pale but bravely she swallowed and asked shakily, "What's all this about, Bev?"

"I've got to warn people, Tanya," I said. "I've got to make sure this doesn't happen to anyone else."

Tanya was keeping her body pressed back against the

wall as she attempted to inch her way along towards me, taking tiny little side steps. "So it's all about the bloke on the leaflets?" she asked, gradually working out what was going on. "It's like Christmas come early down there you know, Bev. You've caused a white-out as far as Bold Street."

That pleased me enormously. Forget the internet, I was spreading my message far and wide without having to "go viral", whatever that actually meant.

"Good!" I said, satisfied that my mission was going completely according to plan. "But it'll take more than that to make sure he can't do this to anyone else. He'll change his name, you see, go on other dating websites. I've got to end it all." It was a poor choice of words on my part, I can see that now.

Poor Tanya almost had a heart attack and she took a wild lunge in my direction and stuck out one hand. "No! He's not worth it, Bev!" she shouted.

I waved her back and reassured her I didn't mean I intended to end my life. I wouldn't have given Scott the satisfaction. I told her he'd made a fool of me, made me a laughing-stock, and I was trying to prevent the same happening to some other poor woman. Tanya seemed to calm down a bit once I'd told her that. She puffed out her cheeks and did some deep breathing for a moment, all while never taking her eyes off my face.

After a while she said something that surprised me. "I don't think you'll be a laughing-stock, Bev," she said. "I think you'll be an inspiration." When I asked her how she worked that one out she answered, "Well, not many women your age would be brave enough to try internet dating." I thought perhaps the altitude was messing with her faculties. She clearly had no grasp of the issues at stake and I told her so in no uncertain terms. She was on her back foot then, or she would have been if there had been any room for her to step back any further from the edge. She attempted to explain what she had meant. "It's just… What I meant was … I know this didn't work out very well, putting it mildly, but at least you *tried* to make something happen in your life."

I could sort of see where she was coming from. She was impressed that a woman of my age had the gumption to try and shake her life up a bit. She probably thought women my age were all knitting nannas so it surprised her I had tried to relaunch my love-life. It was a shame to burst her youthful naivety but it had to be done. "You don't get points for trying, love. Not in this life," I told her.

"Oh, but Bev, listen to me – you can't let one bad experience put you off. You should try again."

I almost fell of the Liver Building roof laughing at that point. "Hahaha… Try again? Are you completely insane?" I halted my hollow laugh and looked at her sweet, innocent face then. It wasn't funny, really, it was heart-breaking. "No … you're not mad though, are you? You're just young and full of hope and possibility. You'll grow out of it eventually." I didn't mean to come over as bitter but this daft cub reporter couldn't possibly understand how Scott's betrayal had made me feel. She clearly thought I was wrong to be so cynical about life but I told her we'd only revealed the tip of my iceberg.

She tried to change tack then, appearing to be worried

that if she allowed me to become morose I might change my mind about ending my life and make a desperate leap towards the Mersey.

"Let's talk about something else, Bev…" Tanya was back to behaving like an eager puppy. "Bev? Are you listening to me, Bev?"

I was distracted by a commotion below, wondering if something was going on down there. I told her to calm down as she seemed to be so jumpy.

"Can we please not talk about jumping?!" she begged.

I decided that, if anything, it was my job then to try and distract her. She was more likely to do something foolish than I was, so I thought it best to keep her talking. I asked her what she wanted to talk about.

"The Beatles!" she said. "Tell me about The Beatles."

Usually, that wouldn't have been too difficult a request to act upon, but after all that had happened I wasn't sure I could summon the energy. "A girl your age isn't interested in The Beatles," I told her dismissively. "I should have grown out of it years ago, too. I'm a grown woman, not a teenager. You know what? Scott has done me a favour; it's time to let go of all this nonsense." With that I grabbed hold of John Lennon, the cardboard version, and flung him as far as I could towards the murky water of the Mersey River.

Tanya let out a yelp of distress. "Bev, stop!" She spoke quickly then, telling me all about how she remembered our first meeting at the auction in The Cavern Club when I'd bought Paul McCartney's old house on Western Avenue. "You were so happy that day," she said eagerly. "You told me all about growing up loving The Beatles. You've loved them for so long, Bev, it doesn't seem right to throw it all away now."

I figured Lennon would be sinking fast in the swirling Mersey, or be halfway to Wallasey by now. I stifled a sob at the thought of what I'd just done with the last of my precious memorabilia collection.

"Did you ever meet any of them?" Tanya asked gently.

Meet them? As if! I told her I'd never come close to even touching the hem of a Beatle jacket. I told her I did manage to get tickets to the big classical concert that Paul did at the Anglican Cathedral in '91. That was magical, a more intimate experience than being at his regular gigs, and so the closest I'd ever got to being in his presence.

"Was Paul always your favourite?" she asked then. She was more perceptive than I'd been giving her credit for, although there was the big clue that the only cardboard cut-out I hadn't launched from the rooftop was McCartney.

I turned and looked at his lovely face as I spoke then, telling Tanya, "Yeah ... it's always been Paul. I'm not one of the nutters though," I added quickly. It was bonkers that I didn't want her to think I was some sort of looney considering where we were and how I was dressed, but I wanted to be clear. "I never sent hate mail to Linda – or even Heather! He was always the one though – always. No one else ever came close." I looked at Tanya and could see sympathy on her face. "I don't hide it very well, do I?" I said. My affection for Paul had always been so strong over the years that it had just become part of who I was.

Tanya chuckled a little as she said, "If you're gonna be

stuck on anyone though, he's a pretty good choice. He's such a nice guy."

I really did have to grab hold of the balustrade then. "YOU'VE MET PAUL MCCARTNEY?" I hollered. Even without my megaphone I reckoned the crowd still watching from below must have heard me loud and clear.

Tanya looked a bit embarrassed at my huge reaction but confirmed she had met him once or twice in the line of duty. Lucky cow.

I shook my head in disbelief. Fancy a young girl like her able to chat away to a real live Beatle. Did she even realise how incredible that was? Then again, they say never meet your heroes, don't they? When I said that to Tanya it was clear she had never heard that advice.

"Who says don't meet your heroes?" she asked, looking perplexed. "Why would they say that?"

"Because you're bound to be disappointed, I suppose," I told her. "And life is already full of enough disappointment … as I think we have already learned today."

We both looked at Paul's cardboard image then and Tanya gave a small smile. "Somehow, I don't think you'd be disappointed," she said.

I managed to smile back at her then. "Between you and me … neither do I," I answered with a wink.

We stood and looked out at the vast expanse of sky in front of us, me and Tanya, with Paul's image between us, standing like the trio of impressive buildings on the Pier Head waterfront known as the "Three Graces" – The Royal Liver, The Cunard and the Port of Liverpool buildings. The majestic, historic, white constructions had withstood wars and times of trouble but remained standing proud and beautiful, symbols of strength and hope. I loved my city more in that moment than I had ever done before. I'd always known Liverpool was an incredible place – the architecture, the atmosphere, and of course the wonderful, warm and welcoming people. Living here in this city was how I was going to be able to survive this, I realised. All I needed was my Liverpool home to help me remember who I was and what was important to me.

Tanya seemed to sense the change in my mood. "C'mon, Bev," she said gently. "Shall we take your Paul home?"

I took a final look out at the view and turned to reach for my last remaining Beatle figure. "It looks like the best offer I'm gonna get today," I answered with a sigh. My rooftop protest was over; it was time to head home.

Chapter Twenty-Two

I'd only been home a matter of moments before there was an urgent banging on my front door. I opened it to find an agitated Jools hopping from foot to foot with an anguished expression on her face and her bright red hair practically standing on end.

"Are you okay, Jools? Whatever has happened?" I asked, ushering her through to the front room.

"What… Has… Am *I* okay?" Jools repeated in explosive stutters, looking at me as though I had grown a second head. "I've come to see if *you* are all right you daft divvy!"

Ahhh, now I understood. Word had clearly reached Jools about my exploits on the roof of the Liver Building. Yep, now I looked more closely she was actually clutching one of my "UNWANTED" posters featuring Scott the scumbag in her hot little hand.

It wasn't that surprising when I thought about it. Her shop was in the city centre after all, and Tanya the *Echo* reporter had said my leaflets had found their way right across the city. I presumed tales of a crazed woman dressed in a yellow submarine costume had also spread quickly through the city streets. Liverpudlians do love a good gawp and gossip and I'd given them something pretty juicy to feast on.

I tried to reassure Jools that I was actually feeling fine. The proclamations I'd made from the top of the Royal Liver Building seemed to have done wonders for my mood. Maybe the altitude and the amazing view had lifted my spirits, or perhaps it was getting all that stuff about Scott off my chest, but I still felt quite exhilarated from the whole experience.

I tried to explain all that to Jools but she remained unconvinced. She peered at me through her scarlet spectacles and asked if I had "taken anything".

"You mean drugs?" I retorted in surprise, chuckling a little. Did Jools seriously believe I was popping pills to get me through all this? Unfortunately, Jools took my laughter as mild hysteria and I had to endure several minutes of her lecturing me on how I should have called her as soon as I had realised Scott was a devious conman.

I appreciated that she was miffed I hadn't turned to her in my hour of need but it was beginning to annoy me that she was making this more about *her* than it was about me, especially when she added, "I knew he was dodgy when he didn't show up at the teriyaki restaurant. I should never have let that go."

That was rich. I didn't remember her saying any such thing at the time.

"Huh, well, it's very easy to be wise *after* the event," I

told her rather snappily. "We could all do that! And what *exactly* do you think you could have done? Burst in through my bay window with a SWAT team when we were having dinner? Staged some sort of intervention?"

I was being aggressive and I knew it, but she was giving me the right hump now. Was she seriously suggesting disaster could easily have been averted if she had just been more involved? That was a cheek considering I was only even *in* this mess because of how involved she had made herself right at the start. After all, the whole internet dating lark had been *her* idea, not mine. She'd pushed me into that, she'd even pressed send on the link to sign me up before I had a chance to think it all through properly. Without Julia Gillespie's involvement I would never have met Scott soddin' Smith, would never have had my Beatles memorabilia robbed from right under my nose, and thanks to Scott's weird remark about my family I would never have found out my big sister was actually my mam and that I'd been lied to all my life. All the pain and anguish I had suffered, the fact that my life had been shaken completely out of shape, was actually *her* fault!

She wasn't best pleased when I pointed that last bit out.

"Is that right?" she said jutting out her chin, her green eyes blinking rapidly behind her specs.

I'd basically just told my best friend that she had ruined my life but I was in no mood to back down. The air had been pretty thin up by the Liver Birds so that might well have contributed to my light-headedness at that moment, but I felt I was actually thinking clearly for the first time in a long while. Despite how Jools was reacting I felt I was completely on top of the situation, if you'll pardon the pun.

I'd let Tanya the reporter believe she had "talked me down" from the rooftop overlooking the dock but, really, by that time I felt I had achieved everything I could from my vantage point and so I'd been ready to come back down to earth. We'd had the presence of mind to take the lift down to the fourth floor and then make our way back down to ground level via the stairs. That way we were able to avoid being confronted by the security guard, who I felt might have been on the warpath once he realised my mission had not been connected to charity after all.

I'd disrobed out of my yellow submarine costume and we'd snuck out the back, away from the prying eyes of the crowd that had gathered out front to witness my protest.

Once I got home, I honestly felt better than I had done in days – stronger, saner and back in control of my own life. I'd taken Detective Constable Levi Collins's advice to warn other women about the despicable doings of Scott Smith, and cleared my own head in the process. But once Jools arrived, full of wisdom *after* the event, I had been brought back down to earth in a rather more depressing way. Now she appeared to be questioning my choices all over again and making me feel I should have done everything differently, both in my relationship with Scott and how I was handling the fall out of his betrayal.

I hadn't even told her about the revelations concerning Deb and Mame and who my real mother was. I considered blurting it all out but thought that would make me sound even more unhinged than she clearly presumed I was.

Jools was still standing her ground in my living room, hands on hips and lips set in a hard line as I gave her a piece of my disintegrating mind.

"It's all very well coming round here telling me what I *should* have done or what *you* would have done," I said as I flung a Beatles cushion from the sofa to the floor. "Shoulda woulda coulda doesn't get us anywhere, Julia!" I carried on de-Beatle-ing my home around her, removing anything with the band's image on from my eyeline. The cushions, the submarine clock on the wall, the pop art Warhol-style framed print, and my stack of vinyl albums by the record player, all got piled in a mound on the floor.

Jools watched me silently for a while, her mouth set in its line while her eyes never left me. "Bev?" she eventually said quietly, but I was fired up and focused on demonstrating how determined I was to move on with my life. The room had been stripped of all the Beatles-themed items that had once advertised my devotion to the band. I needed to purge myself and my home from their influence and I didn't need Jools standing there, judging me, while I did it.

"What?" I whirled around to face her but she seemed to think twice about saying anything else. She muttered something about having to get back to work and I told her to let herself out while I went into the kitchen to see what other stupid, childish, tacky Beatles souvenirs needed to be cleared out from there. I only knew she had left when I heard the front door slam behind her.

After Jools had gone, I carried on sweeping my home for Beatles-related iconography, but my energy levels were dipping fast and I suddenly felt exhausted and defeated.

I checked my phone and saw messages and voicemails had been streaming in. That did it. I simply did not have the strength to deal with anyone else. I fired off what I thought was a reassuring message on the group chat I shared with the boys, telling them I was fine and not to worry. The last thing I wanted was to bother them and I hoped they would simply forget about my drama and go back to their own lives so long as I played it all down. After all, what young lad wants to even think about their mother's love life?

After that I switched my phone off completely, went upstairs and crawled into bed. Amazingly, sleep came quickly and I knew nothing at all until lunchtime the following day.

———

When I woke, my body still felt tired to the bone, despite the deep sleep ... or maybe because of it. My mind was awake, though, so it was impossible to lie there, even though I felt as heavy as a sack of potatoes.

My stomach started churning as soon as consciousness brought back memories of recent events, but my mouth was dry and I was desperate for a cup of tea. I'd fallen asleep in yesterday's clothes – black leggings and an oversize navy sweatshirt – but I wasn't bothered about what I was wearing. I had no intention of seeing anyone or going anywhere. Maybe I just wouldn't leave the house ever again? The thought was oddly appealing.

I plopped myself on the sofa and cradled my mug of tea. It wasn't in a Beatles mug, for a change, as all Beatles-related merchandise – from cushions and tote bags to crockery and tea towels – was still in a pile in the corner of the living room. I averted my gaze from the mound and did my best to ignore it.

The silence in the house was quite soothing but force of habit prompted me to flick on the TV after a while. I wished to God I hadn't. I'd lost all track of time but the two faces that appeared on the screen told me it must be lunchtime.

Actors turned TV presenters Denise Welch and Sally Lindsay were hosting the daytime talk show *Lively Ladies* – you know, the one where a group of gobby women rake over all the news of the day and offer their instant opinions on everything from troubles in the Middle East to the perils of being a middle child. Well, today the topic up for discussion was, quite incredibly … ME!

I'd clearly tuned in mid-way through them telling the audience all about my escapades on the rooftop.

"That's right, Denise," Sally Lindsay was saying, "you must have seen her on the news last night. She was on top of the Liver Building in Liverpool chucking pictures all over the city of a man she claims has conned her. Talk about a woman scorned."

Denise Welch nodded at her co-presenter and then turned to face the camera. "Well, after what she says has happened to her, can you blame her?"

NO. NO, NO, NO, NO! This could NOT be happening

to me. For a millisecond I thought I must be dreaming, that I was still in bed and this was all some awful trauma-induced hallucination, but as I lunged for the remote to turn up the volume the dregs of my tea slopped from the mug still in my hand onto my leggings, and the wet patch of hot tea spreading across my thigh certainly felt real enough. This wasn't a dream; it was a living nightmare.

"In case you hadn't heard," Denise went on to say, "sixty-four-year-old mum of three Beverley Wilson is a Beatles fanatic, and she's so in love with Paul McCartney she bought his childhood home in Speke to live in."

"I am NOT SIXTY-bloody-FOUR!" I yelled as the mug of tea got flung across the room.

Sally Lindsay arched her eyebrows as she commented, "Bit weird," on hearing about my property purchase and then went on to tell the viewers that me deciding to try internet dating as a lonely widow was a "brave" move. There wasn't time to feel complimented by this appraisal of my private life, however, as Denise decided to weigh in with the opposing point of view that it might be seen as "foolish". They were using me as a topical hot potato, tossing the whys and wherefores of my decisions and their consequences back and forth for the entertainment of the watching audience. I could just imagine the stay-at-home mums, pensioners, students and generally jobless the show was aimed at lapping all this up as they watched from the safety of their sofas. Meanwhile I felt violated and exposed while I continued to sit on mine. My sofa was a safe space no longer.

They flashed up some footage of me, dressed in my

ridiculous yellow submarine costume, teetering on the precipice of the Royal Liver Building. I looked like a basket case. If it hadn't been me pictured acting like a loopy-juice looney I would have laughed out loud. But it *was* me and quite obviously that made me a laughing-stock ... a national joke.

The two presenters continued to cover every dot and comma of my downfall, saying I'd had my priceless collection of Beatles memorabilia robbed from "under my nose" and then, dear God, they began to make their own jokes.

"At least he didn't take the McCartney house as well," Denise chuckled merrily, then switched her expression to try and convey some semblance of sympathy.

"Well, she might have noticed if he'd tried to shove a whole house in his back pocket," Sally chimed in, only just suppressing a fit of the giggles. They just couldn't help themselves, sniggering away. Thanks for the female solidarity, ladies!

"Go on, have a right laugh, why don't you!" I was on my feet confronting the screen and two women I was never likely to meet, but who had such strong opinions on me and my life choices.

They'd changed tack again now, switching into sentimental mode as Denise revealed, "The most humiliating part of this story, for me, is that all the time he's wining and dining her, he's using the money he's got from selling off all of her autographed stuff and rare collectibles. What a scumbag!"

"It's such a sad story, isn't it," agreed Sally, although I

noticed her eyes were completely dry. "My heart breaks for the poor woman."

I was rooted to the spot, my heart hammering and my hands balled into fists by my side. "I can see the two of you are positively traumatised," I grunted through gritted teeth.

I wanted to turn it off – I didn't want to hear another word – but I was paralysed. It was like watching a slow-moving train crash. But then it got even worse.

"So today we're asking … what do *you* think of 'Beatles Bev'? Should she have known better before putting herself online and begging 'Love Me Do'?"

I was struggling to compute what Sally Lindsay was now saying… What did *who* think? Surely they couldn't just ask people I didn't even know to call in and—

"Right, we've got Liz on the line," Denise cut in over the top before I could process that I was now the subject of a live, televised phone-in. Yes, apparently any Tom, Dick or Harriet could call in and give their opinions on *my* life! Perfect!

If I thought Sally and Denise were bad enough, that was nothing compared to "Liz from Hartlepool". What a bitch.

"Well, she's clearly a fame-seeker, isn't she?" Liz said. "It's not love she went looking for, it's attention, even before her stunt on the Liver Building yesterday. Buying that house for a start, and d'you know she sells her own autographs to tourists? She stands outside her house posing for photos! Who does she think she is? I bet she's lovin' all this, bein' talked about on the telly."

I sank down onto the sofa muttering, "Oh yeah, I'm havin' the time of me bloody life here." But there was something else nagging at me now. Had bitch-face Liz from Hartlepool got all that from a couple of pictures of me throwing leaflets off the Liver Building and sounding off over a megaphone? I'd never mentioned anything about being part of the Magical Mystery Tour or anything like that. Where was all this background information coming from?

Sally was now winding Liz up, although not as much as she'd wound me up! "Right, well, thanks, Liz, you clearly don't have much sympathy for Beverley. How about a male point of view? Hi there, Brendan, what's your take on it?"

I leaned forward. I didn't really want to know ... I shouldn't want to know ... but I couldn't help but be desperate to know ... what *was* Brendan's take on it?

Brendan was obviously local. His broad Liverpudlian accent gave him away as soon as he started talking. Did I know him? "She's a man-eater, obviously," he declared and I felt like I'd been shot. "It's that Scott I feel sorry for."

BANG! KAPOW! That last one landed so hard I was shocked I wasn't spurting blood across the carpet.

Even Denise wasn't sure how Brendan was making Scott out to be the victim. She asked him to clarify.

"It's well known she went through loads of men before she snared that poor Scott," Brendan helpfully replied as I sat there quietly moaning and shaking my head from side to side. What was this guy on about? Was he one of the disgruntled men I'd endured a disastrous date with before meeting Scott? Was that it? Was it Peter? But he had rejected me at first sight. It didn't sound like Juan ... or Barney... Could it be Andrew the pantyhose pervert? Was it Scott himself? That would take some front but then we knew he had plenty of that. I didn't know who it was but I did know I was having an actual nervous breakdown.

Denise and Sally were hanging on "Brendan"'s every word as though "Beatles Bev" was his specialist subject on *Mastermind.* "Oh yeah, she's thrown herself at every celebrity in Liverpool at one time or another from what I've heard," he said. "From Wayne Rooney to Ken Dodd!"

Now I knew I had lost my actual mind and to prove the point I heard myself shouting, "I'VE NEVER EVEN MET KEN FREAKIN' DODD!"

Sally Lindsay possibly heard me as she told him, "Well in Bev's defence, we can't actually verify that, but thanks for your thoughts anyway, Brendan."

Denise was now looking straight into the camera lens; it was like she could see out from the screen and right into my front room where I sat illuminated by the flickering light from the TV. She started to talk directly to me – I wasn't imagining it, she really was!

"I just want to say to Bev, if she's watching, she musn't let this Scott fella ruin her life."

It's a nice idea, Denise, love, I thought, but it was a bit late for that. Denise hadn't finished though; she was still giving me the benefit of her infinite wisdom. "She needs to put her profile back on that dating website and start building her Beatles collection again," she told me and everyone else, staring out from the screen with her perfectly coiffed blonde hair and expertly arched eyebrows.

Sally was nodding vigorously at her co-presenter, her ample bosom jiggling beneath her expensive silky blouse.

"That's certainly great advice, Denise," she agreed. "Let's hope she's out there listening. Can you hear us, Bev? Come on, girl, you can do it! Don't let that conman win!"

My hand reached for the TV remote then and my fingers closed around the black rectangle as though it was the handle of a pistol. I raised it in my shaky fingers and used my other hand to steady my grip. I aimed it directly at the smarmy, smiling faces of smug Sally and dopey Denise and fired. Everything went black.

Chapter Twenty-Three

I sat there for a long time, frozen in horror and paralysed by abject misery.

My disastrous life and humiliating misfortune had just been discussed on national TV. They'd shown my picture, given my name and even told everyone whereabouts I lived. They might not have given the address and postcode but there was no way I would ever be able to leave my house ever again without people staring and pointing. *"There goes 'Beatles Bev', the woman so desperate for love she let a conman rob her blind."* I must have seemed like an overgrown teenager to normal people. Most girls grow out of obsessing over a band, or a popstar; they take down the posters on their walls as they mature and develop other interests and hobbies. Not me though. Not "Beatles Bev". Oh no, I carried on hoarding memorabilia, surrounding myself with keepsakes, and even moved into a tiny terraced house just because a famous musician used to live there. No wonder they were all laughing at me.

As I realised how the rest of the world viewed me it dawned on me that *Lively Ladies* wouldn't be the only platform discussing my mistakes. Like a moth drawn to a flame I slowly uncurled my body from its locked position on the sofa and went in search of my mobile phone.

Instantly it pinged into life, juddering in my already shaky hands as texts, voicemail alerts and WhatsApp messages trilled and beeped over and over. Switching to social media I realised I was trending on Twitter and – I could hardly believe what I was seeing – my image had been made into a meme. The moment I'd flung cardboard Ringo from the rooftop while dressed as a cartoon submarine was flashing in front of my eyes on repeat with the words *"going down"* and *"dive, dive, dive"* alternating on the screen. That was the least offensive. There were others that were far crueller as they mocked my middle-aged sex appeal … or rather, my lack of it.

There were also already clips of *Lively Ladies'* Sally Lindsay staring down the barrel of the camera lens saying, "Come on, Bev, you can do it! Don't let him win." I supposed those tweets and posts were meant to be supportive, willing me on to overcome my "setback", but it just felt like the final fatal blow.

I didn't think there was anyone who could really understand quite how I felt. Fancy someone saying *"Don't let him win"*, for a start, like my life was some sort of game to be played. Well, I'd decided I didn't want to play that bloody game anymore.

No one had the slightest idea how hard it all was in the first place, not just collecting that stuff, which, let's be honest, took over fifty *fucking* years! There was no way on earth to build all that back up again – even if I could have afforded it. No, what those TV twinkies and the rest of them were seemingly oblivious to was how hard it had been to put myself out there right at the start, where and when all of this trouble began. Didn't they realise how excruciating it was to get out there and parade myself around to a load of men like I was a prize heifer at a cattle show? Like I was an antique being valued on *Dickinson's Real Deal*. That's what I felt like – cheap as chips!

Then, just as I was at my lowest, terrified of facing the world again and desperately wanting to crawl into a hole and hide there for ever, the world decided to come and find me.

It started with sharp raps on my front door and repeated rings of the doorbell. I didn't have a clue who it was and I didn't care; there was nobody I wanted to see, and more importantly no one I wanted to see me. But they wouldn't give up. The door knocking was insistent and it sounded like someone was leaning against the doorbell.

I stayed rooted to the spot until they began shouting through the letterbox and then shadowy figures started peering into my house through the living-room bay window.

"Mrs Wilson? Come and talk to us, Mrs Wilson..."

"Come on, Bev, it'll only take a minute. You might as well talk to us. We're gonna print the story anyway."

"Mrs Wilson, Beverley, love – you need to tell your side of the story. Talk to us, Bev, it'll make you feel better."

"Bev – is it true you've got a yellow submarine tattooed on your arse?"

The national press had descended on Western Avenue and was baying for my blood. I dropped to my knees, crawled towards the window and managed to tug the curtains closed. The action only confirmed to the mob outside that I was home, but at least I'd stopped them actually being able to see into the house.

I crawled back across the living room and went to hide behind the sofa. It was incredibly undignified but since I'd thrown my last shred of dignity away while I was tossing assorted Beatles off the top of the Liver Building, it was a bit too late to be worried about that.

———

Several hours, thousands of tears and a full-scale hysterical meltdown later, things seemed to have calmed outside the house. I'd eventually crawled out from behind my hiding place behind the sofa and fallen asleep on it instead, too terrified to go upstairs in case the reporters spotted me moving about through the glass panels on my front door. The press pack must have eventually dispersed, presumably giving up on an exclusive with "Beatles Bev" and moving on to their next victim, but as morning came things were still far from calm inside the house. I wasn't simply devastated, ashamed and traumatised; by this point I was absolutely fucking furious! With the reporters, with Scott, with the bloody Beatles – for some reason – but most of all I was practically demented with rage at myself!

I paced back and forth across the room, berating myself for getting into this unholy mess in the first place. I needed someone to vent my rage at and as I was the only one there, I was giving it to myself with both barrels.

"You thought you were being so clever, joining an online dating agency, posting your profile ... how very modern. How very fuckin' stupid!" My voice dripped with sarcasm at first and then I really turned on myself. "All your life you've been careful. Okay, so it's not that exciting ... in fact, it can all get a bit bloody boring, to be completely honest. So what! For fuck's sake, Beverley, it's better to be bored silly than to be a national bloody joke!"

My hands were in my hair, yanking at it from the roots as I caught sight of myself in the mirror above the mantelpiece. I looked like a mad woman. I *was* a mad woman, I faced my own reflection and told myself the home truths I needed to hear. "Nothing good *ever* came of being reckless. You know that, you foolish, ridiculous woman. The one time – the one and *only* time – you do something just the tiniest bit crazy, pushing yourself out of your comfort zone, trying to 'shake things up' a bit ... look what happens! Just look what bloody happens!"

My diatribe was rudely interrupted by the sound of the doorbell bing-bonging. "Who the bloody hell is that NOW?" I demanded of the woman with the wild eyes and the even wilder hair who stared back at me from the mirror.

The doorbell chimed again and then came a knocking on the door. "Just piss off and leave me alone," I hissed nastily, although whoever it was couldn't possibly have heard me.

I heard the letterbox clatter then and a voice I recognised

calling through it. "Mrs Wilson – Beverley – are you in? Please answer the door, it's Tanya from the *Echo*."

I sank miserably onto the sofa muttering, "Go away, Tanya, just leave me alone."

I'd thought Tanya was all right. She seemed like a nice girl, a bit naive and full of youthful high expectations, but she'd actually made me feel like a woman of the world when I'd talked to her. I'd even kidded myself into believing we'd struck up a friendly rapport on the roof of the Liver Building. She'd appeared to want to listen to what I had to say and even empathised with my situation, but if she thought that gave her some sort of advantage and I was going to give her an interview she could jog on. I wasn't going to fall for that.

She was persistent though, and the knocking and bell ringing continued. "Bev? Bev, I know you're in there," she hollered. "Open the door, Bev, it's important."

"NOT TODAY, TANYA. JUST LEAVE ME ALONE, PLEASE, LOVE!" I yelled towards the window, begging her to give up and go home. Didn't she understand I just didn't want to talk about it?

"Bev! Answer the door!" Her pleading was louder and more urgent now that she knew I was there. She actually sounded almost desperate. "Trust me, Bev, you will never forgive yourself if you don't open the door! If you never do anything else IN YOUR LIFE as long as you live, you absolutely must – I'm telling you – you *must* OPEN THIS DOOR!"

The sound of the doorbell ringing and ringing was reverberating around the room and inside my head. The noise was going to drive me even more up the wall if she didn't stop soon. I struggled to my feet muttering, "Oh, give me strength," and went to open the damn door.

I wrenched it towards me and got the biggest shock of my entire life. Stood just behind Tanya, large as life and wearing a faintly amused expression on his beautiful face, was the one, the only, Paul McCartney!

Chapter Twenty-Four

I stood there, my mouth agape but Paul just smiled at me and said, "Hi, Bev, I'm Paul. I hear you've had a bit of trouble. D'you fancy putting the kettle on?"

That's what he said. Honest to God. Like Paul McCartney knowing my name and popping round for a cuppa was just the most natural thing in the world.

I simply nodded like a dumb mute and stepped back to let Tanya lead a living, breathing Beatle – a world-famous musician, an icon of our age – into my front room. Oh wait, of course, it used to be *his* front room, didn't it? In my delirium I'd almost forgot that fact.

Luckily Tanya was more on the ball and she chatted easily to Paul about how long it must have been since he had lived there and how much of it did he remember, etc. It was a good tactic on her part, it broke the ice nicely and gave me time to drag myself into the moment. Never in my life did I ever imagine I would meet a Beatle, let alone my most favourite Beatle, and not for a single, solitary second would I have dreamed he would come into my home and sit on my sofa. Dear God, Paul McCartney was sitting on my sofa!

Tanya was over in the armchair, deliberately leaving the space on the sofa next to Paul free for me, and so I went and sat next to him.

It all goes a bit hazy for a while after that. He spoke. I answered. Tanya chipped in on occasion. Conversation flowed back and forth. He seemed to know all about what had been happening to me; about Scott and the Lonely Hearts Club dating website, and the plundering of my memorabilia collection. I can't remember what exactly I said about all that but I did find my eyes flicking over to the sad little pile of remaining Beatle items that were still on the floor in the corner. Tanya must have picked up on that – she really was a most perceptive young woman – as she suddenly volunteered to put the kettle on while Paul and I continued our chat. On her way to the kitchen she dropped a throw that had been on the arm of the sofa over the offending mound of knick-knacks and Paul didn't seem to notice a thing. My full-size cardboard version of my famous visitor was still folded up in my M&S Bag for Life, along with my yellow submarine costume, so luckily Paul wasn't going to be confronted with either of those highly embarrassing items.

By the time Tanya came back with a tray of teas and biscuits she'd miraculously found from somewhere, Paul was giving me the ultimate pep talk.

"The guy sounds like a total loser," he said. "You're well rid of him now though, Bev. You can find yourself someone who'll appreciate what they've got when they're with you."

That's what he said. He really did.

I felt a warm glow start at my toes and begin to spread up my entire body. He carried on blagging me up – like Tanya, he seemed to think it wasn't foolish to try and find love again – and he even told me he admired me for trying to shake my life up a bit. He. Admired. Me. Yeah, you read that right!

As we talked some more, I began to understand where he was coming from. Just think about the highs and lows he'd experienced in his own life. From being in the biggest band in the world, to them splitting up and him having to find a new direction, which of course he did with Wings and his solo work. He'd had to overcome the tragedy of John's murder and the fear that something similar could maybe happen to him. Then there was George's death at just fifty-eight and the painful loss of his own wife, Linda, to cancer, followed by a messy divorce from Heather. All of this in the glare of scrutiny and publicity I couldn't even begin to imagine. And yet, here he sat, on my sofa, talking just like a regular guy and dipping a ginger nut biscuit in his tea while he did it.

I'm not going to go into any details about the things he spoke about – that was private, and thankfully Tanya also understood that sort of stuff was off the record – but it blew my mind that Paul McCartney was sitting there so easily empathising with my life and giving me some bloody great advice while he was at it. If I hadn't been besotted enough with him already…

He started talking then about the loss of my memorabilia collection. "You got anything left you want me to sign?" he asked in his lovely, laid-back Liverpudlian drawl. I quickly glanced at Tanya in a slight panic but once again she came to my rescue. Out of his line of sight, she quickly fished a couple of my Beatles albums out from under the throw hiding the pile of stuff I had been far too quick to discard.

Paul whipped a Sharpie from his pocket and signed them for me. Swoon. He then asked Tanya to pass him a bag she had on the floor next to her feet and presented me with a couple of his own albums, including a new one not yet released – all signed – along with some other assorted merchandise.

It was all a bit much and I felt myself tear up so I was already blinking rapidly when he echoed the advice the presenters on that daytime chat show had given me the day before. "You can use these to start a new collection," he said. "Let go of the old stuff and start over with the new." Somehow when *he* said it, it all sounded much more possible, and I didn't feel insulted or angry at all. When I tried to thank him my voice caught in my throat. He waved my thanks away and told me it was no more than I deserved for being such a devoted fan all these years.

I've no idea how long we had been chatting, but we'd finished our drinks and he'd even shown me a couple of pictures on his phone of his grandkids, who looked cheeky and adorable in equal measure. "Kids, huh?" he said, and then listened as I told him all about James, Richie and Harry. I felt compelled to confess how their names had been chosen and he nodded as if he had already worked that out and told me he thought what I'd done was "genius".

Just after that Tanya suggested we commemorate the occasion of Paul's visit with a photo or two, and it seriously wasn't until that point that I'd given a hoot about what I must have looked like. If you'd told me that I could sit and chat to the man I had idolised my entire life and not fuss or worry about my hair, whether I was wearing any make-up, or that I was wearing yesterday's leggings and a baggy sweatshirt, I wouldn't have believed you, but that is exactly what happened. I reckon it's a testament to the way Paul made me feel, and the way he spoke to me like an equal, like what I had to say had merit. It felt like we just connected in a normal, natural way that put all superficial thoughts about my appearance out of my head. I think I learned that day that a man who is secure in himself, and shows an interest in you and your life, can make you feel attractive and appreciated no matter what you *actually* look like. Men like that are rare, I know, but they definitely do exist.

Having said all that, when Tanya suggested I quickly "freshen up", with a nod of her head in the direction of the stairs, I zoomed up to my bedroom to try and make myself look as good as possible in record time.

Brushed hair, a quick change into clean jeans and my favourite baby-blue sweater, plus a touch of lipstick and mascara made me feel like a new woman. I didn't need blusher, not with Paul McCartney sitting in my living room. That was enough to give my cheeks a hot pink flush already.

They both said I looked really great when I came back down, but not in a way that made me feel embarrassed about how they'd found me earlier; it was just said easily and with a warmth that made it feel friendly and kind. It was amazing how quickly self-confidence can return in the right circumstances. I honestly felt that the time I'd spent with Paul had done more to restore me to my usual self than six months of intense therapy could ever have achieved. I also realised I was smiling from ear to ear like an absolute loon.

Paul put his arm around me as we sat on the sofa and then we both did grinning thumbs-up poses as Tanya snapped away. She said she was going to do a write-up about how my recent trouble had led to me meeting my lifelong hero. She promised it wouldn't drag up anything too horrible and would be a nice, positive piece. I liked the sound of that and I trusted her to do it justice.

I realised Paul was going to have to leave soon, but I was still so thrilled to have had the experience of meeting him, my smile stayed right where it was on my face.

Eventually, I showed them to the door but paused just before I opened it, wanting to give heartfelt thanks to Tanya for somehow arranging this surprise visit, and to Paul for … well, for just being pretty bloody amazing!

Before I could say too much Paul touched my arm and said, "Just remember, Bev, the best revenge of all is to live a good and happy life… They hate that!" Then he laughed and we were all giggling when the door opened.

Suddenly there was a lot of shouting and flashes going off. The mob of reporters was back and they were yelling at us, calling out to Paul and shouting my name too. I was blindsided for a moment; how had they known he was here? But Paul just took it all in his stride, giving them a big wave. He pulled me to his side and let them take a couple of shots of us in the doorway, then, before I knew what was happening, he kissed me quickly on the cheek and whispered into my ear, "Maybe one day I'll write a song about all this, Bev. I won't make it too obvious, but you'll know it's about you." Then he winked and sprinted towards a shiny black limousine that was parked the other side of my hedge and, just like that, he was gone.

I stood on my doorstep, hand raised in the air. "Goodbye ... goodbye ... goodbye, my love, goodbye," I sang quietly and happily to myself. Beatles Bev was back.

Chapter Twenty-Five

A burst of renewed energy consumed me once I'd closed the door after Paul McCartney had left. Maybe I needed to burn off all the excitement the visit had generated or perhaps I was simply so inspired by meeting my idol that I suddenly wanted to ensure I was the very best version of myself.

There was nothing for it, I decided, I had to clean my house from top to bottom. I know, it might seem like a weird reaction but it made total sense at the time. I stuck Paul's new album that he'd given me on as background music and set to work. It was great having him sing to me while I dusted and polished, mopped and hoovered, straightening and tidying everything as I went along. By the time I'd finished the whole place was spick and span, and positively sparkled. I'd erased all lingering memories and evidence of Scott "scumbag" Smith and restored my Beatles trinkets, keepsakes and decorations to their rightful locations.

I lay back on the plumped-up Beatles cushions on my sofa and ran my hand over the seat where Paul had been sitting just a short while before. I hoped the image I held of him in my mind's eye would always stay as clear and sharp, and I thought there was a very good chance it would.

Despite everything that had happened, all the pain of being betrayed and the humiliation of everyone finding out, I now felt like the luckiest girl in the world. Most Beatles fans would give their right arm for a meeting with Paul McCartney like the one I had just had. I'd only had to give up my memorabilia collection, get dumped by a dodgy guy and put up with being talked about on the telly. None of it felt like too big a price to pay for the reward I'd just been given.

Talking to someone like Paul with such amazing life experience had put such a lot of things in my life into proper perspective. Fame and success didn't protect anyone from painful life and death events, so us *normal* mortals shouldn't expect to sail through life unaffected either. Finding out the truth about my sister Deb really being my mother had been upsetting and confusing, but I now realised I was still sure that I had been loved by both Deb and Mame, so that meant double the amount of maternal love, in effect. Wasn't that preferable to the experience Paul himself had endured, losing his mother completely when he was so very young? John Lennon had also lost his mother, Julia, when he was just a teenager, and I'd always thought that shared trauma must have helped the two young musicians forge a special bond.

I also strongly suspected that, if Deb had lived, together with Mame she might have been planning to come clean and tell me. That was definitely what Deb's mate Doreen believed and she'd known Deb well, and been able to talk to Mame at the funeral. I could hardly blame Mame for wanting to protect me from yet more hurt and heartbreak after Deb was killed. If nothing else, I was sure that both of my "mothers" had always wanted to love and protect me and felt they were doing their best. Surely that was all you could ask of anyone.

Somehow, Paul turning up on my doorstep had felt like a message from Deb, and I could feel the connection between us was still there. It was just manifesting itself in different ways now, and I was looking forward to finding new ways to experience that connection in the future now that I knew how closely linked Deb and I really were.

Once I'd had a breather from my frenetic cleaning activity my thoughts turned to the one outstanding issue that was still bothering me. I really needed to make things right with Jools. We hadn't spoken since I'd given her short shrift when she came round after my appearance on the roof of the Liver Building. She may well have sent one of the dozens of messages that had filled my phone after my love life was pulled apart on the *Lively Ladies* show, but I'd deleted all those without reading any of them. If I knew Jools – and I *did* know her, I knew her very well indeed – she would definitely have messaged me even though I'd been so rude to her. She was a tough one, was Jools, but she had a heart of gold and I was lucky to have her as a friend.

She was only ever looking out for me, trying her best to help, and I knew I owed her an apology.

I decided that only an "in person" apology to Jools would do, so I went upstairs to change before heading down to Bold Brides to catch her before the shop shut.

I laid a fresh outfit on the bed – my new black trousers with the white side stripe and a slinky black top. I'd throw my denim jacket and a colourful silk scarf on, too, so if Jools fancied going out for a drink with me, I could instantly be "wine bar ready". I couldn't help but give my favourite blue sweater a little cuddle after taking it off, remembering how Paul had put his arm around me as I was wearing it. I couldn't quite bring myself to put it in the wash just yet, so instead I folded it carefully and put it on the bedside chair.

In the shower I let the hot water cascade over me and used liberal amounts of my favourite shower cream, lathering the scented foam all over my body while my conditioner worked its magic on my hair, bringing back the usual shine and softness. I emerged into the steamy bathroom feeling like a new woman, ready to face the world. Then I remembered I probably needed to get dressed first. The last thing the world needed was to see "Beatles Bev" on a naked rampage.

It was as I stood there in the bedroom, wearing only my bra and pants, one leg inserted into my trousers, that I heard a sudden commotion downstairs. Alarmed, I staggered backwards and then hopped around the room like a demented flamingo in a desperate attempt to stop myself falling over.

The sounds from downstairs, combined with my one-legged jig around the bedroom, had my heart pounding and the blood in my ears making whooshing noises that meant I couldn't work out what it was I had heard. I didn't think it was anyone banging on my door again. No, it sounded like there was someone *inside* the house!

I struggled fully into my trousers and threw my blue sweater back on. Whatever was going on downstairs, it didn't feel appropriate to dress in a clingy top with a low neck. If I was going to confront an intruder, I needed coverage.

Memories of the day I hid in Mrs Malkin's bedroom with her scary dollies came flooding back but I was determined not to get trapped quaking with fear this time. This was *my* house and I'd been through too much lately to put up with anyone else who thought they could come into my space, my home, my life and just help themselves to whatever they wanted.

Arming myself with the nearest thing to hand – a hair-dryer – I descended the stairs warily. To my horror, I saw a large hold-all slung on the floor in the hallway. The thieves were obviously planning to fill it full of anything they could ransack from my home. Maybe they'd read about me in the papers, or heard about me on the news, and thought I might have a few Beatles items left that hadn't already been stolen by Scott, and they could just come and help themselves to the dregs. Well I wasn't about to stand for that.

With a roar I kicked open the door to the living room, flinging myself through it brandishing the hair-dryer as though it was a weapon. The startled intruders whirled around to face me looking even more alarmed than I was.

"Mam?" James spoke first, my eldest boy looking shocked and horrified by the sight of his mother wild-eyed and wet-haired standing in the doorway like a poor man's Charlie's Angel. I froze in my confrontational pose, legs spread, both hands on the hairdryer held out in front of me, ready to open fire.

"What are you planning to do? Blow-dry us to death?" Richie raised an eyebrow and spoke in a mildly mocking tone as my three boys looked at me and then back to each other as they tried to work out why I was bursting into my own front room screaming like a banshee.

It took a little while for us all to explain to each other what the Dickens was going on. They had all been prompted by the lurid headlines about my story to return home to check I was all right. It turned out that the reassuring messages I had sent them had left them unconvinced and they were all very concerned about me. Bless them.

Now they were standing in front of me it was even harder to convince them I was actually okay, completely sane and coping fine, given my high-kicking, Lara Croft style entrance. I could tell they thought I was in the middle of a complete nervous breakdown.

Once Harry put the kettle on, and I put the hair-dryer to one side, we all sat and I was finally able to reassure them their mother was not completely insane. It was tricky when I got to the part about Paul McCartney's recent visit, but luckily Tanya had pinged through a couple of the pictures she'd taken of us that morning so I was able to show them the actual evidence on my phone.

"Cool!" said Richie.

"That's incredible!" said James.

"I can't believe I missed him!" said Harry.

I thought it would be embarrassing to talk about Scott, the whole internet dating fiasco and what had happened in the end, but my boys were a lot more understanding and broad-minded than I expected. I suppose meeting people online, or hooking up with someone via an app, is not all that unusual to their generation, so they took it all in their stride. When I had to go into details about how I'd been duped, Scott managing to steal stuff from under my nose, their anger was only with Scott, not with me. That was quite a relief, I can tell you.

"What a piece of work," James said. "I hope you reported all this to the police."

I told him of course I had but there was very little hope of anything being returned and the chances of catching Scott were slim as "Scott Smith" was not going to be his real name.

"That's why I felt compelled to try and get the word out to other women somehow," I told them.

"By dressing as a yellow submarine and climbing to the top of the Liver Building?" Richie said with a look of amusement on his face again. He always sees the funny side of things does Richie, that's just his way.

Harry said he felt terrible that he hadn't spotted what

Scott was up to as he was the only one of them around. That made me feel bad. Harry is a sensitive soul but I never want my sons to feel responsible for me and the choices I make in my life. I'm a grown woman and I don't want my boys to worry about me in that way. It was bloody lovely to have them all home though, fussing around me and showing how much they cared.

I reassured Harry there was nothing he could have spotted if I didn't, and James, ever the practical, level-headed one, backed me up on that. It dawned on me as we carried on drinking tea and chatting that I had managed to bring up not one, not two, but *three* lovely lads who were kind, responsible and caring. There may be scoundrels like Scott Smith out there in the world, but for every one of those there are men who are honest and trustworthy. I had three great guys of my own right there in front of me, what more could any woman possibly ask for?

Eventually, I managed to swing the conversation around to them and what they were all doing. It felt like Christmas having them all home at the same time, but without the pressure of having to produce a slap-up turkey dinner, and we were able to talk properly for the first time in ages.

James was just telling us about something funny that happened at uni when the doorbell rang. At first my instinct was to ignore it in case it was one of the reporters returning for a follow-up story, but Harry sprang to his feet to see who it was. There was a bit of muffled chat in the hallway and then he led the caller straight into the living room.

DC Levi Collins looked a bit surprised to find me surrounded by a roomful of young men. I was just as surprised to see him and I quickly introduced him to my sons in case he thought I was holding open auditions for a toy boy! He still looked a little embarrassed to be there but Harry offered to put the kettle back on, and James started thanking him for coming before to take my statement, and asking what chance he thought there was of tracking "Mr Smith" down.

As Levi took a seat at the dining table and sipped his tea, he told the boys the investigation was ongoing, but then added, "I think your mum's actions might do more to stop another woman being conned than anything we could do." He explained that the news coverage I had achieved would not only warn women who might encounter Smith but also alert other women to the sorts of things that can happen. "Smith will have to have plastic surgery before going on any other dates now his face has been plastered all over the news," Levi said. "And your mum has really highlighted the problem of dating scammers. She may have done it in, let's say, an unorthodox way, but it was definitely effective."

I glowed a little as he looked at me when he spoke. It almost seemed like he was proud of me. "Is that what you came to tell me?" I asked. "That turning myself into a national joke has all been worthwhile?" I laughed a little as I said that; I didn't want any of them to think I was consumed with regret over my actions. In fact, with every passing moment I was able to believe I had actually done the right thing after all, in the end.

Levi shook his head as he suddenly seemed to remember something and picked up a duffel bag he'd had slung over his shoulder when he came in.

"No, no…" he said. "I wanted to give you … this."

And then from out of the duffel bag he drew a small, cream-coloured plastic guitar edged in red. A toy Beatles guitar. No, *my* toy Beatles guitar that Deb had bought me!

As I sat there in total shock Levi explained he'd been keeping an eye on auction websites and had spotted this one had come up for sale and realised it fitted the description I'd given him when I gave him the list of all the things that were missing. He said an investigation into the person selling it had begun but he wanted to show it to me to see if I could tell if it was mine.

My hands were shaking slightly as he drew the ancient toy from the clear plastic evidence bag it was in, explaining that it had already been dusted for prints. I took the guitar from him and turned it over as I examined it closely. It felt so familiar and looked exactly like mine but it wasn't until I spotted a couple of scratches and a few places where the Beatles' illustrated faces were peeling that I could tell for sure. This guitar had been so well loved by me as a child that it had been impossible to keep it pristine like some of the other things in my collection.

"Yes, it's mine." I breathed deeply.

Of all the things that had been taken from me this tiny guitar actually held the most treasured and personal memories, especially now I knew it had actually been a gift, not from my big sister, but from the woman who was my real mam. I realised I had tears running down my face as I tried to thank Levi. He reached out a hand to touch my arm as I sat there in front of him and a jolt of electricity shot right through me at his touch. My attraction to this tall, dark and handsome policeman was as strong as the first time we'd met in Mrs Malkin's mausoleum, but, with my three boys watching, I didn't want to think about that.

I stuttered my grateful thanks but as I did so I realised the guitar gave me the opportunity I needed to tell James, Richie and Harry all about Deb, Mame and what I had discovered about our family history. I decided I didn't mind at all revealing everything in front of Levi; he had such a wonderfully reassuring presence and I was quite prepared to believe that Levi Collins was another one of the good guys.

My explanation took a little while and they all listened pretty patiently while I sat with the guitar on my lap, telling them step by step how I had found out the truth about Deb. There were a couple of interjected questions and things I needed to clarify further, but on the whole I managed to get through the story fairly unscathed. The boys' reactions varied from surprise and curiosity to polite indifference. It must have all seemed like ancient history to them, and of course they never knew Deb, so it was no skin off their nose if their grandmother was actually their *great*-grandmother.

Levi had said nothing while I made my little speech but I noticed his gorgeous dark eyes never left my face. I gave him a rueful smile and rolled my eyes as if to say, "Can you believe my life?" but he just carried on watching me carefully and then asked softly, "Are you okay, Bev?" I was a bit taken aback at the tenderness in his voice combined with the concerned look on his face. It was obvious he realised that this was a much bigger deal for me than it was for my sons.

I flapped my hand and told him that I was fine, of course. I certainly felt a lot better than I had done. After all, I had recently experienced a close encounter with Paul McCartney, a surprise visit from all my three boys at once and the return of my beloved toy guitar, and now a handsome man was showing real concern for my well-being. To be honest, I've had worse days!

Levi told us he would have to take the guitar back to the station as it was evidence in the crime I had reported, but assured us all he would personally see to it that it would be returned to me. I was tempted to cling to my beloved toy and never give it back but I allowed Levi to gently remove it from my fingers and put it back into its plastic wrapping and then back into his duffel bag. I just knew I could trust him to look after it and I was so grateful to know I would eventually get it back.

James started to quiz Levi then on aspects of police work and crime investigations, and I took the chance to nip into the kitchen to see if I could find anything for the boys to eat. They were always hungry and this was the longest any of them had ever been home without ransacking the fridge and emptying the cupboards of all potential snacks. The best I could find were a few frozen pizzas and garlic baguettes in the freezer. That would do, so I turned on the oven and as I started ripping off the packaging I realised I was absolutely starving myself, and I couldn't even remember the last time I'd eaten.

I was putting the pizzas into the oven when Harry suddenly appeared beside me. "He's a really nice guy, Mam," he said.

"Hmmm?" I replied as I closed the oven door and double-checked the garlic bread packaging for cooking times. "What's that now?"

"DC Collins ... Levi," Harry said, a bit more insistently. "He's a good guy ... and he's clearly got the hots for you!"

I flicked a tea towel at him then and told him to shush as I blushed to the roots of my hair. I was actually thrilled Harry was getting the same sort of vibes about Levi as I was, but the dishy detective did not "have the hots" for me – did he? But Harry had already moved on and was telling me that James had asked Levi why the police hadn't arrested me after my antics on the top of the Liver Building. I stood there in total shock – I hadn't even thought of that! It suddenly occurred to me I must have committed several crimes: Trespass? Breach of the peace? Littering, at least! It seemed DC Collins may have had a hand in things, and it was all thanks to him that I hadn't spent the last couple of days in a police cell! Well I never. To underline his point, Harry went on to explain that a detective didn't need to make a home visit to reunite someone with their stolen childhood toy, it was "below his pay grade", Harry said, pointing out I could simply have been asked to pop into the station.

"How did he even find it?" Harry queried. "If you ask me, he's been trawling eBay on your behalf looking for anything that might come up for sale ... because he lurrrves you." He drew the word out, wiggling his eyebrows at me as he did so.

I ushered Harry out of the kitchen and went to tell everyone food was on its way. If I looked red and flustered, I hoped they would all think it was just because I'd been bending over the oven and not because Harry had made me even more conscious of just how desirable and delicious I found DC Collins.

But as soon as I mentioned the pizzas were cooking Levi jumped to his feet, claiming he had to go. "I'll leave you to it," he said. James and Richie immediately clamoured for him to stay, saying they wanted to hear more of his stories of crime and criminals. Levi hesitated for just a moment and I knew then he actually *wanted* to stay.

"There's plenty," I said with what I hoped was a charming smile. "You're very welcome to join us." Harry was already pulling up his chair next to Levi at the dining table and encouraging him to sit back down. Levi grinned and put his bag back on the floor.

"Well, I do love pizza," he said.

———

As the five of us sat around tucking into slices of Margherita and pepperoni, talking and laughing through mouthfuls, I marvelled at the chain of events that had brought us together for this impromptu meal. Could it be that my signing up to the Lonely Hearts Club dating website had led me to love after all? Levi Collins was definitely the sort of man I could fall hook, line, and sinker for, and this time my three sons appeared to have given their seal of approval before we were able to even have a first date.

I didn't want to be presumptuous but Harry was definitely on to something. I could tell from the way Levi kept sneaking looks at me. The lads seemed to be working in formation, casually finding out that Levi was single and a genuine Beatles fan, a fact, of course, that I already knew after our encounter in Penny Lane and our evening at The Casbah. I figured they were probably keen to hook me up with this kind, good-looking police officer as quickly as possible, before I could get myself into any more newsworthy trouble. That way they could get back to their own lives without worrying so much about their mam hitting the headlines.

Joking aside, I could actually tell that they all liked Levi a lot. He was patient with their questions and entertaining in the way he told them just enough without revealing any details he shouldn't. I'd always imagined that if I'd ever brought a bloke home to meet them they might be hostile and wary, but with the ways things had just happened, Levi wasn't a stranger. It honestly couldn't have worked out better. All I had to hope now was that Levi *did* want to ask me out, but I was determined not to be devastated if he didn't. I wasn't going to let myself be defined by a man ever again. I was "Beatles Bev", I talked a lot, made stupid jokes, and loved to sing along to my favourite songs at the top of my voice. I enjoyed my job, had a cool place to live, great friends and three tremendous sons. Anyone I met in future would have to fit in with all of that and everything else that made me … me. If that was Levi, wonderful; if not, I was more than happy to bide my time. I decided I *was* worth waiting for, after all.

How strange that my journey had brought me to this point, I thought. It had been a long and winding road for sure, but what did that matter so long as I got to where I was meant to be in the end?

Chapter Twenty-Six

The following day, Richie started making noises about having to get back home. Having recently moved in with his lovely girlfriend, Bethan, he was itching to get back to her and he couldn't afford to take any more time off from his job as a mechanic either. James was a bit more flexible as he could catch up on uni work anytime, and decided to stick around for a couple more days. He said it was to hang out with Harry, but I suspected he wanted to keep an eye on me for a bit longer.

I was feeling pretty positive and upbeat so I knew James didn't have anything to worry about. Seriously, they should put visits from Sir Paul McCartney on the National Health! I was so very relieved the boys had escaped seeing me at the point when I was having a total meltdown.

My mood was further boosted by a text from Levi that arrived after breakfast. He'd stayed for a couple of hours after we'd eaten pizza and devoured my not-so-secret stash of salted caramel Magnum ice creams that Richie had found in the freezer. In front of the boys, Levi been relaxed, jovial and friendly, but as I'd shown him to the door he'd become a little more intense as he'd squeezed my hand and asked if it would be okay to contact me, "as a friend". I'd nodded eagerly and then couldn't resist giving him a quick peck on the cheek before he left. I was relieved to note he looked delighted by my flirty behaviour. Hilariously, my front doorstep had seen more action in that one day than it had done for the entire time I'd lived in Western Avenue!

Levi's text the following morning asked if I wanted to meet up for a drink or a meal later on. That didn't need much thinking about and I answered *"Love to"* practically straight away. Before I could look forward to my first proper date with Levi, however, I really needed to sort out the situation with Jools. The boys' surprise visit and the sudden arrival of Levi Collins had prevented my plan to go to Bold Brides and beg my bestie for forgiveness. Our friendship needed to be repaired urgently though, as I would never be truly happy if Jools and I were not back to how we had always been. I couldn't imagine my life without her in it.

By late morning I was pushing open the door to Bold Brides with the biggest bunch of flowers I could find.

Jools was on the phone as I peeped over the petals and as soon as she clocked me and my contrite expression she gave a barely suppressed smirk, shaking her head from side to side as if to say, "What are you like?"

As she came off the phone I began to say sorry but she cut me off before I could even get the second syllable out of my mouth. Instead, she looked straight at me through her scarlet spectacles and demanded to know if I was okay. Typical Jools, thinking of me and wanting to know if I was all right before giving a thought to herself. That girl really is one in a million.

There was tons to catch up on as last time we'd seen each other I'd just descended from the Liver Building rooftop but had yet to be discussed and dissected on national TV by those loose-lipped *Lively Ladies*. Just as I'd thought, Jools *had* tried to get hold of me to see how I was coping with the humiliation and had sent several supportive texts and messages, all of which I had deleted in my rage.

When I recounted how my home had been besieged by reporters she pulled an anguished face and said she wished she'd been there to give them what for. I could imagine Jools telling off a press pack like they were a bunch of naughty schoolchildren.

When I went on to tell her about the frantic knocking on the door and ringing of my bell that heralded the arrival of Sir Paul McCartney himself she almost lost the plot.

"NO WAY! NO EFFIN' WAY!" she shrieked. Thank God the shop was empty of customers at that point. She wanted to know every single detail and I was more than happy to oblige, giving her a moment-by-moment account of everything I could remember. It was wonderful to relive it all again and have Jools share my amazement and excitement.

If Jools thought that was all she had missed out on, however, she began to realise how much more I had to tell her when I started to try and explain what I had discovered about Deb being my birth mother. Intuitive and alert to my change of mood as soon as I brought up the subject, she made a quick decision. As the shop wasn't busy and she had no customers booked in for fittings, Jools said she didn't want to risk interruptions so she flicked the sign to "closed" on the shop door and locked it shut. If we stayed sitting inside we risked confused shoppers rapping on the window to be let in, so Jools suggested we relocate, and she knew exactly the right place to go.

———————

Within minutes of locking up the shop, Jools and I were walking up to The Hard Days Night Hotel on North John Street. I had, of course, been there several times before. The hotel is in a distinctive five-storey building in Liverpool's business district. Decorated with dozens of marble pillars on the outside, and with classical arched windows embellished with ornate stone carvings on every floor, the place must blow the minds of the foreign tourists it attracts – especially Americans, they love that sort of thing. However, it's not the historic architecture most of the visitors come for, it is the unapologetic Beatles branding that defines it as *the* place to stay in the city if you love the Fab Four.

Statues of John, Paul, George and Ringo stand on plinths on the first floor, looking down onto the street below. Inside, the bedrooms are all adorned with enormous pictures of the band, and the John Lennon suite even has a white grand piano. The communal spaces are filled with more photographs, artwork and memorabilia, and fans could easily spend hours inspecting all the fascinating images on display.

I've spent a few great evenings in the cocktail lounge, Bar Four, where the black and red decor gives it a retro nightclub vibe – they have regular live music performances there – but Jools walked me straight past the huge archway of the main entrance. Perhaps we weren't headed to the hotel after all? We stopped at another large doorway on the very corner of the building, directly below the statue of Ringo Starr holding his drumsticks aloft. The illuminated sign above the double doors said "Blakes", which I knew was the restaurant attached to the hotel named after Peter Blake, the artist famous for his work on the *Sergeant Pepper* album sleeve. Now I was excited. I had never been to Blakes before.

Jools swept in like she owned the place and we were shown to a booth – I *love* a booth! As Peter Blake was known as the godfather of pop art, I think I was expecting a riot of colour inside, but the restaurant was tastefully decorated with white panelled walls and polished wooden floors. The large room had an art gallery feel with Blake's work exhibited on the walls. Classical columns rose up to the ridiculously high ceilings, and the enormous windows that ran the length of the room were draped in diaphanous curtains. It was all very fancy.

Jools scooched along the curve of the padded booth seat, giving me room to join her, and ordered us a couple of cocktails from a smartly dressed waiter.

"Well, it *is* almost lunchtime," she told me with a wink

and then explained that she'd been invited to sample the restaurant's new afternoon tea menu so she would be able to recommend it as a possible wedding venue to her customers. "Perks of the job," she said as we clinked our glasses together when our porn star martinis arrived.

Jools arranged for our afternoon tea to be brought to us in a little while so we had time to talk before we ate. There was a lot to discuss. Item one on our agenda was the news about Deb being my birth mother and Mame, the woman I'd always believed was my mam, turning out to be my grandma. Jools listened to the whole complicated story with a look of amazement and then sympathy on her face. "Oh Bev," she said again and again as I described how, once the seed of doubt was sown, I had begun to investigate and how that eventually led to my meeting with Doreen Jordan, who had been Deb's best friend in her Doreen Duffy days, and her confirmation that the story was true.

With her usual perception and common sense, Jools declared that she believed neither Deb nor Mame had intended to do anything to hurt me, a conclusion that I now completely shared.

"Have you told Mame that you know?" she asked. I put my head on one side as I considered that course of action. Was it worth upsetting an old lady who was already confused? If I didn't blame her for what had happened over fifty years ago what would be the point of telling her I knew all about it now? "It might give you both peace of mind," Jools said simply and I knew she might well be right. I said I would think about it.

Jools then asked the question that had occurred to me

from the moment I had found out about Deb being my mam. It had nagged at me immediately but the subsequent events of discovering the theft of my valuable Beatles collection, Scott's betrayal, Levi's advice to get a message out to other women, and my now notorious exploits since had not given me any time to give the matter my full attention.

"So if we now know Deb is your real mam ... then ... who is your real dad?"

We were already on our second round of porn star martinis, Jools reasoning that as they contained passion fruit they could definitely be counted as one of our "five a day". The alcohol had gone to my head, however, so it suddenly seemed completely hilarious when Jools began to speculate that it was within the realms of possibility that Deb could have "got off" with a musician and my father could even be one of The Beatles!

There was something about the suggestion that simply made me want to laugh. I can't explain it properly, but it was as though I felt I would just *know* if I was related to rock royalty. I didn't have Lennon's wit, Ringo's nose or McCartney's eyes. George was always Deb's favourite but surely there's no way she would have headed for London, leaving me behind, if there had been a chance for her to be the first Mrs Harrison? Had George already met Pattie Boyd by the time Deb was pregnant with me? I'd have to cross-check some dates to be sure of that.

Through giggles and hiccups I promised Jools I would try and question Deb's friend Doreen a bit more about who they were knocking around with back then and if she had a clue as to who the likely candidate could be. I knew I'd like to see Doreen again anyway; she was a good connection to my real mam and I'd like to keep that going if I could.

Just as I started to change the subject from my tangled life history to Jools and how she and Mickey were now getting on, the most incredible afternoon tea arrived at our table. Three tiers of finger sandwiches, warm scones with jam and clotted cream, and a selection of fresh fruit fancies and bite-size cakes. Our eyes were on stalks at the sight of it all. The tea was served in beautiful glass tea pots and it all felt incredibly decadent as we sipped from the china cups and made our selections from the tower of treats.

Between mouthfuls of beef and horseradish sandwich Jools told me how she still thought Mickey was acting out of character, or perhaps acting *as* a character, considering his increasing obsession with Elvis Presley.

"You know what he actually told me?" Jools said as she popped yet another morsel of sandwich into her mouth. "That sometimes when he isn't sure about something, he thinks to himself, *'What would Elvis do?'"* She left the revelation hanging in the air while she refilled her teacup. I swallowed down my salmon and cucumber and thought about what it all could mean. Could Mickey be suffering from some sort of mid-life crisis? Why would an ordinary bloke from Knotty Ash think he could identify with the mindset of the King of Rock 'n' Roll? What day-to-day issues facing Mickey could possibly relate to the lifestyle of a world-famous rock star who'd lived in a mansion in Memphis? I doubted Elvis Presley ever had to deal with his car failing its MOT, or damp in the back bedroom. How many life choices was Mickey agonising over? Was he considering a change of career? Did he want to move house? Leave Jools?

The troubling thoughts flickering through my mind propelled me towards the warm scones and I piled mine liberally with jam and cream. Jam first, cream second – controversial, maybe, but let's not get started on all that.

I did my best to reassure Jools that there were worse things in the world than a man who idolised Elvis. I could see she wasn't completely convinced but she said she had a cunning plan.

"On the basis that if you can't beat 'em, join 'em!" she said, suddenly looking very pleased with herself.

I wondered if she was planning to undergo a makeover to transform herself into a replica of a young Priscilla Presley, all Cleopatra-style eyeliner and backcombed black beehive hair. To my relief, that was *not* the plan. Instead, she wanted to surprise Mickey with a trip to Las Vegas, where Elvis had spent the later part of his career performing cabaret-style shows twice a day at a big hotel just off the strip. It sounded like a great idea to me. They could explore some of the places Elvis had hung out, but also spend some time lazing by the hotel pool, take in a couple of shows and experience all the nightlife and excitement the desert resort had to offer. I told her it would be like a second honeymoon for them both.

"Exactly!" she said, cramming the last of her scone into her gob.

We carried on devouring the delicious afternoon tea, chatting about how great it would be to spring a Vegas trip on Mickey, and it felt so good to be back to normal with Jools, giggling and gossiping just like we always do. I was aware that there was one piece of news I had yet to share with her though. I'd been saving the best till last. Before I could begin to tell her, Jools suddenly reached for my hand and looked at me intently.

"Bev, I'm so sorry for pushing you into joining that bloody dating website. If I'd known for a single second the trouble it would lead to…"

Her green eyes blinked rapidly behind her glasses as she gripped my fingers. I could see she was mortified that her actions had led to my doomed relationship with swindling Scott and consequently my appearance on every news outlet from *Lively Ladies* to *Look North*. What she had no idea about, of course, was that that journey had also brought me back into contact with gorgeous Levi Collins, the delectable detective and the very man who had prompted her to push me into the dating pool in the first place.

"What? The cute copper from the house of horrors was the one who turned up to interview you when you reported your stuff stolen?" Jools goggled at the twist of fate that had brought DC Collins back into my life. I told her about our encounter at The Casbah, too, but her eyes practically popped out of their sockets when I told her he'd now asked me out … on a date!

She sat back against the padded leather booth seat as she let the news sink in, and I sipped my tea and tried to look nonchalant as she got her head around the latest development in the convoluted story of my recent life. I could almost pinpoint the exact moment when the penny dropped and she switched from wanting to take the blame to actually wanting to take all the credit.

"Ha!" she exclaimed, leaning forward, her eyes now gleaming. "Didn't I say you fancied him? Didn't I? I knew it! If it hadn't been for that dishy detective giving you the fanny flutters I would never have forced you to sign up to the Lonely Hearts Club. Yes, you'd never have met Scott, but then you'd also never have been reunited with luscious Levi and … yeah, that's right … you'd never have ended up having Paul McCartney come round your house either!" Her face was a picture as she joined up all the dots and realised what I had figured out for myself a good while ago.

"Yeah, that's all true," I said, giving her a huge grin. "Although I still object to the term 'fanny flutters', if it's all the same to you. It's quite a disgusting expression."

Jools then decided the whole turn of events needed to be celebrated properly and called for a bottle of champagne so we could do it in style. The rest of the afternoon was spent in a giggly, happy haze as we toasted all the things we were grateful for, and speculated on what new adventures there might be to come.

At some point we became aware of a particular song playing over the speakers in the restaurant. A Beatles soundtrack had been softly playing in the background the whole time, but our ears pricked up as we heard the words to "In My Life". The song commemorates all the people and places that are so important during a lifetime and it always makes me emotional to think about how The Beatles held Liverpool in their hearts no matter where they all ended up in the world. Every time I hear the song I see the landmarks of my home city – the Three Graces, Penny Lane, The Cavern Club, both Cathedrals, Lime Street Station, the Liver Birds – and I think about the wonderful people who make Liverpool such an incredibly special place to live. Jools is one of those people and as we sang along I could feel that she felt the same way about me, too. We both love Liverpool with all our hearts but as we raised our glasses to each other that day, Jools and I told each other, "I love you more."

I was finally in such a good place, and the only bubble I could imagine bursting was one in the champagne fizzing in my glass. Whatever the future had in store, I knew I'd always get by with a little help from my friends.

Chapter Twenty-Seven

I'd love to tell you that's where the story ends and that we all lived happily ever after. I'd absolutely love to tell you that, but of course I'd be lying. Nothing is ever quite that simple, is it? Strap yourself in, there are a couple more loops of the rollercoaster yet to come.

The very day after my boozy afternoon tea and celebratory love-in with Jools, I was nursing a pounding champagne-induced headache and trying to figure out what I was going to wear for my first proper date with Levi that night. Yeah … I was back to flinging every item I owned out of my wardrobe and onto my bedroom floor, lamenting the fact that once again I didn't have a single, solitary thing to wear. Some things never, ever change!

The plan was to meet for a drink in his local pub and then go for a curry. Nice and simple, it was a straightforward arrangement that I figured meant we could concentrate on getting to know each other rather than be distracted by our surroundings. I was ready for some down-to-earth normal life after the craziness of the last few weeks. Lovely.

But remember what John Lennon said about life? *"Life is what happens when you are busy making other plans."* No matter how closely you keep your eye on the ball, you will never be ready for a spinner that can always get thrown at your head at any given point.

In my case, it came in a call from Mame's nursing home.

I arrived at Wisteria Grove in a tizz and collapsed into a complete mess when they told me she had suffered a stroke and things didn't look too good. I wasn't ready for that. I didn't think I would ever be ready now it looked like I was about to lose her. Mabel Ruth, Mame, was the woman who I had believed was my mother all my life, who had brought me up, made me into who I was, but now I would not get the chance to talk to her about the secrets she had kept.

I tried as I sat for several hours holding her hand. I told her all about the things that had been happening to me, just like I had always done when things had been bothering me at school. I would sit at the kitchen table as she peeled potatoes or shucked pea pods, offloading all my angst and worries about mean girls, tyrant teachers or boys who didn't fancy me. She would listen to it all, taking it in as she bustled about. Eventually, she'd hand me a potato peeler or a teacloth and nod to a pile of unpeeled vegetables or a stack of dishes that needed drying and give me a few wise words of encouragement and understanding while distracting me with chores. Somehow the combination of getting things off my chest, knowing that someone was listening, combined with a menial task always did manage to make me feel a bit better.

She wasn't offering any wise words now though and there was nothing to distract me from the brutal reality of the situation either.

I told her I knew Deb was my mother. I looked at her face as she lay back on the pillows but her glacial expression didn't alter. I couldn't tell if she had heard me, I didn't even know if the Mame I had always known was still in there. I asked her if that was the reason she had always encouraged me to call her Mame, rather than Mam. It was a nickname everyone who knew her well used and I'd never thought it odd before. I'd found out that Mona Best's sons never called their mother Mam either; they'd all called her Mo. I felt oddly proud that our family had a similar tradition. "Mame" and "Mam" were so similar, of course, and I'd always thought it was lovely we had a special name to use. After all, everyone else's mother was called Mam. I'd liked that we were a little bit different, although back then I hadn't realised *how* different.

I couldn't stop the tears from pouring down my face as I told her I didn't blame her for what she had done, but that I wished she would have told me. I sobbed as I told her to tell Deb I loved them both, my two mams, and that I hoped they would be together now, even though I'd be alone.

She died as the afternoon turned into evening and although the nurses described her passing as peaceful, it felt excruciatingly painful to me.

I left the hospital and drove home in a state of shock. I sort of expected to be given some of her things but I left empty-handed after they explained they would sort out her personal effects and call me when they were ready to be collected. It matched how I felt inside, hollow and empty.

I just about managed to have the presence of mind to message Levi to cancel our date. I didn't tell him why. I didn't feel I owed anyone an explanation and I didn't want to see it written down in words on a text anyway. Once I'd done that, I didn't want to communicate with anyone else, not even Jools. I decided even telling the boys could wait. I shut the door, closed the curtains and cried and cried. Not even Paul McCartney could help me now. I was a little girl without her mam and my heart was finally, totally broken.

———————————

Over the next week I pulled myself together enough to let the boys know what had happened to their great-grandma, I got compassionate leave from work and I let Jools pop round with a couple of homemade dishes. A casserole and a lasagne, I think they were, I didn't eat them myself, I just stuck them in the freezer.

Levi sent lovely messages, once I'd managed to explain by text what had happened, and even tried to call, but I just ignored him. It sounds awful and rude but I just could not get my head around the thought of dating and starting something up with a guy. Even if this one did seem nice, I was far too much of a mess. A bouquet of flowers arrived and I didn't even thank him. I was seriously hoping he would get the message and just give up; it was all far too much to deal with.

Facing the rest of my life knowing the truth about Deb and Mame had been difficult enough when Mame was alive. Now she was dead the world had shifted on its axis again and I was seriously off balance. I put on a brave face for the boys and for Jools but when I was alone I spent most of the time crying. The loss of Mame had reopened the wound of Scott's betrayal and the devastation he'd caused in my life, and poured a whole load of fresh salt right into it. I cried because I'd lost a man I was stupidly besotted with, because he'd callously used me and abandoned me. I cried for the precious things he'd stolen from me, the collection I'd spent my entire life building and looking after. I'd foolishly thought I'd come to terms with it all but once Mame died I regressed right back to how I'd felt when it all happened, and of course I cried bitterly over her and Deb, too.

The only saving grace was that I was no longer being written about in the papers or talked about on the TV. But even that didn't console me too much as those headlines had confirmed me as a local celebrity and I knew I risked getting funny looks in the street if I ventured out and about. I decided to stay in as much as possible.

I was never completely alone though, even when the house was empty. I played the Beatles songs that spoke to me in my sorrow: "Yesterday" with all its troubles; "Eleanor Rigby" in all of her loneliness; the visceral pain obvious in John's voice as he sings for his lost mother in "Julia". From "She's Leaving Home" to "While My Guitar Gently Weeps", the band stayed by my side. Surely there cannot be another group of musicians who have succeeded in capturing the gamut of human experience and emotion across their repertoire as well as my beloved Beatles.

The one time I left the house, with my black corduroy cap pulled onto my head, I found my feet had taken me to Mathew Street and the three-storey Liverpool Beatles Museum next door to The Grapes pub. Unlike The Beatles Story exhibition down on the dockside this place didn't attempt to recreate scenes and locations with dressed-up mannequins. That was a fabulous way for fans to experience the story of the band, but this place, a museum run by Mona Best's youngest son, Roag, offered fans a different way to connect with their heroes. It was actually full of authentic historical artefacts and personal items owned and used by John, Paul, George, Ringo, Stu Sutcliffe and Pete Best.

I stood and looked up at the tall building with the grey, overcast Liverpool sky above. I wondered what impulse had brought me here, of all places? But then I gradually realised why I had come.

Inside, I climbed the stairs and wandered through the large rooms, stopping to look at a few of my favourite items on display. A battered pair of round NHS spectacles that John Lennon had borrowed from Pete Best's grandmother when his own broke while he was helping to decorate the basement at The Casbah – said to be the first pair of glasses he had worn with distinctive round frames. A curious wood and canvas lamp in the shape of a wagon from the Old West was in another display cabinet. I was always fascinated by this item as it was one of several given to the band by Elvis Presley's manager, Colonel Tom Parker, when they visited with Elvis in 1965. A gangly cloth puppet, its long legs and arms dangling down from its skinny body, was displayed next to a photograph of the band during their "All You Need Is Love" TV broadcast. The kooky toy, with its tuft of black hair on top of its head and distinctive orange clothing, was clearly visible behind the heads of John and Paul as they performed to a record audience of 400 million. The text written next to the cabinet said the puppet had been gifted to Mona Best by the lads after the broadcast.

There were so many fascinating things in the museum that brought me back again and again to visit, but today I was looking for a particular section.

Inside sealed glass display cases was a variety of vintage Beatles merchandise. Unlike my collection, which had largely been kept pristine, contents intact and boxes unopened, several of these showed real signs of damage and age. But they were the closest I could now get to some of the things I had once been proud to own.

The number of toys, beauty products, kitchenware and personal and household items that had been Beatles-branded decades ago was mind-boggling. The museum had examples ranging from musical instruments, like my toy guitar or a small drum, to a set of Subbuteo figures, glassware and a table lamp.

I found the particular item I had come to see and stood looking at its familiar shape with my nose almost pressed against the glass. My eyes feasted on the red "Margo of Mayfair" logo on the curved canister of Beatles talcum powder and the four snapshot pictures of the Fab Four, with their neat, Beatles-cut moptop hairdos, which decorated the front of the tin. I could almost smell the flowery scent of the powder contained inside, but no matter how much I sniffed I was never going to be able to get the scent into my nostrils. Not now. Not ever.

My eyes stung as I blinked back tears. If anyone saw me blubbing over a tin of talcum powder they would think I was a right daft cow, but I just couldn't help but feel such a huge sense of loss knowing I would never hold the little metal can in my hands again. I grieved for the loss of my treasured Beatles items in a way I knew I never would for Scott. Mourn that miserable, lying scumbag? Sod that! Now I knew *what* he was if not *who* he was, I knew I was better off on my own. Miserably, I made my way home in the rain. I might have decided not to miss Scott but learning to live life all alone again was going to take some time.

The messages from Levi had eventually stopped. I was glad … no, not glad exactly, more like relieved. The pressure was off. I didn't want to risk my heart getting broken again; it was too fragile, and the slightest thing might shatter it to pieces. Why on earth would I want to go through that? No, I was better off not risking anything like that happening ever again.

I was back at work, back seeing Jools and Mickey and a few other friends occasionally, and back trying to keep tabs on my boys' busy lives and helping out whenever and wherever I could. I was still in real mourning for Mame, and for the Deb I'd never been able to know, but life was steady, back on track in a regular rhythm. I was in my safe and sensible comfort zone and that's where I fully intended to stay.

So why is it that just when I think I have my life in some sort of order, something always comes along to shake it all up again?

I should have realised they were up to something. Jools and Mickey had been nagging me for a while that I should do something special to celebrate my birthday. It wasn't a particularly significant one, and I tried to argue that I didn't want any sort of fuss, but they kept on and on so in the end I agreed to let them organise a night out at least. Anything to shut them up.

When the day arrived I woke to a cup of tea in bed from Harry and a bunch of cards slung onto the duvet. He'd got me a lovely scarf and said there was stuff from James and Richie "on the way". I spent the day at work receiving calls and messages wishing me a happy birthday, which was nice, and I was actually really looking forward to my evening out. Jools refused to tell me where we were going but I knew I could rely on her to pick somewhere good. She knew all the best places to go out in Liverpool.

I'm pleased to say I did make a proper effort to look my best for the event; it *was* my birthday, after all. With everything that had happened I'd dropped a few pounds without trying, which meant several items that had hung unworn in my wardrobe for a while now came back into play... Every cloud has a silver lining. Despite it being early September, it was a warm evening and a figure-hugging, summery, turquoise dress I'd rediscovered seemed ideal. I dug out my strappy high-heeled sandals and grabbed my new floaty scarf decorated with peacock feathers that Harry had bought me. It went beautifully and I left the house with it draped around my shoulders, feeling better than I had done in ages.

A taxi was waiting outside to pick me up, as Jools had organised it so that I wouldn't know where I was going until I got there. It was exciting to be off on a mystery trip, and I remember having a few butterflies in my tummy.

We headed for the city centre and I tried to guess where we might be heading. Blakes restaurant or the bar of the Hard Days Night Hotel, perhaps? Jools knew I liked it there. There really wasn't much point speculating though as there are literally hundreds of bars and restaurants in Liverpool and I could have been having my birthday celebration in any of them.

When the car finally pulled up, we were on the opposite side of the road from the famous Liverpool waterfront. The building we had parked outside was West Africa House, a 1920s mansion block. My taxi driver, who'd been chatting happily away during our short drive, turned to tell me I was to head up to the eighth floor. I looked out of the window and up at the building looming over us. Did it even have eight floors? There was nothing for it but to follow his instructions, so I exited the taxi in as ladylike a way as possible in a clingy dress and high heels.

A few minutes later, as I stepped out of the lift on the eighth floor, the sight that greeted me took my breath away. I had been lured to a beautiful rooftop garden with the most incredible view across to the Three Graces lined up directly opposite and the Mersey River beyond. The top of the Liver Building and the Liver Birds I knew so well were at eye level and so close I felt I could almost reach out and touch them. I was so stunned by the view I didn't see the welcoming committee at first, all waiting there to greet me. Jools and Mickey were there, as was Harry and – I couldn't actually believe my eyes – James and Richie were there, too. Hot tears pricked at the back of my eyeballs as I got kissed and hugged by them all and I let myself get pulled over to a table where there was a small pile of presents waiting along with a round of cocktails.

"Goodness me, what a place!" I said as Mickey handed me a mojito and we settled into our seats on jewel-coloured cushions around a low glass table.

Mickey snorted and told me that I'd hit the nail on the head with that remark. I was confused until he explained that "Goodness Gracious" was the name of the cocktail bar, as that was what everyone said when they first came up to the roof and saw the amazing view. Good to know I was totally typical! Richie joked it could easily have been called something far ruder considering the expletive-riddled language of most Liverpudlians!

Jools had thought of everything that night; the mojitos kept coming and were soon joined by delicious little tapas plates of food to stop us all getting too sozzled. The weather was warm with a gentle breeze and I was happier than I had been in a very long time as I soaked up the atmosphere and looked out over the rooftops of my wonderful homeland, relishing the thought that Liverpool really was the only place I would ever want to be.

Every now and again I thought I caught a strange look being exchanged between the friends and family around me, but I put it down to the alcohol skewing my judgement, or just the unusual sensation of being out and actually enjoying myself for the first time in ages.

I think it was James who suggested we go over to the glass balcony to watch the sunset. The sky had turned red and gold and as we all moved to get a better view I looked back across the cityscape, away from the waterfront, and saw the imposing Anglican Cathedral perched high on the hill, silhouetted against the flaming colours of the setting sun. It was like a beautiful painting.

As we stood there in our golden glow I suddenly became aware of a change in the music playing over the sound system as The Beatles' "Here Comes the Sun" began to play. I turned to smile at Jools, betting it was yet another touch my best mate had organised. She gave me a rather strange look, almost as though she was a bit apprehensive about something, but then jerked her head to something over my shoulder. I hadn't a clue what she was on about, but I turned my head to look in the direction she was indicating.

From behind a large potted palm tree a man stepped out. Levi! He was carrying a huge bouquet of sunflowers and had a slightly nervous smile on his face. Oh, but it was good to see him!

Mickey and the boys immediately began to move away, back to our seated area, while Jools leaned closer to whisper in my ear, "Give him a chance, Bev," before she also drifted away and left me standing there on my own.

As Levi stepped forward his dark eyes never left my face. He was obviously anxious but he didn't need to be so worried. Maybe it was the mojitos or because I was feeling so chilled and had my nearest and dearest close by, but I was actually completely thrilled by his unexpected appearance. It felt like the icing on my birthday cake.

He moved towards me as the music carried on, George Harrison singing to his "little darling" about ice slowly melting, the sun coming out, and how everything is going to be all right, and I knew then that it *was* all going to be all right. I smiled encouragingly at Levi, feeling the familiar flutter in my tummy as I did so.

"Happy Birthday, Bev," Levi said softly as he closed the distance between us and looked down at my upturned face. But before I could tell him how pleased I was to see him he quickly added, "I'm so sorry about your mam. I know you needed some space and you still might not be ready, but I didn't want to miss your birthday."

He looked so worried and there were so many things I wanted to say to him to reassure him: how grateful I was that he had let me have some time to process everything that had happened; how I appreciated his patience with me and his understanding; but more than anything how thrilled I was that he had come back into my life. Standing there, on my birthday, literally on top of my world, my Liverpool, with my friends and family, it felt like perfect timing for Levi to show up and let me know that he was still interested in me. I was sure then that I was definitely still interested in him. In fact, "interested" was a rather tame expression for the feelings I was experiencing for my delicious detective. He'd said he didn't want to miss my birthday and I realised I didn't want to miss out on another minute that I could be spending with Levi.

I didn't know how to put any of that into words and so I simply reached up to stroke his worried-looking face and went up onto my tiptoes and kissed him gently on his soft, warm lips. Happy birthday to me, I thought, as with the sound of encouraging whoops and good-natured applause filling the evening air around us, he kissed me right back.

Chapter Twenty-Eight

L evi slipped seamlessly into the birthday celebrations, just as easily as he'd blended into our impromptu pizza evening the night he'd come around to show me my precious toy Beatles guitar that he'd recovered.

The boys all seemed pleased to see him again and he quickly fell into conversation with Mickey about work, football and then eventually music, of course. I heard him telling Mickey all about the campaign to save the Penny Lane Shelter in the centre of the roundabout where we'd had our second chance meeting.

I could tell Jools was taking all of this in, watching the way he was with the guys and how he kept turning to flash a shy smile at me every now and again. He looked great in a simple white shirt and casual chinos, his dark skin gleaming in the light from garlands of fairy lights that had begun to flicker on as the sun went down. Jools clearly thought he was as handsome as I had told her, and at one point she pretended to fan herself while mouthing the word "hot" at me and I knew she wasn't just talking about a menopausal flush.

As the night wore on Levi and I ended up sitting closer and closer together. He was clearly too well-mannered to make our company feel like they were unwanted, and I was mindful of the presence of my three sons, but our bodies kept giving us little reminders of the passion we'd just experienced during our first kiss. Levi's fingers brushed my arm as he reached for his glass and a tiny electric shock shivered through me, and the heat of his thigh pressed up close to mine felt like it would leave a scorch mark on my turquoise dress. We'd inched closer and closer on the bench until we were pressed as tightly together as decency would allow, but I reasoned it was necessary as we'd had to make room to squeeze Levi onto our table. If I'm honest though, we didn't really need to be as conjoined as a pair of Siamese twins. Now and again, Levi touched my back with his hand and it was all I could do not to melt on the spot. I was avoiding turning my head to look at him by this point as I knew if I did I would be consumed with an urge to kiss him again, and I wasn't sure I was strong enough to resist. I was light-headed with happiness, mojitos and desire, but I fought to keep myself under control. We weren't a pair of teenagers, after all.

Eventually, Jools came to our rescue and began stretching like a cat and telling Mickey it was time to call it a night. I didn't argue with her. Richie suggested to James and Harry that they go off to some bar called Django's Riff where a couple of their mates were doing a late-night gig.

Before I knew what was happening a taxi was on its way

for Jools and Mickey, and the boys were saying their goodbyes as they prepared to head off.

Levi's mouth was close to my ear and a tingle ran from the back of my neck down the length of my spine as he whispered, "Do you want to go somewhere else – just the two of us?" Did I? Yes – yes, I did! I hardly trusted my voice so I just nodded emphatically as I sucked the last drop of moisture from the straw in my drink.

Jools gave me a knowing wink as she bundled Mickey into the back of a cab down on the street, Mickey still talking over his shoulder about wanting to help Levi with the campaign to save the Penny Lane site. She lifted her hand to the side of her face, imitating a telephone receiver as she mouthed, "Call me" through the window of the taxi, and then they were gone and Levi and I were finally alone.

I pulled my floaty scarf a little tighter around my shoulders, not sure if the tremble in my body was down to a change in the temperature of the evening air or a nervous shudder of expectation. Levi glanced at me, asking "Okay?" Then he grasped my hand and raised the other to hail a passing cab.

"Hope Street Hotel, mate," Levi told the driver and we were off.

I wondered if he might pounce on me there and then but Levi obviously had more self-restraint than that, damn him! I suppose as a serving police officer it wouldn't look good if anyone should see him necking with a woman in the back of a taxi.

We arrived at the hotel within minutes and Levi took my hand and led me to the large bar area that overlooked Hope

Street. There were a few people dotted around but it wasn't too busy. We headed to a long, low, leather sofa separated from the restaurant area by enormous shards of green tinged glass that erupted from the wooden floor and rose in triangular shapes up to the ceiling, giving the place a cool, edgy vibe. A waiter in a white shirt with black braces holding up his skinny jeans appeared instantly, but when Levi asked me what I wanted to drink I quickly decided I didn't want another drop of alcohol. I was already more than mellow from all the mojitos and I was determined to keep a clear head for whatever might be about to happen next. I didn't feel I needed Dutch courage and I wasn't keen on the idea of dulling my senses either. "You know, I'd love a cup of tea," I said to the waiting waiter before looking at Levi, but he just smiled and nodded.

"Yeah, me too," he said. "Pot of tea for two, please," he said.

It was like a pressure valve had been released and we chatted and laughed and talked about … everything … nothing … I can't even remember, but it was lovely and fun and relaxed, and if I hadn't been sure before, then by the time we'd finished our pot of tea I was absolutely convinced that Levi Collins was someone I wanted to spend a lot more time with. Put simply and in the words of The Beatles, I had to get him into my life.

It was like we'd both lost all sense of time and it felt like neither of us wanted the night to end. I must have said something to that effect at one point because Levi replied, "It doesn't have to…" He left the statement hanging in the air for a moment and I felt a prickle of expectation. I waited for him to continue but then I guessed he didn't want to put any pressure on me and was giving me the chance to set the pace. It was time to take that chance.

"You mean … we could stay here?" I said, turning to look at him and letting him see that I knew exactly what I was saying and doing. It was the perfect solution. I didn't want to take him home tonight when the boys might arrive back at any point in the early hours. The lovely hotel was a neutral place I had never been to before so didn't have any weird associations for me and it's always easier to be a naughtier version of yourself in a hotel, isn't it? Or perhaps that's just me.

Levi went to the check-in desk and made the arrangements and then suddenly we were in the lift heading to the third floor. I was barefoot, holding my strappy heels in one hand as I'd kicked them off a little earlier, and as the lift door closed I was confronted by our mirrored image reflected back at us, Levi a good head and shoulders taller than me standing behind. I looked slightly flushed, my blonde hair a little mussed and my smoky eye make-up making my eyes look sultry. Levi snaked an arm around my waist and nuzzled into my neck, telling me I looked sexy and there was suddenly no doubt that that was exactly how I felt.

We padded down the hallway to find our room, our fingers entwined, and once inside we made our way immediately to the enormous white bed on a raised platform.

We kissed, softly at first, almost hesitant, Levi breaking away to flutter his lips across my face, my neck and down towards my breasts. I stroked my hands around his neck, across his short hair, and then down over his shoulders to where the bulge of his bicep rippled under the white cotton of his shirt sleeves.

He lay me back on the bed, starting to unbutton his shirt until my fingers flew up to take over. His hands then began to peel my dress away, little by little, so that his mouth could find my skin, and I was unable to stop myself from moaning as his lips connected with my tender flesh.

I helped him ease my dress off completely and then my underwear. He stripped naked, too, and my gasps and groans as we kissed and touched and licked and sucked were matched by his growls and moans as we gave in to all the desires we had been fighting for so long.

He was gentle and then passionate, almost reverent and then downright dirty, his sexual skill matched by my desperate need to please him as much as he was pleasing me. Our bodies slick with sweat, we finally let ourselves get carried away to the exquisite point of no return and I clung to him in ecstasy as our bodies shuddered and bucked together.

We lay sprawled in delicious abandon afterwards, our breathing gradually returning to normal, and I wondered if the residents in the neighbouring rooms had heard us. I wondered … but I didn't particularly care.

My nerve endings still jangled from the overload of sensations I had just experienced, I felt energised and alive and a long way from sleep. I couldn't be certain what words had escaped my lips in the throes of passion but I'd never felt like this before. Had I told Levi I loved him? I turned to face him and found him gazing at me, his gorgeous eyes looking straight into mine. "Me too, Bev … me too," he whispered softly, although whether that was in answer to my thoughts or not, I couldn't be sure. Before I could figure it out I fell fast asleep.

Chapter Twenty-Nine

I once came across an article in a fan magazine detailing a young girl's report of what it felt like to be in the audience for one of The Beatles' early concerts:

I was nervous before the show. My stomach kept flipping over and my knees felt like they were too wobbly to hold me up properly. I couldn't believe I was going to be so close to them. I'd spent so much time wishing and hoping and dreaming of this moment and now it was here and I almost couldn't cope.

I was desperate to see them, to hear them, be in the same room as them, and all the other girls around me were all feeling exactly the same.

The sense of anticipation in that theatre was incredible. We weren't jealous of each other being there all together, we weren't even really that much aware of each other. Every single one of us was having our own intensely private, hugely emotional, rite of passage into womanhood. It's not an exaggeration to say that for some of us this was our very first sexual experience. That's the absolute truth.

Whether John, Paul, George or Ringo was our personal favourite, we all knew whichever one you loved the most, that said something about you, about who you were as a young woman, what you found attractive in a man, what sort of man you would date in real life. But at that particular moment in time there were no other men or boys for us, it was all about those four lads from Liverpool.

As we waited for them to come onto the stage we were all consumed with the same thought, the thought that the man you loved – and be in no doubt that we really, truly loved them – might soon look right at you, see you, notice you for the first time. It was enough to make us shake and tremble where we stood. One girl a few rows in front of me fainted at that point. I felt so sorry for her as she was hoisted above our heads by a couple of security men and taken away. Poor girl, so near and yet so far.

I felt, rather than saw or heard, the band appear on stage, and there was a surge of movement through all the bodies in front, to the side, and behind me. I was unsteady on my feet and my view of the stage was obscured for a moment but then all at once there they were. The screaming was ear-splitting but I didn't care, I didn't care even when it dawned on me that I was screaming my lungs out, too.

I couldn't hear a note they played or sang but believe me when I tell you it didn't matter all that much. I knew every beat, melody and lyric to all of their songs and I could hear all that in my head despite the screams that were drowning everything else out. Removing the music meant I concentrated all my attention *onto the details you could never experience when you listened to their records or heard a Beatles song on the radio: the way George bent his knees and watched his own fingers move up and down the neck of his guitar; the way Ringo broke into a grin as he nodded along with the rhythm of his drumsticks; the way John stood with his legs apart and his guitar held up high on his chest; the way Paul shook his hair out of his eyes as he tipped back his head and sang up into his mic.*

The sensations I felt watching The Beatles at close quarters that day were new, exciting and just a little bit alarming. I couldn't control myself. My body shook, I whimpered, I shouted and I screamed. I tingled in places I'd never tingled before, and my entire body was damp with sweat as I grabbed handfuls of my own hair and writhed in ecstasy. I felt euphoric. This was a moment of total liberation and I let myself go. I shook off all my inhibitions and gave myself completely to this incredible moment of frenzied passion and pure rapture.

For some reason this young girl's account of her Beatle concert experience came flooding back into my mind after my night in bed with Levi. For the first time in my life, I completely understood her orgasmic description!

Chapter Thirty

Over the next few weeks, Levi and I spent lots of time together at my home and his modern flat in the city. On my first visit there he apologised for how tiny and basic it was, but to me it looked wonderful. At least he wasn't trying to impress me with tales of a mansion that didn't even exist! It *was* small, but it had great views towards the dock and it was super-clean. Decor was minimal, apart from the tiny second bedroom, which had a rainbow bedspread and a fluffy unicorn sat on the pillow for when his ten-year-old daughter, Rosalie, came to visit. We'd decided to wait a while before we were introduced to each other although I was itching to get to know her and I loved the idea of my boys having a "little sister" to tease and look out for in the future

Levi and I seemed to spend almost all our time laughing, even when we were in bed! Once he found out how ticklish I was, he showed no mercy, but he reckoned my hysterical reaction was what *he* found hilarious.

Considering he was a copper, Levi had a great sense of humour ... or perhaps it was actually *because* he was a copper. An ability to see the funny side of any given situation could be invaluable in that line of work, as I soon discovered. Finally I had met someone who took my tendency to say daft things and blurt out whatever was on my mind completely in his stride. It was great to know I made him laugh.

I knew it would take a while to be able to fully relax into the relationship and not worry after what had happened with Scott, but Levi said we shouldn't put any pressure on ourselves, that we should just enjoy each day, and as time went on my thoughts about Scott would just fade away, *"like an unsightly bruise"*. I liked that analogy; describing Scott as something horrible and ugly was what he deserved, but it was also true that he'd caused a wound that could be sore to the touch every now and then.

At first I questioned Levi repeatedly on how likely it might be that "Scott Smith" would be caught and made to pay for his crimes. I was sure I couldn't be the only woman he had ripped off and I hated the thought of him treating another woman so cruelly. Levi patiently explained, more than once, that Scott would have used a fake name so finding him would be difficult, although he was certain the publicity I'd generated using his photograph would have meant he would be forced to lie low for a while. That seemed appropriate for such a low-life, I said.

One day Levi came home carrying the duffel bag he'd had with him the night he ended up eating pizza with my boys, and I held my breath as he drew out my plastic toy Beatles guitar.

"I explained to the duty officer that it's just as safe here with us as it is in the evidence locker," Levi said as he handed it to me. I couldn't quite read the expression on his face as he said that but I was just so happy to have my guitar back home safe and sound that I decided not to ask any awkward questions. Levi knew how much it meant to me to have such a key piece of my collection returned; I wouldn't have put it past him to bend a few rules to bring me some peace of mind.

I resolved to do my best to move on. "Scott Smith and the Silhouettes" had never existed in real life and so I let them slowly retreat into the shadows where they belonged.

One day when Levi admired the polished wooden box on my bookcase that had once belonged to Mame, we ended up talking, yet again, about the circumstances of my birth. He asked me if I intended to keep in touch with Deb's mate Doreen and it reminded me that I *did* want to do just that. I'd liked her very much and it would be good to keep that link alive. I sent her a message a few days later and she quickly answered saying she would love to see me, too. She'd heard all about the trouble with Scott and so had realised her chance of being reunited with Ringo's leather jacket was long gone but she was dying to hear all about my visit from Paul.

So that's how I found myself sitting with Doreen a few days later, after inviting her round for a pot of tea. I'd even baked a lemon drizzle cake in her honour. She was fascinated to see Paul McCartney's old home and she hadn't been there long before I found myself digging out the old Beatles scrapbook Levi had discovered discarded in the attic to show her.

"Oh, this takes me back," she said as she carefully turned the pages and looked at all the yellowing scraps of cuttings, running her fingers over the tickets and flyers and assorted explosion of papers that were rammed haphazardly between the folds.

She started to tell me all about the nights she and Deb had spent at gigs in and around Liverpool, how they'd dressed up in miniskirts but could only afford one pair of white knee-high boots between them so had shared and taken it in turns to wear them.

"Deb was two sizes bigger than me though," Doreen said, "so we had to buy the larger size and I stuffed them with newspaper when it was my turn to wear them." She shook her head and chortled to herself. It was great for me to hear these sorts of stories about Deb … my mam.

Doreen had been poring over the scrapbook and I'd been listening to her reminisce for ages so I went into the kitchen to make a fresh pot of tea. When I came back into the living room I found her sat with her mouth open holding an unfolded page of notepaper in one hand and a tiny envelope in the other. She looked like she'd seen a ghost.

"You okay, Doreen?" I asked, but she just shook her head from side to side while her mouth opened and closed, no words coming out. I sat next to her on the sofa and gently took the envelope from her hand. It was addressed to Deb Hopewell at our old home address in Mossley Hill, and

I recognised the handwriting straight away. After all, there were dozens of captions in the scrapbook written in exactly the same hand. It was Deb's spidery scrawl, but I couldn't understand why Deb would ever have been writing a letter to herself.

I turned the pale blue envelope over, noting that the notepaper Doreen was still holding was white with an embossed crest at the top of the page.

"Where did this come from?" I asked her. "I've never seen this before."

Doreen gulped down a lump in her throat and told me it had been between the pages of a show programme that had been stuck together.

"I thought the pages felt quite thick," she said, looking from the piece of paper in her hand, to my face, and then back to the letter again. "So I gently eased the pages apart and this fell out." She waved the note around a little. I started to ask Doreen what the letter said but I heard a car pull up outside just then and realised it was Levi, who must have finished his shift.

I let him in, fetched him a fresh mug of tea and offered him a piece of cake. He said hello to Doreen but she just grunted and looked rather irritated by his intrusion.

Levi shrugged off Doreen's apparent rudeness and sat in the armchair, but then he seemed to pick up on Doreen's mood. He was just about to lift a slice of lemon drizzle towards his mouth when he stopped and furrowed his brow in Doreen's direction and said, "Bev, I think you'd better come and sit down." Doreen shot him a grateful look and coughed to clear her throat.

"Do you know what this is?" Doreen asked, looking first at me and then at Levi. I shook my head and Levi put down his cake and leaned forward.

"This is…" She stopped and we waited although I was fighting the urge to go and shake her to make her spit out whatever it was that she wanted to say. "This is a letter from *George Harrison*," Doreen said, and then her shoulders slumped as though the very act of making the claim had taken all the energy out of her.

Levi and I looked at each other and then back at Doreen. What had she just said? I started to say something but Doreen finally found her voice. She said it again, that what she was holding in her hand was a letter from George Harrison, the real one, from The Beatles. That it was written to Deb and sent to her in a stamped addressed envelope that she had obviously included when she had written to him. The letter Doreen was holding was written in George's very own handwriting on a piece of hotel stationery, complete with the handwritten addition of "Friar Park" at the top – the address of his gothic mansion in Oxfordshire – and with his autograph right at the bottom.

"What does it say?" I was stunned beyond belief and I couldn't imagine for a moment what *George Harrison* would have been writing to my sister … no, to my *mother*, about.

Doreen held out the notepaper. "I think you'd better read it for yourself," she said.

Dear Deb,

Always good to hear from a fan. Thanks a lot! I'm not the one to tell you what is right or wrong, but you sound kind and caring. You are right about musicians, we are an unreliable lot! Living the life you are given can be hard sometimes but I'm sure you will do the best for you and your baby. London can feel like a new world, but you'll get used to it. You don't need no Wah Wah. Remember – all things must pass...

Hari Om.

Love from George (Harrison)

I read it out loud – and then had to read it through to myself a couple more times to take it all in – and then we all sat in stunned silence for a while, letting the words from more than fifty years ago reverberate around us.

Doreen spoke first. "Deb must have written to George to ask his advice," she said, although I think that much was obvious to us all. "George did sometimes reply to fans, apparently, even when The Beatles were really famous," she added. The proof of that also seemed to be clear and the fact that he'd written "Friar Park" at the top of the page meant it had to be written after 1970 as I knew that was when he and Pattie Boyd had moved to the country estate that remained his home until he died. The postmark date on the envelope was unhelpfully smudged.

Levi had said nothing but looked thoughtful as he put his mug down on the coffee table. "She wrote to him because she wanted to be reassured she was doing the right thing about you," he said gently, watching me carefully as he spoke.

I looked down again at the letter in my hands. It was so frustrating not knowing what it was that Deb had written herself. The clues were there though. I knew George had always been her favourite in the band and I could imagine that his sensitivity and spiritual nature made her think he would be a good person to turn to. Whatever she had said had caused him to call her *"kind and caring"*, so I presumed she must have told him something about how torn she was about leaving me behind so she could pursue her career in London.

"But what does he mean about musicians being unreliable?" I asked.

Doreen shifted on her seat and pulled her face into a grimace. "I think I might know what that's about," she said. "Deb had been seeing a guy who played in a band just before she fell pregnant with you. He wasn't famous or anything; there were loads of bands around in Liverpool back then," she said, looking worried about what she was about to tell me. "I can't even remember the bloke's name but I do recall Deb had caught him necking with another girl in an alleyway off Mathew Street one night and that had been the end of their brief romance. She didn't know she was pregnant at that point," Doreen said carefully, "but once she found out she was having a baby she was damn sure she wouldn't use it as a way to get him back … not that she could be sure he *would* have come back anyway. Deb must have told George all about it in her letter." Doreen's voice faltered then as though she'd only just realised she was talking about the man who was my father. "Sorry," she said.

I looked from her tortured face to Levi. I didn't know what to say.

"It sounds like your mother was a young woman with a real mind of her own," he said. "From everything I've heard about all this I think she wanted to make a better life for herself so that she could make a good life for you, too."

Doreen nodded. "I agree completely and I'm more certain than ever that Deb's plan had been to tell you she was your mother when the time was right."

"I don't get the 'wah-wah' bit though?" Levi said, looking puzzled. "Although I recognise the 'all things must pass' reference. That's a song George Harrison wrote, isn't it?"

"That's right and 'Wah-Wah' is the name of a track on the album also called *All Things Must Pass*," I told him. "It was actually written about all the tension in the band before they broke up."

Doreen nodded in agreement. "Yeah, that's right, Bev," she said, turning to Levi as she added, "A 'wah-wah' is the name of a guitar foot pedal, but in this case, when George sings about someone giving him a 'wah-wah', he means they're giving him a headache."

I looked down at the letter still in my hands. "The song is about finding happiness by setting yourself free," I said, stunned by how profound Deb must have found these few words from her favourite Beatle.

Levi slowly nodded, with fresh understanding of the meaning behind Harrison's words. "So he's telling her to move on from her troubles and create a new life for herself

… and her baby," he said, as we all sat absorbing this new information.

I found myself reading and re-reading the letter. It was just a few short lines but such an amazing insight into about my background and, incredibly, it had a direct link to my beloved Beatles, to George Harrison himself. It was an awful lot to take in.

Later that night I put George's letter to Deb carefully away in Mame's wooden casket. Bit by bit I seemed to be accumulating unique items related to The Beatles that had such powerful, personal connotations. I might have lost numerous pieces of vintage merchandise, but the things I now had in my collection were worth so much more to me than money could ever buy: Deb's scrapbook, my little cream and red toy guitar, George's letter, and, of course, the photographs and gifts from the day Paul McCartney came for tea. Maybe Paul might even write a song about me one day… Stranger things had actually happened!

As I carefully closed the lid of the old wooden box, I felt Levi's strong arms around me, his cuddle as gentle as his voice.

"Are you okay, 'Beatles Bev'?" he asked as he kissed the top of my head. I turned to face him and saw he was smiling. I laughed with him as I thought about all the reasons I deserved that title – now, more than ever – and how very proud I was of that name.

"Yes," I said, giving him a big kiss and squeezing him tight, "yes, I am."

I'm sure my life will hold many more twists and turns in the future. There may even be days when I will want to scream and shout. But I've learned that "shaking things up" every now and again *can* turn out for the best ... so long as you allow enough time to pass for the dust to settle!

So that's my story ... so far...

With love from me to you,

Bev X

YOUR NUMBER ONE STOP

ONE MORE CHAPTER

FOR PAGETURNING BOOKS

One More Chapter is an
award-winning global
division of HarperCollins.

Sign up to our newsletter to get our
latest eBook deals and stay up to date
with our weekly Book Club!
<u>Subscribe here.</u>

Meet the team at
<u>www.onemorechapter.com</u>

Follow us!

 <u>@OneMoreChapter_</u>

 <u>@OneMoreChapter</u>

 <u>@onemorechapterhc</u>

Do you write unputdownable fiction?
We love to hear from new voices.
Find out how to submit your novel at
<u>www.onemorechapter.com/submissions</u>